MARKED FOR LIFE

Paul Magrs was born in 1969 on Tyneside. He was brought up in Newton Aycliffe and educated at Woodham Comprehensive, then at Lancaster University, where he took the MA in Creative Writing. *Marked for Life* is his first novel, and is followed by *Does It Show?* and a collection of stories, *Playing Out*.

Paul Magrs

MARKED FOR LIFE

V

VINTAGE

Published by Vintage 1996

2 4 6 8 10 9 7 5 3 1

Copyright © Paul Magrs 1995

First published in Great Britain by
Chatto & Windus Ltd, 1995

Vintage
Random House, 20 Vauxhall Bridge Road,
London SW1V 2SA

Random House Australia (Pty) Limited
20 Alfred Street, Milsons Point, Sydney
New South Wales 2061, Australia

Random House New Zealand Limited
18 Poland Road, Glenfield, Auckland 10,
New Zealand

Random House South Africa (Pty) Limited
PO Box 2263, Rosebank 2121, South Africa

Random House UK Limited Reg. No. 954009

A CIP catalogue record for this book
is available from the British Library

ISBN 0 09 959401 3

Papers used by Random House UK Ltd are natural, recyclable products made from wood grown in sustainable forests. The manufacturing processes conform to the environmental regulations of the country of origin

Printed and bound in Great Britain by
Cox & Wyman, Reading, Berkshire

This book is for my sister, Louise Catherine Foster.
With thanks to . . .

(in order of appearance)

Joy Foster, Mark Magrs, Charles Foster, Lynne Heritage, Nicola Clementson, Pete Courtie, Brigid Robinson, Suzi Stephens, Andrea Greenwood, Julia Wiggston, Laura Wood, Steve Jackson, Gene Hult, Jon Rolfe, Antonia Garden, Richard Wilson, Lynne Pearce, Alicia Stubbersfield, Siri Hansen, Joan Diamond, Kelly Gerrard, David Craig, Leigh Pain, Bill Penson, Alan Bennett, Mark Walton, Daryl Spears, Sara Maitland, Tim Donnelly, Fred Botting, Meg Davis, Amanda Reynolds, Richard Klein, Phil Mack, Jonathan Burnham and everyone at Chatto.

One

You never tell me how the kid is. You never mention the kid at all. Why is that? She must be a big part of your lives. Both your lives. You should tell me more about her. I feel like I'm the mother. Funny that, isn't it, Mark? If things had been different, I could have been.

I know. Very different. But still.

Don't give my love to Samantha. It's best not to. I don't know whether she has any idea that I still write to you. Does she, Mark? Do you tell her? When you put the kid to bed at night, when you turn off all the lights in that nice flat of yours, do you scoop your wife into bed, hold her close and tell her that I've been writing again?

I doubt it somehow. And I wouldn't like to interfere.

It's best if she forgets all about me. Whatever she knew. I was just the one behind the wheel. I'm the one she never has to think about again. And that's all right. I'm content to be out of her sight. Out of sight, out of mind. I don't want to be in her mind. I don't like her that much.

Hear that, love? I don't like your wife. I know you'll forgive me for that. I'm sorry. I'd like to say I thought she was worthy of you. But there you are. She isn't. You're pathetic.

They're trusting me to use the library now. Three books a week. I go for the classy stuff. I'm reading up, improving myself. Where was Madame Bovary when she first got the shakes? What colour was Anna Karenina's dress when the train hit her? I'm filling up every corner of my mind with trivia from the literary greats. There's some talk of an Open University course. They're keen on those here. I've got all the answers.

The best bits I read, I copy out onto separate bricks. By my bed, where they can't really be seen. Though I don't mind if people look across my bed and read them. Me and you, eh, Mark? Both of us exhibitionists, deep down. It sticks, that kind of thing. You'll be finding that out, I imagine. We're both gone thirty-six now. The shit has well and truly hit the fan. Stuck there, dried out nicely. The fan goes on spinning.

So, tell me all about the new life. About the kid. One thing I've been wondering about. Was she born looking like you or Samantha?

Was the kid born tattooed?

Much love,

Tony.

Two

'It's such a shame.' Miss Kinsey rattled the staff room's blinds, peering at the driveway. 'He's a nice man, really.'

'Who's that?' Doris Ewart had *Living* magazine out on the table. She was memorising instructions for making cardboard snowmen that really glittered. She thought her class might appreciate them.

'Sally Kelly's father.'

'Oh, *him*.' Doris joined the headmistress to see. 'Poor child. Unfortunate name.' Doris sifted through the mass of parents and children waiting for her to dash out with the school bell and call them in. What a lot of parents wear shell suits, she thought and sighed. You'd think they'd make more of an effort.

'Poor child,' the headmistress murmured.

'Whose class is she in?'

'Miss Francis. Class Two. She's only four. We let her in early. Apparently she's very bright. But look at him.'

Sally Kelly's father was now in full view. From behind their venetian blinds, Miss Kinsey and Mrs Ewart stared at a tall man in jeans and denim jacket. He stood among the school's prematurely aged parents: mothers with twin pushchairs, bleached hair, chapped red hands and faces, all of them about seventeen. The older mothers were dressed to look young, bridging the gap out of what might appear to be courtesy. They were in their mid-thirties, squashed into tight jeans, arses like obscene blue peaches. In their midst, so still he might have been inconspicuous but for the space left around him, Mark Kelly was holding Sally's lunch box and Sally's hand. Sally stood quietly, unbothered by the other children.

You could see from here, Miss Kinsey thought, her intelligence. She held the other children away from her. She would have problems over that. They'd turn on her. At the moment they were too scared to, scared of her father. Heavens, who wouldn't be? Soon, though, their parents would teach them that they needn't be frightened of Mr Kelly at all. But he wasn't a nice man. They should just laugh at him, as though he were deformed. As though those were scars on his face.

'I spoke to him last summer,' Miss Kinsey said thought-fully. 'At Sports Day. That is, when I had a free moment during Sports Day.' Doris Ewart had been found in the staff room at the end of the day with a half-empty sherry bottle and the school caretaker. The headmistress had been forced to begin each race herself. 'And he proved to be an exceptionally articulate young man.'

'You would never think it,' Doris muttered, nursing the school bell, which she had just fetched from the cupboard.

'Perhaps you had better avoid rash judgements?' suggested Miss Kinsey with a hint of kindness. 'After all, he only looks like a thug to most people's eyes. Think of it as a cultural thing. If he was a foreigner we could probably regard him as ethnic. Charming, even. They are quite . . . tribal, aren't they?'

In the morning's pale wash of light Mark's tattoos were pricked out neatly in thick stripes of green and blue. His natural flesh glared out between chinks in the design. From this distance he might have been wearing a Norman helmet. Bold slats crossed his cheekbones, accentuating the thrust of his jawline. The pattern continued down his throat, feather-ing the neck of his T-shirt. The hands that held Sally's lunch box and Sally's hand were similarly darkened. It was largely assumed that his whole body had been done.

'It must have cost a fortune, all that,' said Doris Ewart. 'I'll ring the bell.'

The headmistress nodded absently and watched how the predominantly female gathering kept away from the Kellys. Those sidelong glances. Fear? Ridicule? Miss Kinsey won-dered, Was he really covered from head to toe?

On the doorstep of the main entrance Doris Ewart summoned her already sapped strength and rang the bell with

4

both hands. The crowd broke up and began to file into the school. The Kellys mingled, but remained quiet.

'Such a shame,' said Miss Kinsey again, and closed the blinds.

Each morning the young Miss Francis would stand by the tinkling terrapin pool in the centre of her classroom and welcome her children in. They clustered about her, checking the class pets were still there, crowding her with news. Their parents clutched coats, shuffled about, said a few words to one another, pressed kisses on their children's faces and snuck away.

Mark liked Miss Francis. She beamed at everyone; she wore Laura Ashley frocks, different-coloured flowers all the time. Sally regarded her rather diffidently. Mark was embarrassed by this coolness. The teacher was in turn embarrassed by Mark's attempts at friendliness. He's trying so hard not to seem frightening to the children, she thought.

'How are the terrapins?' he asked.

'All still alive,' she said brightly. 'Thank God,' and shuddered.

This was Miss Francis's first infant class. In a rush of enthusiasm at the beginning of the school year she had bought thirty-two terrapins, one for each child in her care, and named them all accordingly. The children's names were printed in pink nail varnish on the tiny creatures' murky-coloured shells.

Miss Francis bent to point to the sludgy base of a clump of fern. 'There's Sally Kelly,' she said. Mark and Sally watched it basking on the shore, poking in the mud with one flipper. Sally went to sit at her desk, unimpressed with her namesake. Miss Francis looked at Mark.

'Would you mind me asking . . . ?'

His smile was shy, creasing the tidy blocks of colour on his face. 'About?'

'Why did you give her a name that rhymed?'

Mark frowned. 'It's not rhyme. It's assonance.'

'Oh.'

'She's named after Sally Bowles. You know, Liza Minnelli in *Cabaret*.'

5

'I see.'

'As in, "Life is a cabaret, old . . ."'

'I've never seen it.'

'Well, it comes from a novel, really, *Goodbye to* –'

'I think we'd better push her back in. By the looks of things, she's been out of it all weekend.' Miss Francis cupped one careful hand and gave Sally's terrapin a nudge into the viscous green water, where the other thirty-one were having a lovely time, in the laborious, determined way that terrapins have. 'There we are.' She wiped her hands on her print dress.

When Mark left the classroom, he heard Miss Francis clap her hands together and announce that Andrea Fisher had spent the weekend laying Martin Rodgers's eggs on the artificial bank. There was a stunned silence, then uncertain applause.

Peggy, Samantha's mother, spotted him from across the park. He looked up to see her wading across the soggy grass, cursing as she splattered her tights. 'Mark!' she called feebly. 'Over here!'

He was waiting for the bus into town. He was early yet, sitting on a swing in the park by the stop, scraping the soles of his boots on the slimy asphalt. Without kids the park was desolate. Sea birds hurled themselves at each other above the grotesque iron spider that formed the ground's centrepiece. Peggy leaned against one of its legs to catch her breath.

'There's all sorts on that playing field,' she said as he came to meet her. 'It's awful, with kiddies about.'

'Hello, Margaret,' he said, forcing her to look at him and grimace.

'Have you been to school with our Sally?'

He nodded. Peggy was very short and determined, clutching a fur-trimmed coat about her. She spoke vehemently, rapidly, yet rarely looked at the person she was speaking to, as if the distraction would crack her determination. She amused him.

'What are you doing playing on the swings?' She almost followed this up with, 'like a big soft bairn', but Samantha had warned her about that.

6

'Just . . .' Mark's smile flickered; he patted his breast pocket, which crackled with Tony's letter. 'Just waiting to go into town. Shopping, you know, see Sam.'

'She won't want disturbing at work.'

'I often pop in. She likes it.'

'I used to work in a shop. I hated people popping in. It puts you off your stroke.'

'She's got a very professional manner.'

'Yes.' She eyed him, thinking, could plastic surgery do anything? Most likely he'd come out worse than ever. She said, 'I wanted to check with you again – well, with Sam really, but you'll do – about the dinner party.'

Mark nodded and pretended to look blank. The prospect of this do amused him more than Peggy did herself.

'Is everything still on for that?' she asked.

'As far as I know,' he said.

She wished he had more about him. Even with a face like the London A to Z he could look pretty vacant. 'And Sam's quite happy to . . . ?'

'She's coming round to the idea, slow but sure.'

Peggy looked up at him. He was surprised. Uncertainty played about her eyes, tugging the little puckers of fat. 'I want this to happen properly, Mark. I want us all to have a nice time. Now I know dinner parties aren't what the likes of you and I are used to, or Sam for that matter, professional manner or no, but it's the way Iris likes to have things done. And she wants so much to be liked by you and Sam. She's trying hard.'

'Sam'll cook something nice. You'll see. It'll be all right.'

'I'd do it myself, invite the two of you to mine, but Sam wouldn't come back to the house . . .'

'I know. It's all right at ours. Neutral ground.'

'It's hard for Iris too, you know.'

He smiled, thinking the conversation had come to a natural end, and watched his mother-in-law gather herself back up into some semblance of rigour, shrugging her old-fashioned coat stiffly into place. She dabbed the corner of her eyes with one crooked knuckle, overdoing it, he thought.

'Your bus is here.'

Feeling dismissed, he shot off across the grass towards the

7

white minibus purring at the kerb. Peggy watched; he was bright blue against the dull green, vital with a kind of skinhead sexiness. She shuddered.

The town's fairy lights were meagre this year, slung over the main streets and precincts with torpid abandon. The bulbs crackled in tinsel wreaths as the rain came down. The biggest shops had the better displays clustered about themselves, first hands in the tin of Quality Street.

Mark got off at his usual stop in the very centre of town, where the tarmac was sizzling with wet bus tyres and nearby, a student pavement artist threw down his pastels in disgust. On the pavement outside Marks and Spencer his *Hellas and the Nymphs* had turned into a lurid green paste.

Mark went straight to the new arcade. Here everything was lavish, smelling faintly of floor polish and Poison. Mirrors came at every angle, throwing images of unhappily dressed prospective customers back at themselves, and of the gleaming, bullet-shaped elevators that shot up and down between levels of the arcade.

He was reassured by his own constantly monitored presence. He looked like someone drawn in blue biro. A scrawl, he thought, and went for a coffee in the ladieswear department of a store overlooking the main street. You couldn't smoke there, and the frocks pressed in and peered over the tables in pristine, season-coloured ranks.

For her wedding Samantha had worn an immense white dress and veil, tugging it brutally through the narrow hallway of the registry office. Peggy had knelt on the welcome mat to pick sycamore leaves out of the train. Mark held the door and Sam's prim bouquet. She let him keep it. 'It suits your make-up,' she said and smiled.

His eyes rested on the tiny pulse working away at her throat. The sight of that and the softness of the light, filtered through the doors' cracked stained glass, eased his aching eyes a little. He bent to kiss her throat in that spot, and from behind them rose Peggy's voice, warning that they were blocking the way and that there was bound to be another lot in soon.

During the service ('Looks like Gran's old front room,' Sam muttered to her mam, who shuddered) the woman who married them took an obvious dislike to them and kicked up a stink about having only one witness. 'You need two,' she said.

'Mam's got eyes in her arse,' Sam said. 'She counts as two.'

The registrar simmered. 'Could you ask someone to come in from the waiting room, please?'

Peggy, realising the gravity, picked up her handbag to go.

Mark said, 'Couldn't I be a bridesmaid as well?' He proffered his bouquet limply. Samantha giggled and bit his shoulder.

'I don't think you're treating this quite seriously enough, Mr Kelly –'

Sam broke in. 'Ignore him. He's just a camp bugger.'

'You bitch,' he muttered, teeth clenched. 'Can we just carry on through the service till we hit the bit that needs witnessing?'

The registrar groaned. 'Really, they need to see it all. It's a ceremony.'

'Mam'll be back in a minute,' Sam urged. 'She's persuasive.'

The registrar continued. 'And do you, Mark . . .'

'Look who I found across the road!' Peggy cried, pulling another figure in a smart suit and hat into the room. The newcomer's orchid, Sam thought, was a spiteful green. 'Iris was just across the road! What a coincidence! What a godsend!'

'What a godsend!' Sam spat.

'Amen,' Mark sighed.

'Only too happy to oblige,' Iris grunted firmly and bustled into place beside Mark.

The rest of the event proceeded without hitch. Mark and Sam spent their honeymoon decorating their new flat on the estate, and Iris went back home with Peggy.

He went for another coffee. It must be a different girl serving this time, he thought, she's looking at me with renewed horror. There was still half an hour before Sam's lunch break.

The waitress held his cup under the coffee nozzle and it rattled against the steaming grill in the counter.

'And some ginger snaps,' he said.

'You look like a Red Indian,' she breathed.

She was a pretty girl, but wore too much blusher, he thought. An urn must ruin the complexion.

'How?' he asked.

'Are you a skinhead? National Front?'

'No. Where's my ginger snaps?'

'You must get a lot of stick.'

'It comes with the territory. For Red Indians.'

'It must do. Eighty-five pence.' He felt for change. She added, 'Sod it. Have it on the house. I could stare at you all day. You're like *Terminator II* and the Bayeux Tapestry rolled into one.'

He went back to sit among the watching frocks. His eyes were tired again. He hadn't even seen *Terminator II*. A headache was starting up. That's what you get for thinking about your wedding day. He caught sight of the waitress, collecting cups, crumpling chocolate wrappers, observing him.

Women react strangely to me. I've only noticed it the last couple of years. They must always have done, but something made me realise. What?

Oh, I remember what it was. My head-on collision with heterosexuality. You remember, Tony. You were there. You were driving.

I thought, because I didn't notice them, they never noticed me. The child's solipsism. When Sally was younger and wanted to stay in the bath, she'd drape her flannel over her face and go invisible. But we could still see her.

You forced me to come out a second time, Tony. You drove me to it. Literally.

That was a sick joke.

She's still watching.

He finished his ginger snaps, rubbed his eyes again and got crumbs in them, making them worse.

A hangover on my wedding day, not unusual for a groom. Except I spent my stag night alone, in the new flat, with a bottle of whisky. You couldn't come out to play. The one time it was publicly sanctioned and we fucked it up. You should have got me pissed, driven me to the back of beyond, stripped me naked, tied me to a lamppost in the dark, shot arrows at me and left me there. Then you were supposed to come back and get me to the church on time.

But you didn't, Tony, did you? You'd already given me away.

He left a ginger snap to bulge slowly in his half-finished coffee, and a tip for the waitress.

Sam was furious when he showed up early.

Three

Look at him, waiting there. Not an ounce of self-conscious-
ness, standing next to the knickers. He's scaring custom
away. I could let him wait all day, Sam realised. What would
he do then? Would he give up? Look slightly baffled, be
vaguely upset, turn and stroke some lace, examine sizes,
prices, pretend he was a customer, a transvestite? How far can
I push his patience, his utter passivity?

Women were slipping past him as if he were another
dummy, or a lizard in camouflage, blending with the foliage,
stock-still and itching to blink his tender eyes.

Those eyes flickered now across the shop. Sam gripped the
till corners and the thought crossed her mind once more: He
can hear everything I'm thinking.

But that's rubbish. We're still married, aren't we? I've no
reason to believe that.

She steadied her gaze on the black Perspex Christmas tree
beside the till. It was roped in junk jewellery, glistening with
earrings. Sam let the jagged anger draw back, filled her mind
instead with lettuce-fresh thoughts, determined to be relaxed
for her lunch hour. The crossness abated. She had found her
exit. I make myself a Gothic heroine; stonewall myself into
the bowels of my own black castle. And I make my own way
out. When it suits me.

'What's this stack of voids doing?'

Her hand flashed out to grasp tatters of till roll off the
counter.

'Who's done all these?'

She looked at Tracey, who was new and currently making a
pig's ear of wrapping somebody's goods. Tracey was biting
Sellotape.

12

'It was me,' she mumbled. 'I made a few mistakes on someone's Access. I'll sort them out when we get a moment.'

Sam scattered them. 'You'll do them now. Otherwise you'll forget and I'll have hell on balancing the till tonight.'

The supervisor pushed past the new employee on her way to the staff room and Tracey had a stabbing moment of guilt, over that Access bill she hadn't filled in properly.

Would Sam find out and make her pay?

'I don't want to wait long to eat,' Sam warned him as they hit the busy street. He was dawdling behind her.

'Where then?'

'Was Sally all right at school?'

'She always is these days.' He sniffed. 'Takes it in her stride.'

Sally had had a hard time at the beginning of school. The kids were so noisy, everything was so small. Mark remembered the face she pulled on the first morning, confronted by all the worn miniature furniture. She looked stung, as if patronised. Mark wanted to explain to her: It's not a joke, love. This is where you begin to be catered for. Your Local Education Authority takes pains to shoehorn you from this point on; starting with this desk and this chair, horizons to suit your current size. Later there'll be free school dinners, field trips, exams, then either a student grant or a flat of your own. Sally had turned up her nose, burst into tears.

Mark said, 'She's all settled in now.'

'She's going to do well at school.' Sam paused at the street corner, overwhelmed momentarily in the oncoming traffic. Shoppers made their way forwards by brandishing laden carrier bags before them. Everything about them was challenging, alert. All of a sudden Mark felt like giving in. 'We'll go to that vegetarian hole,' Sam decided. 'It's all right if you sit in the cellar and it's rarely full. Vegetarianism will never catch on here.'

'I like it in there.' Mark smiled as they made a bolt across the street.

'Doesn't fill you up, though, does it?' she said, grimly holding her breath as they passed the market's wet fish.

'Not always.'

They found the café busy upstairs, one haggard, hennaed waitress with a glottal Austrian accent tending the customers in an atmosphere redolent of nuts and spices. Everything was olive green and pine. They went down to the empty cellar and sat at an expansive kitchen table.

'You'd think more people would come down here.' Sam drummed her fingers on the pine. 'You can stretch your legs in the cellar.'

'Speaking of meals –' Mark scratched his nose uncertainly and took his jacket off. 'Your mam stopped me in the park to talk about that dinner.'

She had the menu open, running a groove down its polythene innards with her nail.

'Sam. That dinner.'

She looked up. 'I know. I'm sick of hearing about it. It's still on.'

'Christmas Eve.'

'Right. But I'm not having them over on Christmas Day.'

'Right.' Mark still felt that a real reconciliation would involve Sam inviting her mother for Christmas Day.

'She's not getting into my house on Christmas Day.'

'Why the fuck not?'

Her eyes flashed. He flashed his back.

'It's Christmas Eve or nothing,' she said. 'And you did look cross then. See, you can do it.'

'Fuck you.'

'I love you, Mark.'

'Mm.'

She did. But he made her cross. Especially when he was being effete. He hated being called that. The irony was, he had taught her that word himself. He taught her how to curse him.

She had been about to sling a plate across the bedroom.

'You think I'm effete, don't you?'

She swung the missile back. 'What does that mean?'

'Ineffectual. Poncy.'

'Yes.' She threw the garlic-butter-smeared plate, and it shattered against the wall. A startled silence rang between them.

14

'I can't believe you did that,' he said quietly.

'I can. You effete!'

He dropped heavily onto the bed. 'It's an adjective.'

'Oh. You effete bastard.'

'I am. I am. Take me.'

And now he had given in – completely and utterly – to her mother. After all the ruckus, it had been Mark who slunk round to patch things up with Margaret. He never liked rows.

'I don't like confrontations. It's my upbringing.'

'Then you shouldn't have married me, sweetie.'

He was supposed to smile at that. He didn't.

While they were waiting for the Austrian waitress to descend to the cellar, Sam said, 'This is all your fault. I could have been shot of her for good.'

'You've got your independence. There's no need to cut all ties. You've got what you always wanted – your own place.'

She gaped. 'Is that what you think of me?'

'I want to order now. I know what I want.'

'Do you really think that's why I'm with you?'

'It's not often I know what I want so early on. It's quite unusual.'

'You ungrateful bastard, Kelly.'

'What?'

'You think I'm only with you to escape Peggy?'

'Of course not.'

'Good.'

'It's part of it, though, isn't it?'

'It's a side effect. A good one.'

'And we stay together for the sake of Sally, the flat and the absence of your mother.'

'Fuck you,' she said.

'Not to mention Iris.'

'Don't mention Iris. Where's the fucking waitress?'

The waitress was at that moment taking cautious steps towards them. She surprised them both by leaning over the banister.

'Could you please come upstairs and be served there? I am by myself today and cannot leave the till unattended. Thank you very much.'

15

They glared at each other, the menu and the space on the stairs the waitress left behind. Upstairs they saw the café was still full. They pushed out again into the marketplace to look for somewhere else, avoiding the Austrian woman's eye.

'I fancied something meaty anyway,' Mark said loudly.

It was at moments like these Sam discovered to her surprise that she loved him more than he made her cross. When they were being thrown out of places. When they had their faces to the wind, giving parting shots. They could wander about, nowhere special to go. Be children, sexless, with no particular home. They would find one, make a den, play mams and dads.

A market van slewed past in a kerbside puddle, splashing water up their legs. 'Christ!' Her dinner hour was running out.

'I know –' Mark beamed, changing gear – 'just the place.'

The only time Sam had ever seen Mark Kelly completely naked was in family holiday photos. A tubby blond child wading starkers out of the sea. From the first meeting onwards she had known his body; yet as far as she was concerned, it was coated with a different flesh. A blue and green patinaed flesh, a chitinous second skin. The coloured shell of a Smartie. Something she hadn't been early enough to penetrate.

Not that she hadn't tried. It made her giggle. The second night of the crap honeymoon, alone in the half-decorated council flat.

He begged and wept, he had his comeuppance; she penetrated him quite literally, smearing a melted dinnertime candle in rose-scented hair conditioner, ramming it gently up his arse, back again. He begged and wept.

'Now we're quits,' she had said, frowning slightly.

He thanked her, uncertainty rippling through the demarcated contours of his shuddering skin. But they didn't do that again.

'It's not the thing,' he said quite suddenly in the tenderest part of the night, 'to be buggered by one's new wife.'

In an obscure way, she found that touching. In those early

16

hours the candle burned with a tang of rose, and something inscrutable and bloody.

Yet the moment she first clapped eyes on him, he was there in his peacock finery; jade and azure, standing on her mam's front doorstep, the night of the accident.

Immediately she saw that between the slats of tattoo, his face was stark white in shock.

'Who are you?'

She left the catch on. It was past two in the morning. She had sunk half a bottle of whisky, just as the doctor had ordered. Her mother was out with Iris somewhere, or at Iris's posh cottage; there was a strange man at the door, tattooed, in shock, and tonight of all nights.

'I'm Mark Kelly. I was in the taxi.'

She stayed still and reeled within. 'Oh?' She thought she should add, 'Perhaps you had better come in,' but her tongue had turned to sponge in her mouth. She chewed at it cautiously. Her mouth filled with saliva and bile.

'Excuse me.' She squirmed, threw open the catch, dashed past him and vomited thickly on the lawn.

Mark fell to his knees beside her and clapped her on her back – a bit heavily, she remembered thinking.

'Get it all up, love. Nothing to be ashamed of. You've had a fuck of a night.'

She spewed and among it all came the questions she wanted to ask. They crackled inside her skull, scored lines in a dot to dot that never quite articulated itself. Mark drew his arms around her thin cottony blouse, pulled her into the illustrated warmth of his body, fed her a documentary, supplication, apologies. All of which she followed only vaguely.

'You'll be all right. Any more? Come on, have another heave.'

She did – and wondered at herself for trusting him in this most vulnerable of moments on her mother's lawn. Sheer bile and water welled up in her stomach. She pulled with both hands at Mark. 'Mark? Is that your name?'

She felt him nod.

'Look after me for a bit, Mark.'

He whispered against her hair, which, she felt disgusted to

realise, was slicked up with spew. He whispered that he was already looking after her.

A few minutes later he hauled her indoors and snecked her mother's door after them.

Their second café that lunchtime was very small and full apart from one cramped table in the corner, and decorated with a display of novelty tea cosies that were 'available upstairs'. They squeezed themselves in, Sam brushing irritably at the scum of breadcrumbs, dried gravy and sugar crusts that grimed the tablecloth. 'It's horrible in here,' she hissed.

'Stop talking so loud. They'll hear you.'

She fell to watching a family group across the aisle; a young couple with aged parents. The old man was stiffly formal in hat and coat, consenting to be taken out at Christmas. Neither he nor his wife looked as if they got out much. His daughter-in-law scrutinised the menu on his behalf.

'Lasagne, Dad?'

He wouldn't look at her, nor modulate his voice to café-polite level. 'I don't know what the hell that is.'

'It's like . . . pasta.'

'We like things with gravy,' said his wife.

'I don't want gravy when I'm out,' he shouted. Sam thought he must be off his head. Inadvertently she caught his eye but looked away again. The old man dropped his voice to add, 'I won't have anyone's gravy but Mother's. No one else can do gravy, far as I'm concerned.'

His wife glowed with pride.

Sam wondered what her father would have been like by now. Loud, oblivious, wedged into a café in out-of-date clothes, shouting about gravy?

Mark was ordering some coffee. He asked what she wanted. She shrugged and let him plump for toasted sandwiches.

Peggy knew what lasagne was. She had moved with the times. It was something middle-class, something you didn't get years ago because it was too foreign. Package trips with Iris. Her horizons had been broadened like anything.

18

'They're just so nauseating together,' she said. 'Peggy and Iris.'

'They might think that about us,' Mark shrugged. They had been through this conversation before.

'But we're married. We're allowed to be nauseating.' She watched his jaw muscles work in irritation, denting the pattern of his face.

'They're happy, right? Nothing you can say or do will spoil that, so leave it be, Sam.'

'I can't help wondering what Dad would think about them.'

'Just because he's gone, you can't make him the arbiter of all taste and moral judgement.'

The waitress was unloading their coffee cups and milk jugs. 'The management apologises if your coffee tastes like tea,' she said, but remained unheard.

Sam warned, 'Leave my dad out of this.'

'You dug him up again.'

Her hand shot out, upsetting the milk. 'Fuck!'

The waitress frowned. 'I'll fetch a Jay cloth. It's a shame, wasting good milk.'

'I'm sorry I said that, Sam. But your dad isn't here to judge any more, and he hasn't been since you were fourteen. What would he think of me? By your reckoning, he wouldn't approve of me, my tattoos or my past.'

'He wasn't a complete fascist. And he needn't have known anything about what you used to be.'

'So he needn't know anything about what his wife is now. Your mam knows what she needs. Leave her to it, love.'

Sam took the proffered Jay cloth and swabbed the table herself. 'I don't want any funny business from those two in my house on Christmas Eve.'

'Is there no one here to look after you?'

Sam stood swaying by the sink, in case she felt ill again. Weakly she pointed out where everything was kept for coffee. Mark made two strong cups.

'I live with my mam. She's out. She doesn't know about any of this.'

19

'You must be in a right state.' He gave her a mug, which stung her fingers. 'Let's go and sit down.'

Mark sat on the corner of the settee, under a shaded lamp whose orange light turned his tattoos a puzzled grey. He nudged Sam's knees, got her to put her feet up.

'When will your mam come back?' She wants looking after, he thought. Besides, when her mother does come back, I'll have some explaining to do. I'm a complete stranger.

'She probably won't, till morning. She'll stay with Iris. I've told you that once.'

'Oh, yeah.' He was thinking about Tony, driven home in a police car after visiting the outpatients and the station. His taxi left on the roadside to be towed away, with vomit on the back seat and blood up the front fender. It was his livelihood and he had most likely lost it tonight.

'I've thrown up too,' Mark said, and Sam looked at him with muzzy interest. He wondered at sounding so facetious about it. A girl had been killed.

'Your friend's family . . . ? The girl's family . . . ?' He spoke unsteadily. 'Have you seen them?'

She lowered her glance, hair falling across her face in oily ribbons. 'I saw them. I couldn't speak. What do you say? I couldn't say I was sorry, or . . .' She hauled in a shuddering breath and retched drily. Mark rose to fetch a basin but she waved him feebly down. 'We've both been sick tonight, eh?' Sam gave a sudden, conspiratorial grin. 'But they didn't expect me to talk at all, it turns out. I saw them in the station . . . and they said, the mother said, that I'd been through a terrible ordeal myself, that they understood if I . . . I was the lucky one! Her father said that! He held my hand and said how I'd been luckier than their Trisha. I should be glad, he said, and he squeezed my hand. Dead hard.'

She looked narrowly at Mark. He flinched and she saw that his eyelids too were coloured in.

'They said he had a skinhead in the back of his taxi. Covered in tattoos. I saw you. I knew your face.'

Mark made as if to go. 'I shouldn't have come.'

'Why did you?' Sam's voice was hard, her body rigid, feet pushing her away from him like someone clutching in a dream. She was thinking furiously: he was the passenger in the taxi when it happened, when it knocked down Trish. What did he see then? What has he seen?

'I came to say sorry.' He was standing up. His words barely registered. 'I'm sorry. It was my fault.'

Sam was standing on the kerb. She was clutching a bottle loosely around its neck. Trisha, a little ahead, was screaming at her. Her ugly pink gash of a mouth glinted threads of spittle. 'Fucking cow, Sam! That's fucking it this time! How can you do it to your best mate, you fucking –'

Trisha's eyes were glazed over, as if in shock, widened obscenely. She leaped at Sam with wet, red palms in an embrace as sure as sex. Sam wielded her bottle with a shriek, clonked Trish once across the neck, pushed her backwards into the rain-sticky road.

Sam reeled onto the path, cracking the base of her spine as she hit a puddle and the taxi's headlights bore down on them both, sluicing around the corner, sweeping over, swallowing up Trisha's lazy body.

'It was all my fault.'

Mark felt awful saying that. It sounded inane.

'I distracted Tony, the driver. I was ill in the back of his cab. I know him, he was giving me a lift, he can't get the cab dirty, you see, it's his job, he was distracted, and I . . . it was my fault.'

Sam closed her eyes, inhaling deeply. It was all Mark's fault. She felt the thickly padded springs of her mother's old settee rubbing painfully, a dull, throbbing pain in her coccyx. She tasted the wine, sitting in the gutter, shoving her tongue into the bottleneck for the last drops, staring at the street, people from the pub, ambulance, taxi, police, all at dangerous, crazy angles; the mess in the dark. It was all Mark's fault. He had laid his blame before her.

Sam opened her eyes again and spread her palms. 'I forgive you,' she said.

'What?'

'I forgive you.'

His face tightened to a complex mesh.

'She was my best friend. I won't say a thing. She was my

21

best friend. Don't torture yourself, Mark. It's all over now. I won't say a thing.'

'You forgive me?'

She took his hand; she was suddenly, frighteningly lucid. 'Never tell anyone what you've just told me,' she said. 'Never. Hold me.'

Clumsily he gripped her as she bent forward, burying her nose in the front of his shirt, squeezing out tears and mucus into his throat's hollow. Never tell, he thought. Tony won't tell. Tony will take it.

Sam shivered against him. Instinctively he wrapped himself about her, responding with an animal warmth, without thought. He made himself pliable.

'Mam won't be back to listen,' she was saying. 'I've no one else to talk to. Trisha always listened to me. She was my best friend.'

He swallowed an impulse to vomit again and was surprised by Sam reaching up to kiss him. She bore down and burrowed into him, her fingers clattered and jabbed at undressing him. He was stunned; the erection she procured for him was sluggish, merely warmth, but it was the response she wanted.

Sam made urgent, sickly love to him and his head rocked back against the lampstand. He nudged it too far as he came with a confused moan; the lampshade swung and collapsed, smashing, pitching the room into purple. Sam sank to sleep on his stomach, clutching at the whorling patterns of his skin, the vortex etched on his torso. Mark allowed his head to fall back across the armrest. They slept till mid-morning, dehydrating steadily through the night, their headaches knocking uneasily against one another's skin.

Four

I've a feeling that my last letter was strange. A little bitter, perhaps. Was it? I'm sorry, Mark. I only send the better ones. That one sort of slipped through. A waste. I suppose we're lucky to have this contact at all.

I'm content, though. At least on paper I have your undivided attention. These words, for your ears only, can't fail to be taken in. On paper we value each other all the more. If I was there, with you, you would start to fade away. You would have switched off by now. You always did. Does Sam get annoyed with you for that? Your self-absorption. Staring at the backs of your hands, following the tracery of lines up your wrists. I'd trail away speaking eventually, you'd not even notice, and then we'd both be looking at your tattoos.

The most eloquent part of you. Well, maybe not.

I remember your look when you were being tattooed. Impassive; you were brave. It seemed so painful. All that fine shovelling into skin, the deft glutting and smear of crimson and indigo. We used to go weekly, Saturday mornings, and I'd sit quietly to watch. I felt like holding your hand, telling you how to breathe, urging you to push. Did you watch your Sam give birth?

Utter self-absorption, though. You looked so fulfilled while you were being done; this week's bare patch of flesh bright under that noxious yellow light. Old Marjorie, dipping her nibs and scratching away. She never failed to look impressed. Her best customer, you were.

I remember a certain day. She was more concerned for you than she was for her own profit. She unplugged her machine, broke your trance and asked, 'How long is this going to go on, exactly?'

I jumped in my seat, I can tell you. I thought we'd been rumbled.

You just looked at her. 'All the way,' you said. 'I want the whole lot done'.

She cackled. 'Saucy. I'm not sure Eric would want me to keep doing you if that's the case.' I could tell she was unnerved. She went on to warn you about that girl in *Goldfinger*, dying because she'd been painted head to foot with gold paint, which clogged all her pores and suffocated her. In the film and in real life.

'Life imitates art,' you said, as if that was the sort of thing people say all the time. 'Don't worry. I'll breathe.'

She returned to work, sponging your stomach down.

'It'll be ever so painful,' she said.

'It always is.'

'I mean, when we get to your . . . sensitive parts.'

You tossed me a wry look. 'It always is.'

I didn't say anything.

Here, lots of the men have tattoos. It's a real cliché. Criminals, hardened, with tattoos. Roses, scrolls, daggers, Mother. It's like having you here around me, almost; disseminated throughout the hundreds of bodies here. At the thought of that, I could swoon during communal showers. I could run from one illustration to the next, yet never find you. Never hope to reconstitute you.

It's ironic, really. I've no tattoo of my own. No reminder of you, ripped from your flesh, painted onto me. You're everywhere else instead. It's as if you're famous, with your face on every magazine. Bits of you are printed everywhere here. And I am, essentially, only me.

Perhaps this letter is stranger than the last one.

Love,

Tony.

Five

Iris mucked in. She was an imposing presence, drawing attention to herself, wedged standing up against the plush red pew among rows and rows of squirming, anxious children. With her soft pure-wool girth she touched the back of the seat in front and the front of her own.

Doris Ewart, harassed and scarlet, was glad of the impromptu help. Doris passed her a Co-Op carrier heavy with cartons of orange juice, for Iris to dispense along her row. The children about her, parents too, hushed down when the fat woman bent wordlessly to give them each a carton and a straw.

'Sit down, Iris,' Peggy hissed irritably. 'Stop making a show of yourself. Those teachers are paid to do that sort of thing.'

Sitting next to her grandmother, Sally was looking slightly embarrassed, and beside her, Mark was sucking at his own orange juice, waiting for the show to begin.

The fat woman, however, was in her element. Her outdoor coat was fuchsia. She was overripe, a swollen berry of a woman, squeezed into the seething, overelaborate Civic Theatre where, above the bobbing heads of the children, lithe and gilded cupids and satyrs were secreted among florid nips and tucks of cream masonry and scarlet drapings. Here Iris felt supremely comfortable, with everyone swayed by her air of authority, drawn to the gaudy splash she still, in such a setting, managed to make.

Her lips, fuchsia also, were smacked in satisfaction, her mouth sensuous and prim. Hands reached out to her across the rows, sweaty, chocolate-smudged, hot and grasping hands. She passed out the drinks with unhurried assurance, as if daring the pantomime to begin before her task was completed.

25

The air started to dim perceptibly about her; pink, amber, a lambent honey. The audience quietened, slowed their movements, watched the empty stage with its grim ABSOLUTELY NO SMOKING safety curtain. It was almost as if someone had levered off the lid of the theatre's roof and poured the building full of stiff, lucid treacle. The audience were still, preserved. Anticipation was sweet.

Iris took the last drink for herself and sat down with a sigh as darkness set in.

'Just in time,' Peggy mumbled.

'I like to give a hand.'

'You like the attention.'

Iris was staring at the safety curtain as it rose. 'I won't deny I miss it.'

With a bang, a violent glittering of indoor fireworks and gasps of enchantment from various parents, the Good Fairy picked her way centre-stage.

Sally narrowed her eyes. 'She's holding a microphone.'

Mark was scanning the programme's cast list. 'She's been on *Casualty*.'

'Why would a Good Fairy need a microphone?'

'Ssssh!'

Peggy leaned across. 'It's best to be prepared, in my experience. In case people aren't listening properly.'

Sally took the hint and settled back with a tolerant expression.

Last year the pantomime had been *Beauty and the Beast* and Mark had laughed all the way through. Sam had come too; the in-laws weren't invited. It had been Sally's first Christmas in school, her first school trip, a family occasion.

The Beast had been the star of the show. Mark was mortified when they swapped him for the prince at the end; Sally too. Sam was merely reassured. The star was Conrad the Wolf, a veteran TV puppet Mark had once adored as a child. Conrad always sat on a podium without a handler and condescended to the entertainment of children as a vehicle for his own brand of raucous humour. In 1979 Mary Whitehouse, having switched channels one Saturday teatime and been barraged by lupine double entendres, had called him

26

'filthy'. Conrad disappeared from the air forthwith, consigned to the tawdry netherworld of civic pantomime, where the smut still flowed like wine and Mark could laugh himself silly, to the mortification of his wife and child.

Sam refused to come to the show this year, in case the same thing happened. She knew that the first rule in child-rearing was feigned innocence.

The big star in Darlington this year was, however, squeaky-clean Rosalyn, the winner of the 1983 Eurovision Song Contest. Still audibly Dutch, despite brief international fame, she was having an awful time with Snow White's lines, which were, for local interest, written in a Geordie dialect. Iris snorted occasionally as Rosalyn stumbled her way through, looking relieved and happiest when she could sing a song or pretend to be doing some housework.

'Isn't it funny how Europeans never sing with an accent?' whispered Peggy. 'Look at Abba.'

'Dietrich and Pavarotti,' Iris grunted.

Even the dwarfs looked pissed off with Rosalyn. This year it was their turn to make leering jokes for the baffled audience. Mark didn't find them half as funny as Conrad. At the end of Act One they returned from a day's work at the mine, each clutching a can of 7-Up and singing the theme song from *An Officer and a Gentleman*, 'Love Lift Us Up'.

'They never had 7-Up in those days,' Sally complained above the clamour of children and parents stamping out for the interval.

Mark asked, 'How do you know it's not happening now?'

Sally sighed. 'All fairy tales are a long time ago. Wooden houses and people singing. It's obvious. She had a broom and no Hoover.'

Iris ushered them along their row. 'Are we going for a drink?'

'So why did they have 7-Ups?' Sally demanded.

'Um,' Mark began. 'Listen, I'll go up to the bar and order – you go to the loo with Auntie Iris and your nanna. They'll explain.'

'Thanks, Mark,' Peggy hissed as they entered the swell and press of the crowd.

'I think she's a dreadful woman.'

Sam's judgement had been final. Mark wasn't allowed to contradict her, although he had already admitted to a sneaking admiration for the woman who had taken up his wife's space in Peggy's house and made irrevocable changes. A Tuscany patio, with herb garden. The dining room knocked through.

'She acts like she's something.'

'She is something. Your mother's lover.'

They were still newlyweds, this was seven years ago, and Mark didn't yet know how far he could push Sam. She burst into tears as they walked back to their flat. His heart went out to her because he saw she still had a smear of grease on her trembling chin. She chews when she cries, he noted with a shudder.

'You'll have to get used to it,' he said gently.

'I can't. It's so awful. She's so fat.'

Mark sighed in the manner Sally was to pick up at an early age.

He carefully set down the interval drinks. The table was next to squabbling kids clustered about the coloured monitor showing the safety curtain lowered onstage. They were delighted by the idea that they could watch the show up here on television if they wanted. They fought over the best view. One was asking his mother if they could stay up in the bar. She cracked him one.

That evening with the grease on Sam's chin had been the last time they had met as a happily fulfilled foursome, for dinner at Peggy and Iris's. Soon afterwards Sam had started up the feud, with all the zest she usually employed in feeding used boxes to the cardboard crusher at work.

Iris had cooked and then insisted that they watch an American TV movie together.

'Oh, no,' Mark had smirked, 'not the Freak of the Week movie. Which minority are they tastefully handling this week?'

Iris smiled serenely. 'It's called *Mom's Apple Pie*.'

It turned out to be about a single mother who tells her children, in the most tactful manner possible, that she is a lesbian. The children eventually, after about ninety minutes and a good many phone calls, come to accept her as still the same old mom and she makes them a nice pie at the end to prove it.

Mark watched, slightly bemused, soaking up the therapeutic benevolence Iris was sending out in waves as she snuggled massively up to Peggy. Peggy was, however, stiff and alert, watchful for Sam's reactions.

Sam was furious, Mark could tell by the extra-deliberate way she smoked a whole pack of Marlboro Lights and refused to take her eyes away from the screen, even during adverts. When the credits rolled she locked herself in the downstairs toilet.

'Sam, love?' Peggy rattled the doorknob for a few minutes, then joined Mark and Iris over the washing-up.

'We've upset her,' she said, watching Mark's patterned arms wiping suds away.

'Maybe that's what she needs,' Iris said blandly, rubbing plates dry. 'Shocking her into facing the truth.'

Peggy winced. Iris kissed her nose.

'I didn't mean that nastily. It all shows just how much she feels about you.'

Later, under the streetlamp, with Sam sobbing in his unresponsive arms, Mark related this conversation in the hope she would be touched.

'What?' She drew back. 'I was furious – and that showed how much I love her?' She laughed bitterly. 'How fucking typical! Typical fucking selfish, the pair of them!'

Mark frowned at her.

'Couldn't they tell – couldn't they even fucking tell that I don't care that much about them and their doings? I was crying for myself. Too selfish even to see that. Those poor kids in the film – they were just like me and what she's been putting me through.'

Did Mark love Sam?

It was all so complex now. So tied up in vested interests, matters of life and death.

These days it was so hard to get a straight answer from him.

He had no objectivity. If someone stopped him, here in the bar, someone leaned across from another table and asked, as a matter of interest, 'Do you still truly love the woman you married in the eyes of God and the law?', he'd be utterly stuck for words. This was one of his worst-case scenarios, this abrupt question. It was one that must come sooner or later, from some quarter. It was the test he was most likely to fail.

He couldn't say yes or no.

He'd come through with flying colours on *Take Your Pick*.

Like a cassette player with heads so dirty they snag the tape with their accreted scum and release it grudgingly, his words would unspool. Ribbons of excuses, ameliorations, disclosures both shocking and painful. Downright lies, too.

Yes, of course he loved her. She was grafted into the pattern. In the tenderest, most inextricable manner, through the pity and shame their daughter Sally evoked in him. Sally stood baffled between them, dipping her toes in rock pools of their complications. She was growing up, supposedly clearing the decks for complexities of her own. But how could she even start when all this had gone on before? Her own life before it really began was framed in deceit and misalliances. Her parameters were already set in a kind of intrigue; and she was meant to be innocent, surely. Sally's jaded air suggested to Mark that she had a sense of her own inauthenticity; she was not a real child, not, in some way, 'natural' enough. As if she, too, felt she oughtn't be here.

She reminded Mark of Tony.

Tony was somewhere on the edges, somehow unchanging. His integrity made Mark feel false, fickle, hypocritical.

How much had he changed? There was no way of telling. Tony was his yardstick, against which he once measured how much he had deviated from their shared ideal. The charter they drew up for their future lives was still sketched out in his head. Something about not compromising, not being bourgeois, not making money, settling down, selling out, or being shocked, and always being there for each other.

In 1970 they built up defences to guard against the threat of impingement upon the single cell of their friendship. They made the agreement one October night, the Wednesday

30

between their thirteenth birthdays. It was raining heavily as they sat on a bench in a park on their housing estate. Here they sat every night, at an age when anything outside of sport seems inappropriate and boring. Hanging around, they drew up a manifesto.

Over several nights they took a good look at each other, listed faults, failings, tendencies in themselves, and cauterised them firmly, scribbling in the back of a school jotter. They pressed the matter home with smudges of blood. There was a slight shiftiness to this moment of bonding. They were watching for the other's truthfulness.

Is he as serious about this as I am? I bet he isn't. I bet he's pretending. See how far I'll go. He's just doing it to pass the time. He's just doing it for a laugh, and he'll tell everyone about it later.

They tested each other. They picked magic mushrooms and took fifty each. Tony's mother worked through the night sometimes in the hospital. They sat in opposite corners of Tony's bedroom and narrowly watched each other's hallucinations. Until morning their delusions filled up the empty air between them. Neither fell asleep, neither was sick, neither got scared.

They drank a bottle of vodka together, another night at Tony's house.

By now it seemed as if they were as alike as they ever could be. They had gauged each other meticulously and calibrated themselves to one another. If one developed a certain gesture, the other would copy it and soon the gestures they used seemed to have no single originator. Their language became incestuous, knotted up in its own idiosyncratic field of reference.

Tony, though, was the quieter, dark and brooding, broader and with beard-growth already at thirteen. Mark had his first skinhead, inspired by a Richard Allen book they had both read. One night Mark shaved Tony's head to make them more alike.

'We'll never have the same starting point,' Tony complained. 'We can't be identical twins. Even with my hair like

31

this.' He sat in his mother's living room on a newspaper, swamped in dark tatters of hair.

'It looks very nice, though,' Mark found himself saying.

'Nice?' Tony frowned. 'I thought we said that was a bourgeois word.'

The vodka-charged air bristled between them. The discussion of their physical difference, avoided till now, had knocked a chink in their cell's armour. It depressed them and made them aware of themselves as physical presences, potentially uncomfortable with each other. Changes must be made to the manifesto. They needed to appraise themselves in a new way. After the drink was finished, they were reduced to kneeling and measuring their cocks against each other, trying desperately not to touch. It was as hard to balance as it had been to make their erections appear to be in the cause of their science.

'Hold them together,' Mark said with a lucid, calm precision.

Tony looked at him oddly, and, with a slight tremble to his fingers, pressed the two shafts together.

'I'm taller, so we can't measure properly.' He lowered himself, managing to pump Mark gently as he did so. 'Too low.' He rose slowly, then down again.

'I'm a lot smaller, anyway,' Mark breathed.

'You might get bigger.'

'It doesn't matter.'

'If I do this.'

With a sublime nonchalance that won Mark's heart for ever, Tony bent down to suck him off. Mark stared down the line of his back, the crest of soft shining hair rounding his thighs.

It was the first time this had cropped up. They listened to the noises Tony made as he set to work, trying not to laugh. So warm; Mark felt he was bleeding, especially when Tony's teeth jagged on his foreskin.

The manifesto redrew itself in lurid terms, terms that were never articulated except in the wordless press and rustle of that first time. A new language of tenderness was generated between them. Mark looked down at Tony's head, absurd over Mark's opened jeans. His whole body compromised like this, down on Mark as if in worship. Mark put his hands on Tony's head to feel the new-cut hair. The feel of it thickened his cock, the world burgeoned beneath him, a sense of his own potential, as if this made everything suddenly possible. Words crept through his clenched teeth in a whole set of appendices to their original agreement.

He ran his fingers along Tony's throat, the soft quiver underneath. Tony came up to kiss him, and they embraced this particular taboo with aplomb. It was so much more unhealthy and immoral than the action of the hand that stroked Mark's prick until it coughed up phlegm-like semen, Mark pushing forwards, collapsing Tony beneath him as they kissed, squirming the mess between them. After this, Tony tried to fuck Mark. Acquiescing, struggling out of his clothes, he shivered and cried out when entered.

'There'll be lots of other times,' Tony said softly as they lay, a little apart, breathing more regularly, letting surprise settle in and dry off. 'So this is what we were up to all along. I had no idea. Fuck shoplifting. This is really living on the edge.'

Mark tugged his lifeless cock aside, felt the wet, like blood, smearing his thighs. It seemed like everything had been wrenched out of him. Disembowelled, he waited for morning.

Since last year they had done the bar up. It was bigger, wider, Art Deco with arched windows that saw the town roofs. This was the height of the pantomime rush, the week before Christmas, the theatre's grandest moment, with school parties filling the foyer, stairways and balconies. The kids were clustering about gold-framed photos of last year's stars.

'Remember Beauty and the horrible Beast? Remember last year?'

The kids nodded solemnly, gazing at Conrad the Wolf.

Mark saw Iris and Peggy bringing Sally up the stairwell. They noticed him and forged their way through, complaining about toilet queues.

A rush of softness filled him at the sight of Sally's school socks hanging down, the trepidation in her eyes as she eased past school friends who showed no sign of recognising her.

She was so quiet, so meek. She sat next to her father, waiting until he assured her that the lemonade really was for her, then sipping slowly at it. He was scared for her, learning to ride her life like a bike, up crowded theatre stairs. She had grandmothers for stabilisers, but how long before they fell away? Mark wouldn't care so much, but a crappy old bike, every scrap of it in some way second-hand, was all they could manage for her.

He suddenly realised why, at base, he fought so stubbornly against Sam's one-woman feud. It was because Sally needed Peggy and Iris so much. Sam didn't love her daughter enough. Sally needed these surrogates, and she knew it herself.

'Thanks for taking her,' Mark said.

'Are you enjoying the show, Sally love?' Iris bellowed, patting her fuchsia coat as if looking for something.

Sally looked up as she carefully lowered her glass. She beamed brilliantly. 'I just love it. It's all so easy.'

Peggy, who had just been saying how technological the theatre had become, with lasers and whatnot, asked, 'What do you mean by easy?'

Iris smiled kindly, as she often did to soften Peggy's occasional bluntness.

'Life is so easy in there. It's all love and magic.'

The two grandmothers cooed over this until the end-of-interval bell rang, starting a swift exodus to the stairs. Mark slipped an arm around his daughter and gave her a tight hug.

'I'm glad we thought of you, Sally Kelly. You were a good idea.'

She smiled.

During the second act of the show, Mark leaned to offer Sally a wine gum. Her hands were full. Cupped in her palms she held a tiny, sleeping terrapin, her own name etched on its shell in nail varnish.

Mark looked away and forgot all about it until they climbed aboard the school coach to go home.

'Sally,' he said as they sat in place. 'You haven't got a terrapin with you, have you?'

'No, Dad.'

He nodded. The coach pulled away. She had left it in the theatre. Mark was obscurely pleased.

Six

We knew all about each other's inadequacies. It was part of the bargain. We would compensate for each other, cover each other's blind spots as we brazened life through, walking abreast. We were inseparable.

I wonder about Victor Frankenstein. My reading – for my course – has become a little sidetracked; I've read *Frankenstein* twice this week. It was because my library privileges have been temporarily withheld too, mind, and I can't get anything new just yet. But luckily I still had this one. Have you read it, Mark? Have you ever wondered exactly what is going on in that book?

This is the sort of thing you get to thinking about on a course like mine. You start to take things apart, to wonder exactly what they're really saying. Books aren't just decoration, it turns out. They're not just stories, icing on the cake of real life. It's what they don't say that's important, apparently. And something is going on in my copy of *Frankenstein*. It is as if it is somehow infested; this book has bedbugs. When I read, something darts across the yellowed pages, just ahead of my eyes. I read and reread, hoping to track it down, yet fearing infection. Something nags at me.

In case you haven't read it, it's a book about betrayal.

In case you've only seen the film, it's really a book about love. About loving someone so much and having it thrown back in your face, you turn entirely the other way; meticulously, systematically, you take to bits and pieces the circumstantial impedimenta that hedge in and create the beloved's life. Hatred takes over; hatred is the dark, glossy, bloody obverse of a love that is fused by another's obstinacy. Fused into molten rivulets, as in welding.

It's a difficult book; I haven't figured it out yet. Franken-stein makes the monster; he wants to take him apart. Yet it is the monster who also hates and wants to take his creator's life apart, bit by murderous bit. I think, perhaps, they are in love.

Somehow they can't cope with it. This is a long time ago, this book. Still, I am told by my study notes that it is widely regarded as the world's first science-fiction novel. Surely in science fiction the wildly outlandish is permitted existence? Couldn't they have come to some kind of settlement up on that mountain; faced the truth, in the teeth of the tempest, about their feelings for each other?

We did, didn't we, Mark? In the early seventies. It was different from the nineteenth century. It was easier, perhaps, to feel easy about messing about with each other. Everyone was queer, it seemed for a time. You only had to turn on the telly. Or maybe we just saw it like that. We created the world we wanted to see, in the glorious haze we set up in our nonchalance for convention.

Who created whom? That's what it comes down to, I suppose. And, I suppose, we could say that we at first attempted to create each other, each in the image of the other. Naturally it couldn't work, but it got us together. It worked in as much as it got us sleeping together.

I could never believe how easy it was. I never thought, at first, that you were being natural. I thought you were putting it on, to please me, to come up to my level, that you were submitting to some glorious image of ourselves. But you seemed keen enough. I was, despite our wanting to be twins, the elder brother in that respect. I brought you on by hand, you might say. You had no idea what I'd already been up to. For me, there had never been a first time. I seduced you, Mark; the innocence was all yours. There was no mutual ground-breaking or discovery; nothing natural about it. And perhaps this was the first betrayal: mine.

But yours was the bigger. Oh, yes. You grew to fill up the mythological space I had cleared for you. We both outgrew the twins thing. Sticking together, walking abreast, or sleeping squashed together with secretions gluing our flesh, we matured enough to realise we still had separate agendas to fulfil. You started your tattoo thing when you were sixteen. A rose across one nipple, huge and garish. You had been reading Genet. I watched. But I had seen you naked. And as the weeks stretched by, taut as your stomach, the artist's head poised above it, scrawling away, I thanked my lucky stars that I had been there first. Now, I thought to myself, whoever came after me, because I knew they would, would never know you as wholly as I did.

Samantha lives with you. Samantha has given birth to your child. You and Samantha have a home and she sees you every day. She has the luxury of growing bored with you. She can afford indifference to Mark Kelly, and from what your letters say, indifference is the word for it. I oscillate between extreme emotions, but maybe that's just me. But she will never know you whole. I imagine you sleeping together. You are in armour and, in the end, impervious to her.

Seven

Tracey came off her mid-morning tea break feeling stunned. She had been allowed ten extra minutes. Sam's voice crackled through the intercom into the breezeblocked corridor where they were allowed to smoke and informed her that she could have a bit longer; Sam was enjoying herself on the floor. Tracey lit another fag in celebration as the music in the shop – a Madonna compilation – doubled its volume and could be felt vibrating in the brick at her back. The extra fag made her feel sickly, but she went back to work smiling and surprised.

'You're cheerful today,' she told Sam, whom she found rearranging a display, jogging lightly on her toes to 'Vogue'.

'All you need is your own imagination . . .' sang the supervisor. When Tracey looked carefully, however, Sam's eyes were hard and she was singing through gritted teeth. Her handiwork with the display, too, was inaccurate and seemed to be more for the sake of something to do. She wielded a staple gun ferociously and said nothing when a woman, right in front of them, knocked a number of slips off their hangers and left them lying there on the mustard-coloured carpet.

'Are you all right?'

'I'm on my break now.' Sam grinned, slinging down the tools of her trade. 'You'll manage if I take a little longer than usual, won't you?'

Tracey nodded dumbly, gazing at the wreckage of the display. It was of winter scarves and shawls, all of them pinned to the walls. Sam had wanted a Bedouin-tent effect and had ended up with a jumble sale.

'Yes, I might take a little longer, because I'm going to take those boxes down to the crusher. It'll save you a job.'

Samantha waltzed off, singing again. Tracey sorted out the fallen slips and went to the till. Almost immediately a queue

39

started to form and, as she served, she phoned Letitia, the supervisor in the Bishop Auckland branch. Letitia had trained here, under Sam, and occasionally had helpful hints for Tracey.

It sounded as if they had Prince on in Bishop Auckland. 'It's bad news, I'm afraid,' Letitia warned. 'That's *exactly* what she's like when something *really* bad is about to happen. You watch yourself, Tracey.'

At least, Tracey thought, fiddling with the Access machine, and her customer watched anxiously as it ground across her precious card, they don't have intrigues like this going on in McDonald's. They're rushed off their feet at Christmastime, but they don't get time for anything personal. Her boyfriend Hugh worked across the road in McDonald's. Usually she thought she was one up on him, working here. He had a big boil coming on the back of his neck, from the grease.

As Sam stomped her way down the back corridor, footsteps resounding ahead and behind, she felt herself growing lighter on her feet. She felt superpowered; it took the merest effort to open the steel concertina doors of the lift to the basement. With a deft flick of the wrist she wrenched them open, and set about slinging the useless cardboard into the dusty alcove. This should have been done weeks ago, but it was fitting to her present mood. A good pile built up inside the lift of partly collapsed boxes spilling cellophane and tissue paper. Even, she noticed as she climbed in with this detritus (having to stand on the pile, there was so little room), a number of delivery notes and seconds, strewn about. Today she couldn't care less. Sam slammed the doors and jabbed ferociously at the buttoned labelled B.

What had made her feel light and strong like this was the shedding of guilt. Too often had she stolen into the basement for an extended fag break and felt creepily guilty about it. While she was down there, with the cardboard crusher glinting its metal teeth, the cardboard riding up under the wire mesh as if in some ghastly parody of copulation, she often saw Mark staring at her from the jagged shadows, his tattoos pricked out in the scant light. But not today.

The lift shuddered and jolted. She thought she'd just die if it stuck now. Already she was slightly late. It would be entirely typical if she were late. Thanks, God. But the lift resumed its surly descent. Sam had a horror of God. It was because of God that she still thought, in her heart of hearts, that she had killed her father at the age of fourteen. And that was where the guilt sprang from.

Her father was a religious maniac. When he drew pictures for Sam it had always been scenes from the Bible. She never had annuals for Christmas; she was given instead, in annual instalments, his masterwork, a lavish comic-strip adaptation of the Old Testament. It was all disasters and fingers pointing out of tempests. Her mother hid the carefully bound volumes each Boxing Day, in case they gave Sam nightmares.

They still did and, when her father was dying, during her early teens, Sam found herself digging out the complete cycle of his work to read to him as he lay in the back parlour, coughing. The wallpaper was peppered with large red roses. Blood clots, she thought, retched up in the night. When she reread the captions of his comic strip and described to him the pictures (his eyesight went first) he had meticulously painted years before, she found that the pictures, glimpsed only once by her, each year after Christmas dinner, had been printed indelibly in her memory. She remembered each nuance, each twisted expression, each burning branch. She never knew what her father was dying of, painfully and inexorably; she still didn't know. When she reread the Old Testament comic strip to him, she found that he had mixed his captions up in places. Here and there, the fervour of his religious convictions had gripped him so hard that he had the wrong people saying the wrong things. Several balloons were attributed to goats or servants, and the hand of the Old Testament God tended, at times, to point in arbitrary directions.

Peggy never warned her how little time there was. The day he died, Sam was arguing with him about Moses, annoyed by a wasp in the airless room. As she ranted about the burning bush having the lines that the lawgiver ought to have, and her father rattled his final imperatives, she stalked the insect to the windowsill and brought down this particular hardbound

41

volume, crushing it, with a loud bang. Her father expired with a gasp of holy fright.

Guilt dogged Sam, but not today. When the lift reached the shrouded basement, she hauled the cardboard across the concrete towards the corner where the inert crushing machine bulked. Piece by piece she worked; fastidiously yet rapidly, eventually pushing down her first load and standing back against the railing as the machine screeched into action. Then Bob stepped out of the shadows in his Prussian-blue uniform. He even had his helmet on.

'In case I get seen by one of your security guards,' he explained as she stroked his blue-black chin. 'I can pretend to be on duty down here.'

The security guards could appear at any time. When Sam had first learned to use the crusher, one had taken to creeping up behind her with handy tips.

'But I also left it on because I know you like it.'

He had neglected to shave, because she liked that too. He disengaged and set about making a rough bed against the wall out of cardboard and polythene. Sam resented Mark's continuous shaving. It was because of his tattoos. Everything went; she had been startled, at first, at the sight of him, one arm raised, peering in the bathroom mirror, seeing to an armpit. Then they took to shaving each other's legs in the bath, and it had been fun. But now she understood it was all narcissism. Bob had said as much, said Mark sounded queer, really, but Sam had let it drop at that. She found, though, that she resented having a hairless husband. His missing pubic hair weighed especially heavy here. She still felt bewildered and a little odd about that. Who was going to see the markings there anyway? Why had he had them done in the first place? It made him almost like a child and it gave her the horrors sometimes. She thought about the colours growing fainter as he grew erect, like a balloon, then turning brighter again in detumescence.

So here it was reassuring, it felt real, to have Bob's hair ground and pressing to her own. She savoured the rasp of their markings of maturity. The cardboard sagged and buckled beneath them, adapting to the shapes they threw on the floor, shoes scraping the dust, raising little clouds. Bob was spread right across her and she luxuriated in the sense of him covering her, a voluptuous, darkly uniformed wrap that worked and worked at her, prising open sections of her clothing with blunt fingers while she pressed herself down on his eager, clumsy prick. It was different, this shocking, abrupt sex with a police officer. When Mark made love to her, she was an object in space, almost free-floating; his possibilities, at their best, seemed endless. Here she was a front, an assemblage of female parts crammed on her back in musty-smelling garbage, for Bob to ease himself into and rummage against. Sometimes she found this preferable, however. She caught the tip of his cock with her hand, guided it into herself and found he altered the rhythm of his thrusts very little. He was nearly oblivious to her; for him she was a tender wall at which he could throw himself, time and again. Quickening his already ridiculous pace, he mistook her anger for excitement.

The guilt was missing today and she thought that it was the guilt and the thought of being found out that had made this rough, easy sex with Bob worthwhile. There he was, running through and through her, and she had no sense of what that ludicrous organ was doing inside her walls. This pleasure was, perhaps, a numb one; so near, so far. She had a sense of the inside of herself, moist and aching for simply the right touch; and Bob probing uselessly like a cack-handed water diviner, an inept xylomancer, bless him; but he was trying. She imagined the terrible pleasure of being starving, yet not able to eat from a sumptuous buffet. The saliva creeping up your 'gums' tidemarks, threatening to spill. Despite herself, she chose to ignore the numb throb of Bob's workaday fucking and concentrated on the bizarrely tender rustling of his hair.

He came with a wrenching cry that filled the entire basement, which used to be a fairly sizeable car park. He collapsed to one side, slick hips still juddering to a faint pulse, trapped in his bones as if he were an overheated engine after a strenuous run. His shirttails were glued to his stomach, his eyes shrouded and misty. Sam felt the dusty chill of the basement running right up her cunt, so she hooked free her arms to pull up her knickers. Her fine blade of anger had lost its thrilling edge as a consequence of their swift tumble, and she felt able to deal with its cause. She jabbed Bob back to life and handed him the letter from her blouse pocket.

'I found this,' she said in a voice she thought was astonishingly clear. 'This morning. It came this morning.'

He struggled up, still panting. She saw his penis retract almost completely inside him as he took the violet notepaper. She stared at the red, rumpled foreskin in its fluffed-up setting of hair and thought, He's so natural and unspoiled, this one.

Bob had cropped up initially in the line of duty. Soon after Sally was proclaimed imminent, Mark vanished.

They had been at the fair. Sam was driving a dodgem car and Mark was clinging to the rod that stuck out of its back and brushed with the ceiling, showering blue sparks. Sam drove recklessly and unfairly, barging into everyone, even when the proprietor screamed at her to stop. He looked unwashed; a Gypsy type by the look of him, so she took no notice. Mark clung on.

'We're pregnant!' Sam howled as they collided with two rough-looking lads in a bright pink car.

Mark inhaled deeply; burning rubber and undercooked hamburger. A desolate sense of danger overtook him. 'Take your fucking foot off the pedal,' he yelled, trying to grab the wheel. 'What do you think you're doing if –'

She cackled and veered wildly, trying to shrug him off. The steering wheel jammed and they were thrown out of the congested whirl at the centre of the rubber floor, rebounding gently to the side. The motor cut out beneath them. 'Look, they've stopped our go now.' She cursed, clambering out. He tried to take her arms. She frowned. 'That's you, messing about on the back. They don't like that.'

'How can you tell me you're pregnant when you're driving a dodgem car?'

She hopped off the wooden platform, allowing the next lot through. He followed.

'Have you got no sense of responsibility? What if . . . I mean, how do you think I feel, being told . . . ?'

Sam was already in another queue; she wanted to be put in a

dark cage and whirled about in the sky, far above everybody's heads.

'What are you trying to do?' Mark cried, seizing her hands.

'I *was* trying to enjoy myself.'

'What if you damage . . . our child?'

'And what about *me*, Mark?' she flashed dangerously.

Mark waited by the rifle range when she went up in the cage. They went up in a group of ten, each strapped into place against a black grating that was silhouetted gruesomely against the murky evening sky when the cage was sent up to revolve, at first slowly, then faster . . .

He vomited round the back of the amusements, and played on fruit machines till she had finished. Let her look for me, he thought.

'Mark, isn't it?'

He kept his eyes on the one-armed bandit until the fruits stopped whirling and he knew he hadn't won anything. He looked round to see a young bloke in a blazer, longish hair, white shirt and jeans. He was very pale. 'Yeah?'

'We . . . I mean, I'm Vince. We met, um, a while ago, one summer in Darlington. Um.'

'Oh.'

They stared at each other blandly, Vince kicking at the grass, which was flattened here inside the hot marquee. He smiled, a little shyly. 'What are you doing now?'

'I'm married,' Mark said. 'I'm really happy.'

'Right.' Vince shrugged. 'Well, it's funny seeing you.'

'Yeah. A coincidence.'

'See you around then.' Vince couldn't resist a parting shot before swanning off. 'Have a nice life, love.'

Mark rested his head against the cool metal of the one-armed bandit. He couldn't even remember sleeping with that bloke. He remembered his face . . . but never . . . but there were all sorts of things that had gone on. He remembered certain times, gruff and apologetic encounters in the open air . . . nothing to warrant abstracted reminiscences like that one, though. That Vince obviously read more into whatever went on. Mark was rueful; tattooed, he couldn't help standing out. Especially naked; there was no anonymity for him.

And here was Sam, breaking into his reverie and nausea with a whiff of brandy on her breath and gloating over her triumph. She was surprised at him, making a show of himself, slumped over the amusements. When he looked at her, it was through tears.

'Listen, the baby's fine. We're both fine.'

'I can't . . . it's the responsibility, Sam . . .'

Gently and coaxingly she had lectured him on how he was eminently suited to taking up that responsibility. He knew that already; what he meant was, Sam's recklessness terrified him. It was almost more than he could take.

Three days later he disappeared. At first Sam thought it had nothing to do with the baby; she gave him a fraught twenty-four hours and then called the police to list him as a missing person. That was when Bob came to the house to take her statement.

'He just popped out to the all-night garage for cigarettes,' she began, as they both sipped their tea. She was hugging a cushion to her stomach, she realised; for comfort and practice.

Bob nodded at her, hung on every word, writing down every scrap she uttered. She was fascinated by his chin and the livid red of his hands. You could see the white flex of his knuckles working beneath as he scribbled. I'm going off my head, she thought. It's all too much.

'You hear this all the time, don't you?'

Bob smiled reassuringly. 'Every case is different.'

'No, but the "he just popped out" bit.'

'Well, it turns up quite often, yes. But how else do people disappear if not by popping out? They never have a fanfare. They all do it quietly.'

'But you think he's upped and left me.'

Bob carefully brought her round to describing her husband and mentioning any distinctive marks he might have. It was ten minutes later when she suddenly burst out, 'But he's got all-over body tattoos! You're bound to find him!'

The policeman was young and eager and very considerate. Sam told him about the pregnancy and, as time passed, about

Mark's evident qualms, their story, their song, his bisexuality and her doubts that he could hack it. Bob was appalled.

'How could he go after anybody else with a beautiful wife like you?' he said, in the high-pitched voice people often put on to denote incredulity. On Sam it worked and she smiled tearfully. 'And as for going after –' he shuddered perceptibly – 'queers, well, that's revolting. I shouldn't say this, but I think you're well shot of him.'

Sam was torn. 'You think he's gone off with someone, with some man?'

Bob shrugged diffidently; a man-of-the-world shrug, a we-see-all-sorts-of-queer-buggers-down-the-station shrug. And here he was, six years later, shrugging at her again as he tucked himself into his trousers and stood up in the basement of the shopping arcade.

'It's off some bloke?'

'It's off *the* bloke. The fucking love of my fucking husband's life – Tony. I thought we'd heard the last. He's been writing to him the whole time.'

Bob handed back the letter. Suddenly he looked sick. 'You think he's still . . . seeing this Tony, on the sly?'

She snorted. 'Hardly. Tony's in prison, has been since before we were married.'

She watched what she was saying; not 'almost at the same time as we were married'. She never told Bob that their getting married in the first place could be attributed to an imprisoning offence of Tony's.

'Your fucking husband!' Bob spat. He had met Mark only once, and hated him. Mark had returned after three days of hitching around the country, 'getting his head together'. He came back filthy and found his wife being comforted by the law. Luckily the law had his clothes back on.

'I couldn't have lived if Tony hadn't been away,' Sam said. 'I didn't think they were in touch. I didn't even know they let prisoners send letters out into the outside world.'

Her policeman nodded wisely. 'Oh, yes.' He watched her crumple the letter.

'He's so vile about me.'

'Twisted.'

'Prison must turn them . . .'

'Turned from the start, if you ask me.'

She sighed. 'Don't start on that. I've accepted Mark. He's safe, we're all safe . . . if I can accept his . . .' She gasped; Bob had seized her wrist.

'I'll tell you one thing, pet – you don't get lilac-coloured notepaper and envelopes in prison.'

'You what?'

'The bastard's lying or he's mad as a bloody hatter – but he's not in gaol; I'll tell you that for nowt.'

Eight

The world is very small, or so it seemed to Iris. She was peeling vegetables on Christmas Eve. She whittled and rolled a smooth yellow potato round in her hands, until it disappeared almost into nothing.

These were preparations for tomorrow's dinner. Tonight they were eating out, but Iris liked to have things ready.

Yes, it's all so small and, really, if one puts one's mind to it, well, anything can be accomplished. We arrive at the states we are in through a simple matter of choice, whether conscious or not. Iris believed that all her choices had been conscious and rational. Her life had been a ragged and bumpy, but ultimately safe, progression towards this point: living happily with Peg in this cosy house on the outskirts of a new town in the northeast. It was a small, ossified and provincial corner of the world, but she had chosen it, she thought.

The idea of choice is a terrifying one. The roads not taken are dizzyingly profuse. People choose too early if they are lucky enough to panic and choose at all. They pick one turn-off and stick with it.

Iris liked to think of her style of living as rather like the way she had observed working-class people eat spaghetti. Not teasing out and winding up strands, but using knife and fork to chop it into shreds, then wolfing the whole lot down. Certainly that was the way Mark Kelly had eaten spaghetti, at their last meal together.

In the end, though, you have to limit yourself. God knows, life imposes its own limitations, but you must make your own, too, so you don't send yourself bananas in the vertiginous buffet of lifestyle options. So yes, she could see that she was, in a sense, exiling herself to this place and this life, but she thought that was probably all right. She was happy and she was aware she was limiting herself for the right reasons; she was in love.

Iris plunked the shaved potatoes one by one into the pan to save them going brown. She gave a self-deprecating chuckle. Still in love; a miracle in itself.

In this town she behaved as if in exile. She moved through the shopping centre unsure of the language. In the bakery and the newsagent's they looked blankly at her because of her accent, which was perceived as posh. Her clothes were old but of good quality. That showed in the way they had worn and *were* worn. She was a Liberty-print island adrift in a town where people wore shell suits to shop. And yet, originally, Iris's family had come from this place, had owned a farm on the flat, slightly boggy land where Mark and Sam's council estate had been built. She ought to feel quite rooted.

One morning, about a year ago, Iris had taken a walk with Mark and little Sally to a broad patch of waste ground at the back of that estate. The wind whipped the long yellow grasses as she hunted around for evidence of rubble beneath the undergrowth. She gained her bearings from the trees that were still standing and soon found the ragged foundations of the farmhouse, partially collapsed into the mildewed cellar.

'It's intact,' she breathed, hands on knees and peering into the hole. She wished she had brought a torch and could explore the dank space where she and her brothers had held Hallowe'en parties, ritual sacrifices and pretend opium dens with stolen cigars.

Keeping Sally back at a safe distance, Mark said, 'It's terrible. Somebody could fall and break their neck in that.'

Briskly she chopped broccoli and carrots. She had a heavy chopping board and a good knife so sharp it whistled. 'Expensive utensils,' she heard Mark say. 'You can't beat the best.' He would say it as a double-edged compliment; he thought her middle-class and complacent, she was sure. Probably because she went on about Florence and Paris, and so on. In conversation sometimes she could feel Mark cringing and wriggling about.

Iris continued to wield her expensive utensils with aplomb.

When it comes to quality, we have to wrench the best we

can out of life. She couldn't have an ill-equipped kitchen if she tried, and what point would she be proving if she did away with her six-speed blender and coffee-bean grinder? Would it make her more authentically a part of this town where, as far as she could see, salad dressing was as rare and fabulous as homosexuality?

No, there were choices to be made and decisions to be stuck to. Iris dedicated herself to being bourgeois, happy, and loyal to those closest to her with every fibre of her expansive being. Mark might think she was wrong, attempt to spread his own conscience and meagre largesse a little thinner, further afield, but she felt she must be true to her own essential self.

Peggy joined her in the kitchen as Handel's *Messiah* began once more – the fourth time that day – on the radio.

'For heaven's sake, put some clothes on. The windows are open. And isn't it sacrilegious to prepare Christmas dinner in the nude?'

Hallelujah!

Outside it was pattering on to snow; dry flakes skittered across the box hedges and settled on the grass. The opened windows bloomed on one side with kitchen steam, the other with frost. Their house was warm and fragrant, and surely Peggy could see the bliss in preparing dinner in the nude with the joyous certainty that here she was happy and safe?

And, as the afternoon swept into an evening of a grainy matt grey, Iris took Peggy into her arms and kissed her slowly, not, as she might have liked, under traditional mistletoe, but just beside a vast blue vase of hot-pink lilies.

'You must spend a fortune on flowers,' Sam had sneered, the last pre-feud time she deigned to visit. It was true; in each corner nodded the extravagant heads of the season's most expensive blooms.

Iris had whirled about. 'Yes! I want this house to be like a living Georgia O'Keeffe exhibition! Cunts everywhere you look!'

That remark hadn't gone down at all well. Only Mark smiled politely, half understanding.

Today, outside, the dry snow was clogging the narrow

paths and silting up the window ledges, where its crust was starting to melt from the heat of the oven.

Iris is as old as the hills. Except, in this landscape, there are precious few of those. It is one brisk gallop from the North Sea in the east to the Pennines in the west. Let us say, then, that Iris feels herself to be one of the oldest standing objects in that flattish expanse.

When it comes to official documentation she is extremely cagey, avoiding personal details whenever possible. When a few particulars are required, she uncaps her gold fountain pen with an expression of disgruntlement and fabricates a pack of lies. A number of times now the cottage has been visited by besuited young men with clipboards, come to clear up the discrepancies left in Iris's wake.

As her partner, Margaret worries about all this. She feels that somehow Iris's statements about her date of birth, parentage, nationality and other things will land them in hot water. Iris's insouciance when the subject is raised infuriates Peg. These games Iris plays nag at Peggy late at night, not so much for what they might bode in her own relationship with Iris, but because she fears the consequences. Surely one can't get through life without being to some extent accounted for in official files?

Peggy imagines the baying of wolves – pencils, clipboards twitching – all around the magic circle of their cottage. It is as if Iris is refusing, quite literally, to be penned in.

Peggy worries that apparent illegitimacy only compounds the problem of their being lovers. Because, secretly, this is still a problem for Peggy. She would never admit this, but she hopes that maybe authority would turn a blind eye if they were fully documented. Two old women living together; it's for the company, they don't want to end up going into sheltered accommodation. They're supporting each other. It's sensible, even touching; it's a solution to the problem of single and unwanted pensioners. Peggy and Iris would agree that they do not want to be written off, but Peggy would prefer that they were both adequately written up. If only for the extra pension.

She doesn't know how old Iris is and daren't ask in any way other than jokily. And jokily always gets the reply, 'Four hundred and seventy-three years exactly.' She knows that her partner must be of pensionable age. Iris's flesh bears the signs of a dignified depreciation. Like wood that has been refined with continuous use into an elegant, very nearly baroque, curvature. A wood strengthened by the giving and taking of bodily oils; a tensile strength lovingly transmitted. Her skin has the texture of vellum so expensive you could ponder your opening sentence for ever. Touching this is a luxurious possibility, endlessly deferred, richly indulged. Its mature flawlessness brazenly exhibits a zero degree of writing; Iris reclining naked presents her lover with a fabulous display, a promise of an experience beyond words, beyond language. This is why the pair of them – at least, while at home and with the windows on winter mornings shut – are nudists. Peggy's body is not quite so smooth and inarticulate. Wrinkles, stretch marks and various scarrings speak volumes. Although it is as brazen a body as Iris's, it speaks a very different story.

So, how old is Iris?

Hallelujah . . .

She is still holding her in the kitchen on the morning of Christmas Eve.

She is still holding her. Iris mulls this phrase over as she continues to hold Peggy, rocking gently back and forth to Handel.

When Iris used to be a novelist, many, many moons ago, she never really hit upon this problem of pronouns and representation because of the simple fact that she never wrote explicitly about lesbian relationships. And in fiction, especially when documenting anything more casual than carnal knowledge, it is easy to separate the pronouns out – like sifting flour – and not to let them clash in ambiguity.

It might prove a problem, should she take up the pen again some day and, in this much more enlightened age, dabble with a spot of authentic realism. She might relish the quandary of pronoun etiquette.

She finds herself stroking the flesh of Peggy's forearm. She hadn't realised she was doing it, and when she does she starts to consider the elasticity, the durability of flesh and how it will decide what it fancies doing. Her own has seen her through a great number of scrapes.

As if in response, Peggy starts up the old, jokey conversation.

'How old are you tomorrow then, Iris?'

She murmurs this into Iris's shoulder. Her skin smells of brandy as if she has been using it as a scent.

Christmas Day is Iris's birthday. Even this sounds implausible to Peggy, though she submits to it as a mutually convenient fiction.

'Let me see. Well, I believe I'm four hundred and seventy-four this time.'

'I thought you might be. And when do I get a proper answer?'

'Was mine improper?'

'I mean, true.'

Iris looks at her with a frown. Concernedly she asks, 'Have you ever read *Orlando*?'

'Yes.'

'Well then, prepare yourself for a shock.'

Peggy read *Orlando* a couple of years ago because Iris told her to. All her reading has been directed by Iris these past few years, and Iris knows it.

'I'm like Orlando,' Iris declares, and Peggy is embarrassed by her earnestness.

'You mean heterosexual?'

'No.'

'You mean transsexual?'

'No. Yes. I mean . . . I'm four hundred and seventy-four years old.'

'Is that how old Orlando was, then?'

'That's beside the point,' Iris snaps. 'What I mean is, I'm very, very old.'

'I see,' Peggy says flatly.

Iris asks gently, 'Is that what you wanted to know?'

'I suppose so. Yes.'

'Why now?'

'Oh.' Peggy buries herself in their embrace once more. 'The census people have been round. We're going to have a hellish council-tax bill.'

'Oh.'

The hallelujahs on the radio have petered out by now.

'Iris?'

'Yes?'

'Have you changed sex, too? Like in the novel?'

Iris nods solemnly. 'Four – no, five times.'

We'll leave them for a little while. As I said earlier, Iris knows all about the multiplicitous choices available in a lifetime, the absolute terror of the roads not taken. The reason she knows is that, on the whole, she has taken most of them.

Let us draw a veil of darkening air and random clots of wet sleet to allow Peggy to digest the idea of so many decisions in one, terribly prolonged lifetime. Or, alternatively, to digest the fact that her lover is insane. There is a lot to take in.

In any event, whether old or mad, Iris has abruptly declared her seniority.

Imagine Peggy in this situation.

When your lover is so much older than you, older than the hills, and really, you had no idea, no conception, that you had been hoodwinked by a flesh that is vellum and rich in a manner you thought only youth could possibly be, you feel, perhaps, a little dwarfed in the complex shadows cast by these hypothetical hills.

Nine

Christmas Eve's afternoon saw Mark with a glass of gin in one hand, watching a rerun of *Rebecca* on Channel Four. A pale orange light, refracted through the messy weather outside, shone off each of the living room's mirrors in turn and, for a good half-hour, rendered the TV screen opaque. Mark stared at the grey cube, listened to the voices, and waited for the light to die. He sipped his drink and dangled his other hand in a carton of Turkish delight. The powdered pink and yellow sweets rubbed icing sugar onto what now seemed to him startlingly blue, mimeographed hands.

Only at particular moments did he remember his blueness. Not that he was wholly blue; closer inspection revealed him to be intricately multicoloured, as a number of people had found. However, from a distance, Mark read as simply blue.

He was worried about getting tonight's dinner ready in time. Not that it was his responsibility. Sam had taken over the whole affair and was insisting on dealing with it by herself. He was pleased, really, but time was creeping on and the kitchen was still clean-smelling and dark. Sam was in the bathroom and, to judge by the periodical squawk of Sello-tape, wrapping her presents. Her manner today was one of grim efficiency, a mood Mark had learned to slink away from. He had consented wordlessly to her supplying him with the *Radio Times*, the gin bottle and the best seat in the house for the afternoon's duration. His wife was set on getting things together at her own pace, and Mark knew his place in that scheme. So did Sally, usually. But Sally was with her mother.

Sam winced as she stood up, listening to her knees crack, watching the black circles give her momentary tunnel vision for rising too quickly, and gripped the cistern for support. The toilet flushed by accident. She was a bit shocked by her sudden apparent decrepitude, but she had, after all, spent a full hour kneeling on the bathroom floor, stooped forward in concentration in a mound of crumpled wrapping paper. Enough to give anyone tunnel vision. She rubbed her cold nose.

'Who is it?' she asked, and the knocking came again.

Rapid, impatient knocking; a child's, but that could mean Sally or Mark, really. Sam had been enjoying her peace. The heating had just come on, shuddering through the old radiator, seeping in waves through the carpet. The only carpet with decent pile in the whole flat. The heat brought out a faint aroma of piss. Why can't men aim properly? she wondered.

'Mam, it's me.'

Sam opened the door and Sally shot in, slamming it behind her.

'He didn't hear me come in, I don't think.'

Sitting back on the carpet, Sam rested herself against the side of the bath. 'What have you got there?' she asked.

Sam detested that tone in her own voice when she spoke to Sally, whenever mother and daughter were together. It was part parodic baby talk, part wearied rhetoric; as if she could barely conceive of this being before her as capable of replying. Indeed the logic of it seemed absurd; it was like addressing one of her own hands or feet and expecting an answer. This set up a tension whenever they were on their own together. A tension that Sally responded to by casting down her eyes and mumbling. Not shyness, exactly, but in sympathetic appreciation of the absurdity of her speaking.

'I need help. Wrapping this for Dad.'

And she held up for Sam's inspection a cellophaned bar of pink soap from the Body Shop. Sam sniffed. Strawberries.

'Do you think he's dirty?' Sam asked with a laugh, pleased with the easy naturalness of her question, but thinking at the same time, Has she bought me something too? Is this where Sally declares her allegiances?

'We can't tell if he's dirty or not,' Sally said. 'Because of his make-up.'

'Tattoos,' Sam corrected, reaching for an appropriate scrap of paper and the roll of tape.

'Do tattoos mean you don't have to wash?'

Biting tape, Sam shook her head. 'Your dad is the most obsessively clean person I've met. It's a wonder he hasn't washed himself white again. But you would never be able to tell if he was dirty, would you?'

'Turtles are dirty. They bask in mud at school.'

Sam was about to ask one of those adult-to-child questions which flatter the child with a semblance of genuine interest. She was going to ask, 'Would *you* like to be a turtle, Sally?' but she ditched this and asked instead, 'Would you like to have tattoos when you grow up?'

'Do girls have tattoos?'

'Some girls do. They don't show them off so much, I don't think, as men do.'

'Dad has them all over.'

'Yes.'

'I wouldn't like that. He stands out.'

Sally was looking past her mother now, at the carefully stacked wrapped presents. She said, 'I like that idea. The bows. Making them out of toilet paper.'

Surprised, Sam looked at the bows she had spent ages fiddling with, folding and securing with tape. Now they looked tatty and, where they had been somehow splashed with water, ripped through.

'Oh, it was just an idea I had.' She shrugged.

Turning to her mother, Sally smiled. 'I've got a very clever mam,' she said, stepped forward and hugged Sam. A chill ran through the mother, as if she had bumped into something fragile, realising too late.

Peggy was reassured by the fact that she and Iris were walking in step, although wordlessly. The brisk scrape of their heels sounded on the tarmac. They both knew the way to Sam's flat, even though the paths on the estate twisted, turned, doubled back, and they had only come this way a handful of times. It was as if they had separately rehearsed this walk in their minds' eyes and now when it came to it, the evening of reconciliation, their feet carried them firmly, deftly, almost instinctively. Peggy stole the occasional glance backwards, to see their footprints etched black in the sleet. This feeble deposit was both the colour and texture of pepper. As the council streetlights popped on, one by one, the air changed to the shade of bruised lemons.

Their footsteps carried out a calm and measured conversation, it seemed to Peggy. Iris's, of course, resounded more earnestly, as if her reverberations were felt more deeply into the earth beneath the tarmac, as if her musings simply went further down. Was this because she really was, as she claimed, about nine times as old as Peggy? Or was it because her shoes were patent leather? Peggy's had rubber soles.

But this was ridiculous. Peggy was all for a little mystery, a little light romance to perk up life together. Iris had gone too far, though, this time. She had had her joke, made herself a tad glamorous with all that talk of Orlando, but ever since then she had been sunk in what seemed to Peggy suspiciously like gloom. The atmosphere between them sagged with an indulgence on Iris's part. Since that particular conversation they hadn't touched at all. Iris had swanned off upstairs, leaving Peggy to finish chopping tomorrow's veg, then returned swathed in layers of violet and ostrich feathers. She had sat about the place until it was time to leave, silent, like a fagged-out Isadora Duncan.

Right now Peggy was nervous about the impending interview with Sam. She was about to enter a fortress barbed and set by her daughter at her most duplicitously welcoming. Peggy had to be calm in her mind and, above all, alert and undistracted. With Iris's funny mood pressing in, she would have a hell of a job on and already she could picture the resultant scene, should a foot be put wrong tonight.

'Why are you so quiet, Iris?'

Iris stopped for one moment in her tracks, her mouth pulled down in scorn as she looked at the black windows of the council houses. The streets were quite silent, aside from a distant, frenzied barking. Where had everyone gone? They seemed to have crept away, turned their lights off, hidden behind their settees, as if Christmas Eve were an alarming visitor, best avoided. When Iris walked on, Peggy noticed she had fallen out of step. Iris's words were punctuated by their dissonance.

'At the moment I'm thinking about my parents' land. The land here used to be a bit of bleak pasture. Christmas Eves past, say in the thirties, the grass would stand high and hard as the branches of trees. We'd have to fight our way to the frozen pond. The swans slept, those ridiculous, slender necks knuckled back onto their bodies. They looked like white fists, poking through ice. And the air smelled of clay, whitening out into bizarre shapes. Until spring the ground remained like pottery; my brothers and I walked on what we called china, sculpted by our own feet when the ground was still soft.'

'Oh,' Peggy said. 'Mind the dog shit,' she added, too late, but that was frozen, too.

'They've ripped the heart from this land,' Iris sighed. 'And replaced it with an alarm clock. Which doesn't work because the punctured chest keeps bleeding, pumps blood to this inadequate mechanism, rusts the metal and the inauthentic ticking has stopped quite dead.'

Now it was Peggy's turn to stop in her tracks. 'Iris, what the devil are you talking about?'

'I'm talking about a sense of history,' said her lover levelly.

'And you'd know about that,' Peggy sneered, 'Mrs Orlando.'

'Why are you being like this?'

'If you must know, I've had it up to here with your pretentious bloody twaddle. You could at least have a little sensitivity and see that I'm in for a hard time tonight with our Sam and all. Just shut up about yourself for a bit. I couldn't give nick about the land or your farm or bloody alarm clocks. Just think of me for a while.'

'Peggy, I . . . do nothing else'.

'Right.'

'I mean it. It's just that I've been thinking of everyone I've left behind in my past. Living as long as I have, I've had to forget about a good many loved ones. Owning up to my true age today . . . well, it's made me have to face my own immortality.'

Peggy gave a short, bitter laugh.

60

'Don't laugh at me! I'm standing here, telling you, I can't bear the fact that, whatever happens, I will live longer than you will, and I'm scared by that.'

'Bloody nonsense!' Peggy snapped. 'Don't talk to me about death.' Peggy had had her share. A thought struck her. 'Anyway, you've just said again, about growing up on this very land in the thirties with your brothers.'

'Yes,' Iris said glumly. 'The fifteen-thirties.'

'Oh, bugger off, will you?' Peggy had stopped at a garden gate. As she reached for the latch, she clumsily broke a series of icicles from the wood. 'We're here now. No more talk about history. This is now, and it's terrifying enough.' A child's silhouette appeared in the door's glass panel. 'Merry Christmas!' Peggy cried, swinging her shopping bag aloft.

'What have you been wrapping for me, then?'

Credits were rolling over *Rebecca*. Sam sat between Mark's knees. He was a bit dizzy from the gin. Smells of cooking bloomed all around them. He was impressed by Sam's sly competence in getting it all together. She rested her elbows on his thighs, drummed an ironic tattoo on the crotch of his jeans with her fingertips.

'You'll just have to see, won't you?'

'And will I be happy?'

Drink always did this to Mark. His most complicated sentiments flattened out into *faux-naïf* statements and he spoke with primary-coloured words. Always rather pleased with the effect, he felt that only then, pissed, was he expressing himself fully. Now he waited on her reply.

'I hope you'll be happy,' Sam smiled, drawing herself back slightly. 'With the way it all turns out. Now. Hold still. This is Christmas Eve, and I want to touch my husband's heart.'

Quickly she unbuttoned the front of his shirt, briefly exposed his chest, kissed his left nipple. Right in the centre of the blue clock face he had printed there.

Ten

I am an awful ironist. Actually, no; I am a wonderful ironist. It's just that I get carried away and do it a bit much. I'm sorry, Mark. You know how I am, that you have to take a pinch of salt with the way I pitch my salty wit. I'm not sure that Sam knows, however. In fact, I imagine she takes me pretty much at face value. And believes every word I write to you. Oh, dear.

I am aware by now that she reads the letters I send. It's something I've picked up on. I even tailor certain things for her delectation. Like my last one, full of raving insults hurled straight at her. I wonder how she took that. I picture her flat on her back in the basement of her shopping arcade with her policeman stooped above her, and she's mulling over my nasty missive. I wonder if that's how it really happened.

Did you know that she sees a policeman behind your back? Behind the cardboard crusher beneath the dress shop?

No, take it from me, and with a pinch of salt. It's all ironic, Mark. I'm pulling your leg. I'm taking the piss.

Observe those two euphemisms for verbal wit. Both are bodily. Is irony, my irony, quite so penetrating? Does it have a physical manifestation? Believe me, I am not malicious; my wit is meant to strike glancing blows only.

And you are armoured, Mark.

And me, I have decided that enough is enough.

Christmas is coming and I don't want to spend this one alone.

I think the time has come for some straight talking. I want to sort a few things out. Here I am – Jim'll Fucking Fix It – and I'm going to sort out our lives. All our lives. Watch me pass into the present; I'll insinuate myself into your current lives and I'll cause a disturbance. I'm moving in on you all.

Too long, too long I've been a disturbing memory, a ghost somewhere on your horizon. I want to make myself imminent. Sam, I assume you are reading this first, as usual. Let me warn you first. You, to whom I am an obscure, invisible enemy. I shall manifest myself from Mark's past, subtly as a virus. Here I come.

You, Sam, you and your jolly policeman friend were right. No; they don't hand out lilac writing paper in prisons. My lilac paper was a little scam, another piece of irony. I wondered how long it would take to click. It was, literally, a piece of textual irony. Fingering those delicate sheets, I wanted both you, Sam, and you, Mark, to reach separate and horrifying conclusions. The conclusion that, no, I wasn't really languishing at Her Majesty's leisure. She would never waste her pastel paper on convicts. No; I was languishing at Sam's leisure instead. I was waiting for the realisation to click and then, then I would strike.

Now, in fact.

Rest assured, Mark, I'm coming back for you.

See you soon,

Tony.

Eleven

'They're just darling,' Iris gasped as she fondled one of Mark's proffered golden cherubs, adding, 'darling' once more with affection.

'I thought you'd appreciate it.' Mark and Iris gazed together at the Kellys' Christmas tree, which Mark had arranged the previous afternoon. His chosen theme had been angels and fruit.

'Haven't the false grapes got a funny texture?'

'Plastic,' Mark grinned.

'Yes, but quite pleasant.' She weighed a pendulous clump thoughtfully in one hand.

'Let me take your coat,' he suggested and waited till she put her bags down. They were bursting, he noticed, with crackling parcels. Sam would have another go about the old dykes ruining her daughter. He took Iris's heavy fuchsia coat, under which he saw she was wearing an extremely baggy scarlet cardigan.

'Got to keep the chill out,' she said, 'I know; I dress like a bag lady, don't I?' Almost nervously she hugged that expansive girth and Mark felt ashamed of his staring. 'Peggy always ribs me about the number of layers I wear.'

'Does she tell you that you'll "never feel the benefit" when you won't take them off?'

'Something like that.'

Mark was surprised; he had never seen Iris anything less than skilfully and dynamically sure of herself. Here, in the corner of the flat's sitting room, dwarfed by the silver tree and cast in the magenta haze of its fairy lights, she was . . . well, flinching at almost everything he said.

He decided to put her at ease, as he would any visiting old dear. (But Iris, surely Iris never needed putting at ease? Once, even, he had seen Iris eat a whole half-pound of Quality Street as she shopped in Gateway, and throw away the box, unconcerned, before reaching the checkout. Iris lit cigarettes in libraries and complained there were no ashtrays. Nothing that was known could put Iris off her stroke.)

He said to her, 'Why don't we both dig our feet in and keep our many layers on for the evening?' Saying this, he winked broadly, and she saw, with a jolt, the bright green iris and blue pupil drawn on that eyelid.

'I think we shall need thick skins tonight.' She smiled, returning to fondle his fake fruit.

This was the cause of Iris's perturbation. Part of her was worrying at the door into the kitchen. As she exchanged Christmas chitchat with her ostensible son-in-law, the protective and responsible part of herself was prying its way through the serving hatch, under the door, into the damp heat of the kitchen, trying to listen in. She wanted to interpose her layered bulk between mother and daughter, and yet the sensible remnants of her scattered thoughts suspected strongly that this was simply not on.

Mark caught her glance. 'Don't worry.' He smiled. 'I'll fetch Sally in a moment. She's been in her bath long enough now. I'll get her ready for bed and bring her to see you both.'

And that would ease the tension they both could feel building up through the wall. Sally could become the focus for a while and teach them the true meaning of Christmas. Iris cursed herself inwardly. She remembered a swift jab of spite she had once felt towards Sam, newly pregnant and espousing the most banal of her views on Christmas: 'It's for the bairns, really, isn't it? And New Year's for the grown-ups. That's how it's always been.'

Iris had nearly choked on her own venom. I could tell you, she thought, of other Christmases. When children rarely existed as such; they were merely young animals, dressed and fed almost for amusement's sake. Those were brutal winters and the creatures often died. Here in the north we huddled by candlelight in halls and the music was rich and the dances were regimented. And Christmas – the solstitial rite – was all for adults. It represented the sharp end of the wedge, the frozen hinge of the year, and it was all about self-gratification.

Only adult human beings know fully about gratifying themselves. There is a vocabulary of sensuality acquired only by living and if childhood is anything, it is a bodily progress towards bearing the full weight that learning this language involves. Perhaps, Iris might have told Sam crossly, Christmas ought still to be for adults; a time for drinking themselves and fucking each other stupid. The New Year might better be for the as yet inarticulate children. They need the new year more than we do, surely. The articulate – the sensually articulate – tend to fall back into a satiated torpor. This is the meaning of decadence. So why not set the little bastards off on their own quest for decadence? Set them down on January the first, with the first crisp breeze in the air, the new orange mists rising. Let them begin their own search; leave us with our Christmas hangovers.

Iris meditated solemnly on the irony of herself and Mark relying on a child to deliver them from a sticky family situation. Like something from a sit com. The two queerest people she knew, and the most motherly by far.

The two real, natural mothers were meanwhile beginning to raise their voices behind closed doors.

Sam went wiping round the kitchen surfaces as they talked. Peggy restrained herself from commenting, though Sam's dishrag was making some surfaces dirtier than ever.

They had once had a terrible row about this. At sixteen Sam had left home for the first time because her mother accused her of deliberately spreading germs in her kitchen. Now this was Sam's own kitchen and it really wasn't Peggy's place to mention hygiene, not even if she was eating here tonight. She listened to Sam talk, but her gaze was fixed narrowly on the tannin-stained sink, which was wrist-deep in greasy brown water. There were tea bags bobbing about in it. Peggy had a wistful glimpse of Iris's kitchen, with its sanded, hard-worn surfaces, its glittering utensils.

Still, there was something touching about all this mess. It was the mess created by her younger family's daily lives.

Wallpaper, tablecloth, pictures on the wall, all clashed in uncomplementary shades of pink, mixing gingham, stripes and floral patterns. What made it cohere was the notion of family. Blood relationships, Iris would insist, always encourage bad taste. There, above the sink, hung a calendar made at school by Sally. One of those fluorescent-paint jobs, where they make a butterfly by folding the painted paper down the middle, opening it out again. Peggy wondered why she hadn't been offered a new calendar made by Sally. Sam's earrings, clumpy and fake, from her last day at work – this afternoon, in fact – lay at rest on a shelf, by the scales, like golden insects. On the table by the washing machine – which was on, as it always was here, drenching their little chat in consoling noise – was splayed open a Jeanette Winterson novel of Mark's. Peggy recognised it, Iris flicked through her books occasionally, a box of chocolates on her knee.

Seeing her mother notice this last item, Sam snatched it up on her next lap round with the dishrag and flipped it into the gap between washing machine and work surface. Then she flung open the oven door and went jabbing at the spitting roast potatoes with a fork.

Peggy couldn't help advising, 'Turn them over; those sides are done.' She added, 'You've made your own Christmas pudding!'

Sam, turning the roasties over, nodded with her head in the oven.

'I don't know how you've found the time. All that messing about, all those ingredients . . . I've seen them make them on daytime telly, and it looks an awful job. And you a working mother!'

Her daughter straightened up, saying, 'Oh, I quite enjoyed making that. And the Christmas cake. I made a huge, fuck-off Christmas cake, do you want to inspect it?'

Peggy held up her hands. 'Perhaps we can try a bit after dinner.'

'After dinner you'll be stuffed,' Sam promised.

'Oh . . . good.'

'No, I had a wonderful time making all that, a few Sundays ago. Getting my hands into the mixing bowl, all those

67

squelching ingredients, getting really dirty . . .' Fastidiously Sam turned the heat up on the cooker's rings.

'I've never been one for cooking,' said Peggy.

'Banana sandwiches.'

'Pardon?'

'I've just remembered,' Sam said. 'Banana sandwiches. Left on the table with crisps, when I used to come home from school. When you were up at the hospital with Dad, or when you were working. Sometimes a Mars bar, too.'

'Fancy remembering that, pet.' Peggy hesitated before glowing over fond memories.

'Didn't you used to call them "funny teas"? Those snacks we used to have, sometimes even when you were home? They *were* fun, I remember. I used to look forward to them. I even preferred them to sit-down, cooked meals when Dad was well. It was as if we were – I don't know – girls together. With banana and sugar sandwiches . . . and stuff . . .' She refilled both their glasses.

'Nursery food.' Peggy smiled. 'It's amazing you've ended up so slim. By your age, I'd gone to pot. Pot-bloody-shaped.'

'Do you know, it took me years to realise that those "funny teas" weren't just for fun? I realised they must have been when you were quite . . . when you were really hard up.'

'I can't really remember,' Peggy murmured into her glass, squinting as if at dregs.

'You were making the best of things. Making a virtue of them. I mean – sugar sandwiches! When I think back at all that, I can see clearly what you did. I was thinking about this the other day. It's just heart-breaking.'

The cooker's buzzer went off. Sam shrugged herself up from leaning against the linen closet and went to see to it.

She went on, 'I suppose I can only appreciate this now, the way you had to struggle through, salvage things, keeping me in the dark, because of my being a mother now. We're bonded in a particular way. We share things like that. I find myself struggling, keeping Sally in the dark, shielding her from the hard stuff, trying to make the visible stuff better.'

'You're doing a grand job with her.'

'There's so much, though, to keep her in the dark from.' As

68

she took the warmed dinner plates out from under the grill, they clanked and jarred on Peggy's nerves. 'It's why, Mam, I wanted you round tonight, really. Why I wanted us to talk again. Do you see? Because it's so hard.'

Peggy was itching to go and give her a hug. It was a visceral sensation, a welling-up, as if she could take three steps across the lino, enfold Sam and stroke away the size and age of her, cuddle her daughter back out of competence and adulthood. But Sam had two fistfuls of cutlery and was thoughtfully wiping each piece with the teatowel.

'I've messed up the timing a bit with the dinner. I think I've fucked the vegetables.'

'Never mind, pet. What's important is, we've had this talk.'

'Perhaps I'm not so domesticated, after all.'

Her mother was fixated for a moment by the green and purple butterfly calendar. The paint was so thick it had cracked in places; little chunks had dropped onto the draining board, where Sam's dishcloth had turned them into garish streaks.

'I think you're doing fine. And Mark's doing fine, too, considering. And don't worry about keeping Sally in the dark from things. Children find out . . .'

'But I do worry about that.'

'Trust your own feelings. She'll turn out how she turns out. You turned out all right, didn't you, with me?'

Sam dropped knives and forks loudly onto the pile of plates. 'I don't fucking want her to turn out like me.'

Something beat feebly at Peggy's inner ear. The aftershock of ringing cutlery, her own startled heartbeat. She swallowed, waited for Sam to continue.

Sam looked her mother in the eye. 'You, Mam, to be quite frank, never kept me in the dark enough.'

They sat down to dinner. Mark carved the turkey standing up in the candlelight, making it clear that he was doing it under duress and, as it were, between inverted commas. The women applauded likewise as he passed neat slivers round. Iris dished out more wine.

'Oh, what's this music?' she exclaimed, banging down her

glass and slopping a little on the cloth. Mark looked from the purple stain to Sam.

Sam said, 'It's a compilation tape Mark did for me, a few Christmases ago.'

Iris was shifting about in her seat, waggling her hands in time to the music. 'But this particular song – what is it?' Without waiting for a reply, she went on, 'You know how some pieces of music, some songs, the first time you hear them and every time afterwards, they make your insides jump up inside you? And want to be out?'

'Oh, yes,' Mark said.

'It's "Heroes",' Sam muttered, tactlessly dabbing at the stain, 'by David Bowie.' But a new song had begun – Marlene Dietrich intoning 'Give me the Man' – and the rest of the main course was taken up by a long story from Iris about the decadent nightlife of Berlin. Sam gritted her teeth all the way through; Mark was politely interested – and genuinely so, at one or two points; and Peggy looked down at what she was eating, wordlessly. She glanced fiercely at her partner only once, when Iris let it slip that she was talking about Berlin of the nineteen twenties, and had once appeared in the same cabaret as Dietrich herself.

'It was fabulous. You would have loved it.' She patted Mark's hand and crammed her mouth with sprouts.

'Shouldn't that make you about the same *age* as Marlene Dietrich?' asked Sam icily.

The ensuing pause fell unfortunately between tracks on the tape. 'Darling,' sighed Iris, 'you should never ask a lady her age.'

They lit cigarettes between courses. As if on cue, Iris produced a ridiculous holder which, they found, had a spring strong enough to catapult dead filters across the length of the table. They were beginning their fourth bottle of wine and moulding little balls out of melted candle wax when Mark went to deal with the pudding.

He reappeared in the doorway, sucking his fingers. 'Have you doused this in petrol, Sam? It almost blew up in my face.'

'Just light it,' she snapped, getting up from her seat. 'What's wrong with you? Oh, I'll do it.'

'Sit there,' Mark said, cross more suddenly than if he hadn't been drunk.

'Oh, *this* song!' Iris cried, toddling over to the hi-fi to turn up the volume. Nimrod boomed out of the speakers. Peggy felt, quite distinctly, the glass tremble at her lips.

Moments after Mark returned to the pudding (finding the sauce smouldering in the pan), Sally appeared in the dining room in her dressing gown, her hair fluffed up with static and clutching a stuffed koala bear to her chest.

'Darling!' Iris predictably burst out and went scuttling for her carrier bags. Sally looked a little alarmed.

Sam slammed down her glass and growled, 'Would you once – just once – say something without the words "fabulous" or "darling" in it?'

Yet it was Peggy who looked as if she had been slapped. And what made it worse for Peggy was that Iris didn't respond at all to Sam. She simply stopped in her tracks, clutching her bag and smiling foolishly.

Sam added, 'And could you please stop talking about yourself all the time?'

'Have you . . .' Peggy began tentatively, turning to Sally, 'Have you come to see if Santa's been?'

Taking a deep breath, Iris smiled reassuringly and asked, 'Sam darling, are you always this fabulously premenstrual?'

'Dad!' Sally cried, coming to life as Mark carried the lit pudding in the room. He held it level with his shoulders so that his face and forearms were polished with a spectral gleam.

'Ta-dah!' he announced. 'And I think clever Mam's gone and put coins and fortune cards in this, too!'

I'm going to choke on this, thought Peggy, as Sam plopped a large spoonful of pudding into her bowl. Dimly she recalled all the other moments in her life when she thought something was going to choke her, and almost all seemed preferable to this one.

'Aren't you having any, pet?' Mark asked Sally.

'Leave her. She's opening her prezzies.' Iris pushed her own bowl under Sam's nose and they all turned to look at Sally, on the rug in front of the television set, in piles of shredded colourful paper. She unwrapped her gifts as if still dreaming. She had decided to herself that she *was* still dreaming; Christmas had come hours early this year. If it was real Christmas, the grown-ups would be watching her more closely.

Sam finished dishing out and uncapped a bottle of gin. One of the comfortable, square bottles, the girth of which neatly fits the palm.

'I've got a fifty-pence piece!' Iris shouted out. 'Sally, you really ought to have some pud! You get free surprise money with every portion!' She waved the coin and the square of lilac paper it had been folded into. 'And what's written on this? Is it my fortune?' She read aloud, '"Age before Beauty." What's that supposed to mean? What have you got, Peg?'

'Two pence.' Peggy shrugged. She looked at Sam, who shrugged too, and poured herself more gin. 'And this says, "There's no place like home".'

'They're not fortunes,' said Iris, 'they're mottoes. We got it wrong. They don't tell your future at all.' She paused in one of those curious moments of lucidity and doubt often brought on by alcohol, and added, 'These aren't about the future; these are about the way things *are*.'

Sam let out a sharp yelp of laughter and raised her glass to her mother's lover.

'What do you have, Mark?' Peggy asked him gently.

'No money.' He smiled sadly. 'Just a piece of paper. Lots of writing, though, by the looks of it.' He began to unfold it.

'What does Dad's future say?' Sally asked from the carpet. 'Mam, what's Dad's future tell us?'

Sam slipped back into the kitchen with her glass and the bottle.

In the oven the lilac paper had turned brittle and crisp. It was charred slightly at the edges and blotched with alcohol and grease stains. It was a letter that began, 'Dear Mark,' and continued the length of the sheet in Tony's customary scrawl, the black ink burned a deep brown.

'What is it, Mark? Quite a long, involved one?' Iris stopped, noticing his expression.

Behind them all, the back door banged shut. Not loudly,

not with any particular finality, but with a breezy negligence that left an awful silence in its wake.

Twelve

It has been dark for hours and there is still a long way to go till morning. On Christmas morning, traditionally, everyone tries to get up before it is fully light anyway. Parents are harassed into waking early. All over the estate tomorrow morning, lights will click on, orange squares of windows, beaded with frozen black dew, competing with frail red streetlamps, which buzz indecisively, wondering whether the night is really up.

All over the estate, first cigarettes will be shakily lit, kitchen doors creak open to let eager dogs out and dogged cats in. First pots of tea will be brewed, too weak and too milky, poured in haste and abandoned to cool as other rituals exert their demands.

Here, houses are very close to one another and the same rituals are gone through a thousand times over, within a few hundred square feet. Yet each family, still in their pyjamas, exchanging presents with the TV on and unwatched, will be entirely unaware of their neighbours that morning. Neighbours will have wished each other a merry Christmas the previous afternoon, when they were out with their kids to see the council Santa Claus come by their street on his lorry decked out with fairy lights. On Christmas Eve they locked and bolted their doors and will emerge only once tomorrow morning, to crush armfuls of used wrapping paper into their wheely bins.

The council won't remove a wheely bin that is too full to shut. The neighbours press down the paper harder, reflect on the waste, maybe even stand on it with their full weight. In a quiet moment, perched unsteadily on top of their binful, they might reflect upon the silence of the streets. It will be about eight in the morning, say, and although it isn't a white

74

Christmas, the tarmac is bright with untouched frost. Then they'll go in, back to their hive of activity, nervous hilarity, disappointment and torpor. They won't emerge properly until Boxing Day when, perhaps, it will be time to visit relatives across town.

In the darkness before that dawn, it is almost like any other night. Even the twenty-four-hour garage opposite the flats is still open. The garage is new and under the white lighting its brickwork is a sickly colour and seems fake. As Sam wades over a churned-up field of long grass and brackish, part-frozen water towards it, she remembers the garage in the Noddy books and how it had been made of alphabet blocks or something. She recalls Noddy stopping off for petrol, before he was hi-jacked and joy-ridden by the golliwogs, taken to the forest and ceremoniously gang-raped. Reading the sanitised version of this story to Sally recently, Sam had been disappointed by the changes. How much gin has she drunk tonight? She shudders and stamps her shoes clean on the garage forecourt.

Inside the shop they're playing Cliff Richard's Christmas album and the girl at the cash desk is looking oddly at the man facing her. He taps his plastic card on the desk in what Sam would take to be a threatening manner.

This shop is much too large for what they have to sell. This is all she can think in her state. Large white bottles of oil and pop, and about four flavours of crisps. And cigarettes, of course, which is what she is here for, but she takes one of each flavour of crisp anyway. When she is miserable sometimes, crisps seem the only thing. She thinks it has something to do with the noise; there's nothing like stuffing yourself with loud food.

She waits blearily in turn, eyeing herself in the mirror to one side of the till, behind the sweet racks. She looks a blotchy mess, of course, and begins to suspect she is looking into a two-way mirror. Something to do with safety, crime prevention, probably, since garages are so often in vulnerable spots. Into this mirror she mimes, 'What the fuck are you looking at?' and to herself, insides lifting up in a pang of lust, 'Crime prevention! If only I could find him now!' At this moment, having escaped the home, what she needs is someone entirely other.

Luckily there is one other; an Other she has prepared earlier.

The conversation between the cashier and the card-tapping motorist has begun to seep towards her now. The man's vehemence has been reaching out, trying to draw her attention.

'Fucking bastard. Fancy lying in wait. Lying in bloody wait. It isn't on. Skulking in dark corners like a fucking pervert.'

'They're having a clampdown,' says the cashier a little nervously, yet managing to insinuate a you-should-have-known-better tone. 'A clampdown on drunk driving. Haven't you seen the adverts?'

'Drunk! I'm not drunk, though! I'm steady as fuck! Look at that!'

He held his hand still under her nose and enlisted Sam. 'Am I pissed or what?'

Sam, who was absolutely pissed, said, 'Yes, but it shows up in your bloodstream. Or in what you breathe out . . . in the fumes. It shows up all right. The policemen always know best. They know what you've had.'

'Don't get me wrong,' said the man, 'I agree with what they're doing. Shouldn't let lunatics at the wheel arseholed, knocking over bairns and what have you, but a decent, respectable man like me being pounced on, fucking *pounced* on in the night as I'm coming home – well, it makes me want to throw.'

The cashier looked alarmed.

Sam asked, 'Where was this?'

'What?'

'Where are they lying in wait, did you say?'

'That's right; you'd better know where to slow down, too, lass. You've had a skinful as well, 'an't you? They're down by the Burn. In the layby before the bridge. There's no bloody streetlamps, so you can't see them sitting up there all night, as if they've nothing better to do on a Christmas Eve, the bastards.' He looked down at his hand suddenly. 'I've snapped me fucking credit card now.'

Blanching once more, the cashier looked towards Sam, who had taken the opportunity of slipping unnoticed, for the second time that night, out of the door.

'Let her cool off, Mark,' Iris said, sobering quickly when they realised that Sam had stomped out.

'She's probably just gone out for a quiet cigarette,' Peggy added, as between them they ushered Mark over to the green settee. He was still clutching the letter from Tony in two hands before him, and both grandmothers were tactful enough not to ask what it was and why it should have whipped up such a storm.

Mark couldn't quite take in what the letter actually said. The fact it was a letter from Tony and that Sam had got to it first, and then served it up in such lavish circumstances, was enough to render him well-nigh catatonic.

Solicitously Peggy hurried Sally back to bed to wait for morning. She whispered a few things as they went about magic letters from Father Christmas, and how Sally had witnessed part of the mysterious night-time magic that went on behind the scenes, unnoticed by children, each and every Christmas Eve. Sitting up in bed, Sally's eyes widened in interest. Peggy improvised, 'Yes, it was a magical letter from Santa saying that his sleigh has run out of petrol just out of town, and your mam had to go and help him get it started again. She's good like that.'

Sleepiness overcoming her, Sally repressed an expression of extreme scepticism and lay down.

Mark's eyes flickered backwards and forwards across the crackling sheet of paper, until he came to the phrase, 'I'm coming back for you now.' It repeated itself over and over to him, making no sense whatsoever, until Peggy rejoined them and quietly put on another tape.

'There's another bottle of gin,' Mark mumbled. 'Open it, would you?'

'Two bottles of gin!' Iris exclaimed, and went to find it.

'Mark, we'll give you your present now,' said Peggy, reaching into one of her carrier bags. 'It seems the thing to do.'

'The thing to do,' Iris repeated, 'at this particular juncture.'

'Right,' said Mark, with a forced smile, making himself fold the letter away into his jeans pocket. Iris passed him a full glass. I've been drinking for nearly twelve hours straight, he thought. What a long day! Then there was a heavy parcel on his lap and he mustered his smiles, flexing his fingers to unwrap it.

'It may need some explaining,' said Peggy as she watched him work.

Inside the parcel there was a leather case with a zip. Dismayed, Mark assumed it was shaving things. The way Sam seemed to discuss his shaving habits with everyone always dismayed him. 'Thank you,' he said.

'Open it,' prompted his mother-in-law. Over the rasp of the stiff new zip she and Iris exchanged a tense smile.

Mark found his own eyes staring back at him from a compact mirror set into the opened case's lid. They were surrounded by little squares of pastel colours, and beneath these were strapped a series of dainty brushes and tubes thick with what felt like some kind of unguent. Mark stared dumbfounded at his present.

'We thought you might appreciate this,' Iris smiled. 'We made sure we got most of the colours in suitable flesh tones'.

'What's it all *for*?' he asked at last, completely at a loss.

'You see, Mark.' Iris sighed. 'We understand that conspicuousness, while sometimes being a wonderful thing, can also at times conspire to be a drag.' This was a prepared speech, delivered with great aplomb. Mark blinked and reached for his glass. 'So now, basically, when you want to move about the populace undetected and unremarkable –'

'You just slap on a little foundation, blusher and so on, and off you go!' cried Peggy, stealing Iris's thunder.

Realising what they were on about, Mark looked down again at the make-up case. 'That's so sweet,' he said and promptly burst into tears.

'More drinks!' Iris called out, as if she were the sort to be embarrassed by overt shows.

'There's freezing mist on the river,' Bob said, wiping condensation off the windscreen.

'It's so parky,' said his friend, who was in the driving seat.

'It's too cold to snow,' Bob added.

'It's always too cold to snow.' His friend looked disgruntled. He poked about inside his lunch box for a while, then looked at his watch. 'Nearly midnight. Happy bloody Christmas, Bob!'

'Yeah; same to you.' Bob poured a drop of brandy each into their flask-tea.

'I suppose what I mean, Bob, is that, just when it seems as if it's cold enough to snow, it suddenly gets too cold and then it can't snow. Like the sky needs unblocking.'

'Yeah, right.' Bob looked at his watch. 'Not much traffic.'

'Just as well.' Bob's mate sniffed, loud and long. Bob, who wasn't usually sensitive about that kind of thing, shuddered. Sometimes it was hard work, traffic duty. Sitting long hours over the dashboard together, out in the night. Even tonight. Some of the married blokes down the station said they saw their wives less than their traffic-duty partners.

It was a long, lonely job. Traffic duty does not encourage a vital inner life. But partners on these jobs developed a different rapport and adapted to one another's bodily presence. They, for example, knew how often the other had to go to the toilet. Tonight Bob and his mate had been taking turns to nip off down the road to piss in the Burn. Traffic police even have to learn to fart without compunction sitting next to each other and, on cold nights like this, unwilling to wind down the windows. Luckily this night was a quiet one; it was a widely held belief in the force that the more exciting the car chase, the greater amount of farting went on. That's something they never tell you on the telly, Bob thought.

He said, 'This road'll be icing up tonight. Look at the mist. God help them if they come speeding down here tonight, the piss-heads. They'll be straight in the bloody Burn.' Thoughtfully he rubbed at his itching chin; his five-o'clock shadow was now seven hours old.

'I hope they don't bump into us,' said his friend.

'We can nip out of the way.'

His friend looked sceptical.

'I've been in the thick of some nasty dos,' Bob insisted. 'Not a mark on me.'

Nervously his mate went on fiddling with the remaining item in his lunch box, a very large orange he had left till last because it had an unpromising look about it. He unpeeled it morosely, stopping to whisper 'Shit!' when the all-in-one-piece rind fell to pieces in his hands. He asked, 'Do you reckon I could get the whole of this orange in me gob, all in one go?'

Bob sighed. 'Shall we see what's on the radio?' he asked as his mate prised the fruit into his mouth.

Two women were talking.

'. . . hairy. I know. I said. You know what it's like.'

'Where does she live then?'

'Up the posh end. Past Shildon. Near that pub where you sit outside and they bring you sausages.'

'Like the continentals do?'

'She's had a conservatory put on.'

'Has she, now?'

'But when you go past on the bus you can see right the way through her house because of it. All the way to her front passage. Silly cow! How they could make her detective inspector when her house is a burglar's paradise . . .'

'It's a select area, isn't it?'

'I'd never have selected it. There's horses and all sorts in the fields there.'

Irritably Bob switched them off. Beside him, his mate was moaning. He's having a heart attack, Bob thought. Fuck! I wanted an exciting life on the force and here it is. Gossip and coronaries; fucking hell.

Bob looked at his friend, who was now sitting quite still in the driver's seat, staring straight ahead as if he had seen something breathtaking in the middle of the black windscreen. Bob might have been tempted to check that nothing was out there, but he could see straight away what the problem was.

'You've locked your bloody jaw, haven't you?'

His mate gave a terse nod, eyes bulging out only slightly less than the waxy orange half stuck out of his mouth. His lips were stretched like elastic bands, looking as if they were about to split. Bob felt like just getting out of the car and walking away.

'You're not having me on, are you?'

Bob's mate looked at him with the first signs of an angry panic snorting up in his throat. He stopped short, as if realising how close he was to suffocation.

'Bloody hell! We'll have to go to casualty.'

His mate waved his hands no and spent some moments finding a pen to scribble on the back of a charge sheet, 'You'll have to suck it out.'

'It's an orange, not snake fucking venom.'

The rising panic in his mate's eyes, made worse by the dashboard's baleful glare, seemed almost pleading to Bob. With an embarrassed cough and a glance around, Bob repositioned himself in the driver's seat, cupped a hand round his mate's neck for support, and hesitated, inching forward, over where to bite in first.

Waiting up for Sam, Mark, Iris and Peggy were becoming a touch maudlin.

'The thought I can't stand,' Peggy was saying, and the others listened carefully, 'is that we . . . oh, I dunno . . . *fool* ourselves into making compromises. You know.'

They all thought about this. Somewhere at the back of his mind, as he rubbed a forefinger into a square of eyeshadow, Mark was wondering how appropriate a conversation this was to be having just now. It wasn't the sort of thing to be discussed between partners with others present, and he felt it might touch too rawly on his doings with Sam. Nevertheless, as these conversations most often tend to, it rumbled on under its own momentum.

'What do you mean?' asked Mark, greasing the cogs.

'Well . . .' Peggy stirred herself to be self-revelatory, quite forgetting that even as recently as this morning she had thought of Mark as less than trustworthy. 'What I mean is that whatever we assume is good, whatever we think works, what we think we're happy in . . . What if, really, we're lying to ourselves?'

'Oh, God!' said Iris, quietly aghast for a number of reasons.

Mark bided his time, expecting to hear the groans of a very old chestnut being rolled around the room. He sat back and said, 'The way to look at compromise is that it's salvaging something, when if you didn't, you'd probably end up with nowt.'

Peggy blinked. 'You needn't tell me about compromise, Mark.' She bit her lip. She had overstepped the rules. Here, in this game, they were all equals. There could be no rank-pulling. 'I'm on about something worse than simple compromise. That's a day-to-day activity. If you didn't compromise all the time, then you'd have no character, no personality, no body at all. Identifying yourself, specifying yourself is all compromising; of course it is. You put up a good shopfront and flog it for all you're worth.'

'Hear, hear,' said Iris.

'No, what I'm talking about here is fooling yourself. We've just been on about sex, right?'

'Right.' Mark nodded, though he couldn't remember. He hoped, vaguely, that he hadn't put his foot in it.

'That moment, think about that moment when you at last succumb to the charms of a new lover, wherever it is, in whatever circumstances.'

Iris and Mark both thought hard.

'What do you feel? Beside all the lust and anxiety and so on? Underneath it all?'

Her audience looked blank. What was it they felt? As persistent and obvious as their own accelerated heartbeats? They both had their own ideas, yet were content for Peggy to vocalise them.

'What you feel then is relief. That's part of it. Like that ache, like a nostalgic ache; homesickness. It's a parting grief, right at the start of an alliance. As if you were living your life backwards and the first moment of intimacy is experienced as the last ever. You know that ache? Your chest drum-tight inside? At this particular moment you invest so much that you make your own entire bodily and mental fabric drum-tight. You pull it all together in a vulnerably taut net for the other to fall onto. You feel relief that they are prepared to fall; fear that they'll rip straight through.

82

'But the thought I really hate,' said Peggy, and a tear slid down her stoic face, 'is that the feeling I've called relief or fear is really only gratitude. That we are pitifully glad to make ourselves so vulnerable. We're only too happy to see some-one, anyone, fall in our direction.'

She put down her glass. Mark and Iris put down their own glasses, as if following.

'It's warm in here,' said Peggy. 'We need to take a walk around the block.'

'Go *out*?' asked Mark.

'We often go out walking at night,' Iris told him.

'In the nude,' Peggy added. 'You know we're nudists?'

Mark knew, but he was still shocked.

'Would you mind awfully, Mark?' asked Iris. 'Since Sam's not here? We'd hate to miss our nightly ritual.'

Dumbly Mark shook his head and Iris, beaming, stood and took off her scarlet cardigan. As Peggy went on talking, her lover removed layer after layer of woollies. Talking, Peggy was undressing too, folding her clothes and putting them neatly on the settee.

'It's like getting rid, for a little while, of the excess baggage. You've really no idea what it feels like, Mark.'

'I'm sure I don't.' He poured himself the last dribble of gin.

'We all carry so much stuff around with us.'

More shocking than the sight of Peggy's bare breasts and limbs, to Mark, was Iris's apparent shrinkage. Beside the messy heap of garments she had rapidly made, Iris was a shadow of her former self. The fat lady had dwindled away before his eyes and Iris herself was quite unaware that this might be surprising.

She can only weigh about seven stone, Mark thought. Both grandmothers were now looking at him with blasé, almost bored expressions. And, despite Iris's bodily revelations, Mark found nothing shocking about their nudity. They were just another part of the family, and this scene tested that feeling. Their pale flesh was no more alarming than a glimpse of his own bare feet.

'Would you let us out, then?' Peggy smiled.

Mark stood, carefully setting aside his make-up case and

his glass, and, also careful, now that he *wasn't* embarrassed, not to *look* embarrassed.

'Mark,' Iris said. '*You* carry a lot of baggage with you.'

He nearly laughed. 'I know I bloody do.'

'Why not, just for an hour or so, drop it?'

Mark found it odd, in a way, speaking to this new, terribly thin Iris. He frowned for clarification.

'Why don't you join us, out tonight?'

'What about Sally?' he asked immediately.

Peggy waved a hand. 'She's asleep. We won't be far. And naturally, we're both witches. So I'll cast a protective spell.'

Gratefully he said, 'I think you already have, Peg.' He gave a brief sniff of a laugh, looked down, then took off his shoes and socks.

He said, 'We've talked about making yourself vulnerable; and we've agreed that we do it all the time. But we still find it hard to do, don't we?'

'Yes,' Iris said. 'Don't come out tonight if you don't want.'

His bare feet could mean equally that he was settled in for the night, or the opposite.

'No,' he said. 'I feel warm . . . and a bit, well, quite a lot pissed. If I can't take off all my clothes and go for a walk in the middle of the night with two old dykes, what else would I do?'

'That's the spirit!' Peggy grinned as he pulled his shirt over his head and unstrapped his watch. 'Absolutely cynical and absolutely sentimental at the same time. That's the combination we like.'

Peggy and Iris grasped hands for a moment, almost in pride, as Mark concentrated on stripping off his jeans and underpants. Almost a moment, too, of solidarity in the face of something alien to their nightly ritual; whether alien because his was a naked male body, a sexual other to them, or because his body was thoroughly tattooed, they wouldn't have been able to say. But when Mark looked at them both with that silly, shy grin, and glanced quickly down at his own, oddly boyish body with its gangling limbs and quite small and sleepy cock, they felt a blush that was merely the envelope of warmth released from the private space around him, and it included them.

'Ha'way, then,' he said. 'Let's hit the town.'

Thirteen

She found her policeman busy in the line of duty.

Skidding on sheer ice, Sam hurried down the hill to the layby. Relief glowed through her, making the gin in her belly bubble up in anticipation. Here was the police car she had been looking for tonight and, odds on, her Bob was in it, traffic-watching. She knew they put unmarried bobbies on the job during sacred holidays; they were missed less, they had fewer family ties. But Sam wanted Bob tonight.

As she tottered closer to the panda, she peered in through the dark windows, hoping for a glimpse. She saw the white cords of his neck twisted round, the Adam's apple working, as it did when he talked to her. She could watch the muscled intricacies of his body work all night and never hear a word he said. She loved to watch him talk. And the dark fingers of hair spread down his neck; definitely Bob.

Relief and savage joy picked her up like a weightless doll and flung her the last remaining steps to the car door. Her frozen fingers clutched at the handle and, with a swift scorch of adrenaline, she wrenched it wide open.

This was a police car she was attacking! Imagine doing this if policemen were fully armed! She was risking her life and flouting the letter of the law, but only because she wanted to see Bob.

Bob was caught at work, delicately nibbling away at segment after segment of the orange. For a quarter of an hour now, with his mate squirming and moaning beneath him, he had been popping the tiny cells of flesh between his teeth, sucking out the volume of juice slowly, painstakingly.

Sam stared dumbfounded at this revealed tableau. Bob had swung round, mouth dripping orange juice, his whole face smeared and pith stuck in rags on his stubble. His mate still lay prostrated with the bulk of the fruit wedged solidly in place.

'What the fuck is going on?' Sam demanded, appalled but unsure what, exactly, she was looking at.

'What are you doing here?' Bob asked.

She couldn't figure this out at all. Bob's amazingly serene tone and the stillness of the other man conspired to make her believe that she was the one out of the ordinary. For a moment she was about to close the door again, say goodnight and slip away.

'I came looking for you,' she said. 'I needed to see you.'

'Right,' Bob said. 'Get in the back.'

Sam was watching his throat work out of habit as he talked. She could see he was angry, and so she complied.

'I'll see to you next,' he said as Sam got in and sat quietly on the cold back seat. 'I've got this stupid fucker to sort out first.'

His mate gave a low growl of complaint, but Bob shot him a warning glance. At last Sam asked, 'What's happening, exactly?'

Bob ignored her and examined his friend again. 'I think I've made it worse.' His mate whimpered a single note of enquiry. 'I think I've pushed it further in.'

Sam was beginning to wish she had braved it out at home. She wasn't up to having another facet of Bob revealed to her tonight.

'Sit back,' he told his mate. 'We'll have to change seats. I'll drive you to hospital.'

'Hospital?' echoed Sam.

'Put your seatbelt on,' Bob snapped at her and climbed out of the car, motioning to his mate to move seats. His friend looked glum, acquiescent and, as he struggled over the clutch, supremely uncomfortable.

We're going to hospital, thought Sam woozily, and settled back in confusion. Bob took the driver's seat and started the engine. As the wheels ground into the hard frost of the layby, Sam concentrated on the pleasingly aggressive noise of the motor and was content to be borne along for a while, slumped in the back seat, during somebody else's drama.

*

'It's so warm!' Mark grinned, linking arms with the two old dykes. And it was; he couldn't work out how. They were walking the perimeter path of the estate, quite sedately. As they passed under each streetlamp he felt they were giving off a radiation as gentle as the lamps.

'It's just the gin,' Peggy said.

'And the female bonding!' cried Iris.

The houses were dark and built like shoe boxes. At night they seemed the size of shoe boxes, as if, driving past, you could stretch out a lazy limb and scatter them across the ground. There was no one around to notice the walkers tonight.

Beside the estate, the fields rolled dark and static with frost, pressed under a weight of violet cloud. The town clock rang out the odds and only then, as the hour reminded Mark of Sam's running out, and of Sally being in by herself, did he give an involuntary shiver. The soles of his feet were hard, glass slippers on the tarmac, his fingers so cold that if he bit his fingernails now he would expect them to snap, and his balls felt as if they'd knotted right up inside out of consternation, as a plane taking off retracts its wheels.

They passed into the older streets with their bristling high hedges and patios left alight for Santa Claus. Once, a dog came sniffing out of an alleyway, saw them from afar and bolted. They were approaching the town centre and still hadn't seen anybody real.

'I never meant us to come out this far,' said Peggy. 'Isn't it a pleasant night?'

'I can't believe we've walked so far into town like this,' Mark breathed.

'It's quite a coup,' Iris cackled.

'But naked!' Mark was starting to be shocked by himself.

Iris stopped to look him up and down. He was suddenly acutely conscious of his shrinkage. 'Just look at yourself,' she told him. 'You're no more naked now than anybody ever is when they're out.'

She left him to absorb this as they walked on in their threesome. Through the town centre, Mark glanced less and less covertly at himself in the darkened shop windows.

There he was, as he imagined himself in his best dreams, authentic in a public space in his own private markings. Iris and Peggy exchanged another of their swift, proud glances as he looked over his shoulder to see the extent of the drawings down his back.

'I look wonderful,' he said to the twin pale figures who had led him to this. They were outside the subdued window display at Woolworth's and Mark gave a slow twirl. 'It all looks wonderful. I never thought I'd ever see all of myself, together.'

The three of them breathed in their spiced moment of epiphany. They knew these things didn't come about too often.

Then, without particular displeasure, they realised the moment had been broken by the hum of an approaching car.

'I don't believe this!'

'Mmm?' asked Bob's mate.

'All bloody night sitting with nowt happening.' Fiercely he swung the car to the left.

'What is it?' asked Sam, sitting forward, stomach lurching with the panda.

'First him and that orange, then you, Sam, and now this. All hell suddenly breaks loose. What a bloody nightmare!'

He hauled the car to an abrupt stop in the middle of the street. His headlights picked out three luminous bodies outside Woolworth's.

They stood in the mesmerising glare of his discovery, not in the least bit startled. 'Look at this lot,' Bob spat in disgust.

Sam began to throw up nosily on the back seat. Bob's mate gagged on the fumes and the stuck remains of his packed lunch.

Sally has always slept with her window open. Of course it is a chancy business on this estate. The last thing Mark does each night before going to bed is to check each window in the flat, especially the easily forgotten one in the bathroom. But ever since she was old enough to argue, Sally has insisted on having hers open while she sleeps. She can't breathe otherwise, she says.

Late at night Mark goes through the routine of sealing up the flat, locking the door and putting a kitchen chair behind it, and sometimes he will stop and listen to, perhaps, the low moan of the wind through Sally's window.

Tonight she is awake and the air is cool and still. She is thinking over the whole business of Christmas Eve, and starting to regret that she doesn't have a stocking set out for Santa Claus. At school some of the kids were talking last week about leaving out wine, mince pies and some carrots for the reindeer. Sally kept her mouth shut, wondering how the kids didn't work out that reindeer would never get through the door to eat the carrots.

The moonlight is flat on her rows of cuddly toys; bears, gorillas, koalas, cats. Its progress across the room is stilted by piles of books. She has no bookshelves yet and her collection is scattered, some resting open, ready for other bedtimes.

Perhaps the kids at school last week had got it right. Iris clearly believes in Santa Claus. Even if she was using him as an excuse for Mam running out of the flat. For a moment Sally imagines the night as Iris pretended it; her mam calmly discussing Santa's engine parts with him. The sad old man and the reindeer watching in head-shaking consternation. Her mam can do things, sort things out, Sally knows this. She calls her dad cack-handed and pathetic because he can't. That was why he stayed at home while Mam ran out.

It is real, then. The whole thing is true. Sally wishes more strongly than ever that she had a stocking to leave out.

She turns over to look at the frozen window and wonder what Santa really looks like. At school they spent a morning drawing pictures of how they all thought he would look. Everyone gave him bright red clothes. A number of scuffles broke out in the classroom because there wasn't enough red crayons to go round. It became quite a heated issue.

Sally couldn't see the problem. She hung back and complacently coloured her Santa Claus a deep midnight blue. There! Then she gave him a glorious hat woven from emerald holly leaves, and gloves a startling white like those of her talking Mickey Mouse, which was propped at the end of her bed.

At lunchtime Miss Francis pinned up all the Santas and the class stood back to admire the effect. Sally's dashing and brilliant Santa was consigned to the edge of the display. Probably because hers was faceless and this had made Miss Francis shudder, but Sally had drawn him that way because she couldn't imagine what face he should have and didn't want him to be an old man the way they said God was, and anyway, she didn't know any old men to copy it from.

Which Santa, if any, will come tonight?

'Sally?'

The voice is oddly familiar. She won't wonder, yet, who it is. If it is someone she doesn't know, she doesn't want to know about it yet.

'Sally? I'm here to tell you a story.'

She is still watching the window. Soundlessly she shrinks down inside her duvet. White hands creep up through the opened window. They have three black stripes up the back like Mickey Mouse's gloves. They pause, unsteadily, on the sill cluttered with Sally's toys, tottering on their fingertips as they find a space. They turn slowly about and then, with their ten digits as little feet, do a rapid dance. Sally laughs aloud.

'I'm here to tell you a story and then we're going to go to the North Pole,' the voice tells her, and Sally realises that it is the gloves talking.

'I see that you read lots of books, Sally. You know lots of stories already. Far more than the other kids at school. That's why you hang back, isn't it? When the other kids rush in, you hang back because you know what happens to people who are heedless. You've seen what goes on in the world, in stories. It also makes you think about things more, doesn't it? But it makes the other kids difficult to talk to sometimes. I know that. I know how hard it is for you. They seem like babies still, don't they?'

The gloves have jumped lightly down from the sill and independently they clamber across the strewn book covers. The pale, tapered fingers caress the titles as if, in this way, they can read.

'I imagine, Sally, that you've read lots of those books where people visit magical and mysterious lands. Where they *explore*. There are lots of books like that, and those are the best ones, aren't they? That's what it'll be like when we go to the North Pole.'

'Are you Santa?' she asks levelly.

'I can be anyone. As you see, I have no face. Put on any you like, but we're going to the North Pole nonetheless.'

Sally considers this. 'Good,' she replies.

'When you grow up,' the gloves say thoughtfully, coming back together and steepling their fingers, 'you don't have to stop having adventures, going into those magical lands. But it's more difficult. The magical lands are more . . . ambiguous. Do you know what that means?'

Sally shakes her head, sitting up now.

'It means complicated. They might be one thing or they might be another. You can't be sure. The land you go into could be bizarrely magical or it could be completely ordinary. And these grown-ups find it harder to get there in order to decide. They have to depend on each other believing that the place they have found is special. If they were alone, as Alice was alone in Wonderland, then Wonderland might never have come about. It might have fallen to pieces in an instant.'

'It does fall to pieces,' Sally complains, 'at the end of the story.'

'Exactly. When grown-ups are there, they need two of them and between them they sustain the illusion. Do you see what I mean?

'My story now is about Sam and Tony. They went into a land that might have been magical, it might have been quite ordinary. They never really found out. Before they both went in, their paths had never crossed before. They would never have known each other if they hadn't set out to explore this particular place.

'This place was a park, like those old-fashioned Victorian parks that are ringed around by iron railings, crowded in by trees and sluggish streams that wend down gentle hills to seep into bronze lakes.

'When Sam and Tony went in, their hands came away from

the heavy iron gates smudged with rust, like bloodstains or pollen. When they entered this enchanted parkland, it seemed to them like a wonderful child's playground, inhabited only by the stillest objects. They went exploring.

'What looked from outside the railings like a perfectly ordinary old park, inside proved to be stuffed with wonders. As they passed, the flowerbeds shook out and displayed the most exotic hothouse flowers, densely whorled and brilliant heads which nodded and followed their progress. In the trees, gaudily painted banners were stretched out with slogans printed in archaic languages. Fireworks speared the sky and hung there all afternoon.

'A rickety wooden bridge, bright scarlet, led them to the blue castle in the centre of the park. From a distance it had looked like a castle, a monument, but as they entered through a head-high number six and climbed inside, up a staircase of moving clockwork parts, they saw it was really a giant alarm clock. Here within, the metal building shuddered with ticks like heartbeats, passing inexorably towards the moment the bells would ring, as if alert to intruders.

'From the top of the clock, sitting on top of the shiny gold domes of its twin bells, Tony and Sam looked down on the spread extent of their discovered land.

'It stretched in five vast directions: four branches of solid, intricate geography leading downwards from the clock in the centre, and one promontory to its north. This northern realm bore two limpid ponds, open to the sky. Tony left Sam for a while, climbed down the clockface, and headed off up to this realm.

'All that night he roamed labyrinths of golden brick, trying to find those lakes. The brick was real gold, oily and soft to the touch. Sometimes he would meet dead ends; occasionally he came to a small, neat garden where the flowers never looked quite real. They were drawn with the expert haste of a Chinese watercolour; the pink flowers a single broad stroke, branches a twist of black.

'At last Tony found one brown, oval lake. He shielded his eyes and looked to see if Sam was still watching from the safety of the alarm-clock monument, and she wasn't. She had gone to discover things on her own. Quickly Tony undressed and slipped into the pool. It was cold but, as he swam, the viscous water began to warm and support him. It was like the Dead Sea, it kept him buoyant.

'Elsewhere Sam was leaving the clock at the centre and then she was running through a field of ornate, abandoned, pale-blue statues. A horse twisted its marble wings back, rearing and defending itself against the onslaught of a frozen gryphon. Angels and saints watched solemnly from atop wonky pedestals; some lay crashed sideways in the dust. Tearing the length of this cemetery of icons, Sally realised none could harm her, but she never stopped for breath till she reached a kidney-shaped field of poppies.

'At the other side, drowsy and careless, she reached the orchard she had seen from afar. The air was rank with overripeness, but Sam loved the smell and the squash underfoot of the flesh of fallen, wasted peaches. In the shaded, autumnal alleyways the colours were high; she ate the fruit and smeared herself in juices. This kind of thing often goes on in these stories.

'In their separate ways, Tony and Sam had decided that they would both be quite happy to stay in this place. They roamed and ran wild all that night, and each subsequent night for a month. Tony would return most often to the pools that warmed him as he swam; Sam to the orchard where, each evening, new fruit would grow for her. Every now and then they would meet in the centre, at the alarm-clock monument, as the bells rang out over the landscape. They would tell each other what they had found.

'They never told each other, however, that they had both resolved never to leave this land. They pretended to each other that they would leave, separately, quite soon.'

Sally asks, 'Were they in love?'

'Not with each other,' the gloves tell her sadly.

'Why not?' Sally can't see any other point to a story for grown-ups. It's what they're usually like.

'In the end they met on the other side of the world.'

'What?'

'Well, one night they both went too far. Tony swam too

deep in the pool, and Sam ate her way too far into the delicious forest. Without the other knowing, they both sank so deep through that they came out on the other side of the world.

'More places to explore! And here there were words, pricked out in blue flowers, blue bricks and clipped into trees. Words they couldn't read because they were too small to fit all the letters into the proper perspective.

'At last, that night, they met each other on the rocky spine of the land, from which vantage point the spread of the country was laid out once more. Their current position was high above the rest and the realms flung themselves out, it seemed, in languid abandon. A storm crashed all about them, obscuring the extent of the land they had both made their own.

'And then, when Tony and Sam saw in each other's faces the determination not to leave this place, they both resolved that the other must be made to leave right then.'

'Why?'

'Because . . . even though a grown-up knows it takes more than one to keep the illusion up, they always want to be the only one. The single Beloved. And so . . .'

'And so what happened?'

'A terrible battle ensued.'

'Who won?'

The hands drummed a gentle tattoo on the top of a pile of books. 'No time now, Sally,' they whisper. 'It's early Christmas Day. Soon it'll be too late to catch up with the magic of the Eve. We've got to leave for the North Pole right now. Come on; get ready.'

Sally hopped out of bed and started to dress. 'Will you tell me on the way who won the terrible battle?'

'Maybe later. Stories aren't always in the past. I still don't know how this one turns out. It is still unwinding itself in the storm. It's happening somewhere else. We'll just have to see. Come along now; it's time.'

Fourteen

When the phone rang, Iris was just coming in from a long walk. Peggy snatched up the receiver and gave her a curt nod. 'It's Sam,' she mouthed, watching Iris heave her snow boots off.

'I want to talk to Mark.' Sam's voice was hard.

'He's here,' Peggy told her. 'He's in the bathroom.'

'Would you get him?'

'Get Mark,' Peggy hissed to Iris. 'Sam, where are you?'

'I'm staying with a friend.'

'That policeman?'

'Yes, that policeman.'

'Shouldn't either you or Mark be in the flat . . . just in case?'

'Don't tell me what I should do. Why isn't Mark at the flat? Why is he at yours still? Why can't he be at home?'

'We're keeping an eye on him. You saw what he was like. He's completely off his head.'

Iris had come back. She tapped Peggy on the arm. 'He's coming. Let me speak to her.'

Peggy handed her the receiver. 'Sam? Listen,' Iris took a deep breath and weighed in. 'Sam, we have to let the police know *now*. It's been a whole day. This is madness. If we want –'

'Keep your fucking nose *out*!'

Mark stood behind Iris. He was deathly pale, expressionless. As he took the phone, Iris gasped. He had blanked out the tattoos on his face with thick white foundation.

'It's me,' he said.

'Iris has been telling me we have to phone the police.'

'No,' he said. 'I've . . . heard something.'

'What? Who from?'

'We had a call.'

Iris shot Peggy a look. A call? Peggy nodded quickly.

Mark went on. 'Tony phoned me. Sally's safe. She's with him.' He could even hear Sam grip the receiver tighter.

'Where? Where has he taken her?'

'Sam . . . Sam, we have to be careful about this . . .'

'She's my fucking kid, Mark.'

He breathed out slowly. 'Mine as well.'

'She came out of *my* body, Mark. My body, not yours. You've tried to keep me out the whole way along. But not even you can change this fact of nature. That bairn came out of my body, and . . .' Her voice snagged and she stopped.

Mark repeated, 'I think we have to play this very carefully. I don't know what's going on exactly. I don't know what's going on in Tony's mind.'

'I wouldn't put it past the pair of you to have planned this together.'

'Sam, I . . .'

'Oh, don't flounder. Look, just tell me; tell me you didn't have this planned.'

'No. It –'

'What did he say then? Where is he? Where's he taken her?'

'They're in Leeds.'

'Leeds? What the fuck for?'

'I don't know. It's just where he went.'

'Are we going to get her back?'

'Yes.'

'Should we get the police in now? If he –'

'No. Now listen, Sam. We had twenty-four hours without getting them. What if we did now? What would they say? You know what happens with these *Home Alone* cases. That's the way to lose Sally for good.'

Sam kept quiet. He heard her breathing. He thought she was calming down.

She said, 'I don't know what the fuck you thought you were doing, leaving her, parading about with –'

'Don't go into all that now.'

'I don't intend to. I don't want to know. I just want my daughter back safe. What did he say on the phone?'

97

'He wants me to go down. Tonight, to Leeds. To see him, and talk.'

'I'm coming with you.'

'No, you're not.'

'Don't try to –'

'We can't fuck this up, Sam. I don't know what state he's in.'

'What does that mean?' She sounded frightened.

'I don't know. But he says that Sally is safe and happy. He wants to see me tonight. Look, I'll sort it out.'

Sam was silent. He went on, 'Where are you now?'

'I'm . . . staying with a friend, still.'

'That copper?'

'Yes, that copper. Bob.'

'Right.'

'He wanted me to report it. We've rowed about it all day. This could really foul up his career.'

'Tell him to keep his fucking nose out.'

'I'm not going to talk about this now. We'll keep the police out of this, right?'

Mark felt himself sneer. 'We're no strangers to that, are we, Sam?'

She simply repeated, 'I'll keep the police out of this, so long as you bring my daughter back from Leeds with you.'

'And afterwards?'

'What?'

'When we get back to normal? Will you keep the police out of our lives then? This Bill, or Bob, or whatever you call him?'

She gave a shuddering laugh. 'I don't believe you. Just get on that train, Kelly, and sort that pervert out. *Now*!'

The phone clicked off.

Iris said, 'I don't understand.'

'While you were out,' Peggy told her, 'we had a phone call.' Mark was tying his shoelaces. 'It was Tony.'

Peggy took hold of Iris by her elbows. Over the past day it seemed at times as if Iris had been worst hit by Sally's disappearance. As dawn came up on Christmas morning, she had been sitting among the abandoned wrapping paper in Mark's flat.

'My fault. I put her to bed. I never closed her window. It was my idea to go walking like that . . . like bloody . . . like . . .' Sitting naked still in all the rubbish, she had looked pathetic. Peggy had been caught between the sight of her, Mark slumped on Sally's bed, and her own panic.

Now Iris was asking, 'Who is Tony?'

Mark was stuffing things into an overnight case Peggy had found for him. 'Someone I used to know. That note in the Christmas pudding was from him.'

'Why is he doing this?'

'I don't know. I don't know what he's doing.'

Bob's house was a pigsty. Sam had never seen it before. She sat down on the green settee, on a tangle of stale blue shirts. She'd never dreamed this would be the way to leave Mark, nor that these would be the circumstances of her escape.

On the wall there was one of those mass-produced paintings from the seventies showing a child with a tear rolling down his cheek. These paintings were rumoured to be jinxed and the cause of house fires. Bob's mam, he said, had pressed it upon him when he moved out to his own home. That and his tea service. He put by her feet a cup of thick, greasy tea.

'You made me sound so bad just then, on the phone,' he said.

She took her head out of her hands. 'What?'

'You told them that I wanted you to report Sally's disappearance just because of my work.'

'Does it matter?'

'It matters if I come out of this looking like a complete shit. I care, too, you know. I want to do something.'

'You hardly know the kid. She's mine.'

'But if we . . . carry on, if you stay here; she'll be mine, too, then.'

'Leave it for now, Bob. Don't fuck it up by talking about it now. It's like tempting fate. Just don't do it.'

Bob had seen Sally only once before. It had been one of those rare days when Sam finished work early because Mark had a job interview in Darlington. On the spur of the moment she asked Bob to come with her to meet Sally, instead of keeping their usual rendezvous. At the bottom of the school gates Bob had carefully shaken Sally's hand.

'Are you being arrested?' she asked her mother.

Sam was watching the other mothers watching them. Let them, she thought. She liked to be thought of as an unusual family. 'He's a friend of ours.'

'Are you giving us a lift home in your police car?'

'We're catching the bus. Bob has to go back to work.'

The child had given him a long, appraising look. Bob had been pleased; he felt himself being measured up as a replacement father. Sally had smiled briefly and then walked slowly past, dismissing him.

'She likes you,' Sam told him afterwards.

'Mark's going to Leeds tonight,' Sam said. 'Tony's in Leeds.'

'Tony?'

'His ex-lover. Remember? He's got Sally.'

The blood drained from Bob's face. 'Christ!' He looked completely helpless. 'What's going to happen, Sam?'

'I wanted to go down to Leeds with him, but he wouldn't let me. He's got to sort this out for himself, he said. A man's got to do what a man's got to do. Ha!'

'Is there an address?'

'He wouldn't give me one.'

'So we just have to sit?'

'Looks like it.'

'While those two faggots discuss the future of our family?'

Sam looked up at him with the greased tea cooling in her palms. 'Our family?' she asked.

'Please, Mark,' Peggy had said, 'phone us. Tell us what's happening.'

On the bus all the way to Darlington her words kept coming back to him. What did she think? That he'd just up and leave them in the dark?

'Will you come back tomorrow?' Iris had asked. Her voice was broken. They were in the kitchen just before he left. He hoisted the bag over his shoulder, knotted the scarf at his throat. Iris looked exactly what she was: a little old woman, distracted by fear. She had never struck him that way before. It was as if, after her ritual disrobing on Christmas Eve, she had remained a pale shadow of her former self. Then she had appeared pared down, vital; the essential part of Iris. Now she just looked stick-thin and frail with anxiety. Mark couldn't bring himself to reassure her.

'I don't know when I'll be back,' he said truthfully. 'I've got to see what Tony wants.'

Neither Iris nor Peggy knew what Tony was like; they hardly knew anything about him. But Mark did. Until a certain age he had known everything about Tony, and Tony everything about him. Perhaps this was Tony's way of bringing him up to date. He was being summoned to a résumé. That was the way to look at it. That was the safer version. It was the benign version of Tony he had fed Iris and Peggy, and now all three were depending on it.

The bus was empty and Darlington was stark, almost Gothic as they slipped in through freezing fog.

He was surprised by the reflection of his own face. He had forgotten about the make-up, and now registered how natural it made him look. He still wasn't quite sure why he had done it. In the small bag he was carrying, he had packed the leather case. It was a kind of talisman, because he had been given it just before the disaster.

The make-up was also a means of going incognito tonight. As if this were a spying mission. He barely recognised himself.

There was also another possible reason for it. But he pressed that down as soon as he thought it: the notion that he was making himself look as much like his old self as possible. Tony would remember him the way he was before the tattoos were completed. And suddenly Mark realised what Peggy and Iris hadn't said. The words they hadn't dared to speak as he left tonight had been clearly etched in lines of worry.

They thought he would end up going back to Tony. The suggestion had hung in the air of that kitchen. They thought it was obvious that, faced once more by an ex-lover, off he would go.

But the idea had never occurred to him. It had never seemed

real enough to become an idea. He was concerned with Sally. It was Sally he was going to see, it was his daughter he was out to find tonight. If he started thinking now about seeing Tony again, it would be too much to handle. This trip was for Sally. He couldn't see Sally and Tony in the same scene at all, not at all, not yet. Their existences were mutually exclusive, just as a multiple-choice question couldn't have two answers ticked. He couldn't picture Sally and Tony together, not even on a train station platform, waving him down.

Preoccupied with Sally, Mark had given little thought to the questions of why Tony wasn't in prison, how he had found their house, how he had managed to abduct the child. Sally's absence was the only real thing. Mark had been devastated by the sight of the scattered books on her bedroom floor, the dawn light fingering their dust covers on Christmas morning, her bedclothes mussed up.

To Mark tonight, Tony was merely the vehicle of this disaster. Not a real person; nothing to do with the person Mark used to know, used to love. For the moment, Tony was nothing more to Mark than the sneezing and grinding of the bus as it crawled into the station stop in Darlington.

'What a Christmas!' Peggy sighed as she sat down. She had washed everything in sight in Iris's kitchen. They had completed a dispirited meal. This was the first time in years that Iris's cottage had seemed unfamiliar to Peggy. Washing everything in sight seemed a way to reassert her ownership and to quell the bouts of panic.

Sitting still for the first moment since Mark had left for Leeds, all she wanted was to turn things back.

To before Christmas, say, when they were at the pantomime together. To before Sally was born, even, so they could have all those years again; have her novelty and newness, the bewildered charm of her. And even, if they could, turn time back to before Sam and Mark married, before that accident, before Iris and Peggy were together, when Peggy was alone in her own home. So many wrong turnings they'd be able to reroute. How much effort would it take to achieve all that?

Yet it seemed that all the effort in the world was being wasted right now, by Peggy herself, holding her tears back.

'Oh, God, don't cry,' Iris said. 'I thought you were keeping strong for us.'

'Just shut it for now, would you, Iris?'

Iris put the telly on. Christmas programmes. Something brash on ITV, foreign cartoons on Channel Four, opera on Two, and on One a sit-com Christmas special shot abroad. She turned down the sound and listened attentively.

'He'll be on the train by now,' Peggy said.

On the coffee table between them stood the teapot, cooling slowly, and the phone.

Sam tried, but she couldn't see herself finishing work every day and coming back to Bob's bleak kitchen with its cracked lino. And who would pick up Sally from school? A policeman couldn't stand each day at the gates. He had odd hours. He'd never consent to being the househusband Mark was.

She still couldn't see a life without Mark. The future had come down like venetian blinds. Bob's venetian blinds covered every window – it seemed fitting for a policeman, she thought – and their slats were bent and buckled by his impatience when opening windows.

The house had no reverberations for her. Not like the warm pinks of her own kitchen. The air here was dank, chilled. Was Bob mean with the central heating? That wasn't a good environment for bringing up a kid. Sally would catch her death.

He had come into the kitchen after her. She heard his footsteps, hesitant, respectful, on the yellow lino. This was his house; she could imagine him alone, crashing heedlessly from room to room. He put his arms around her.

'What are you doing?' His voice dripped with pity.

Her spine stiffened slightly. Patronising bastard.

'I don't know,' she admitted. 'Putting the kettle on?'

'We've drunk gallons of tea today.'

'Some Christmas,' she said. 'I'm sorry, Bob.'

'If this hadn't happened, we'd never have spent Christmas together at all.'

103

'It's not how I would have wanted it.'

Bob said, 'We've smoked nearly eighty fags between us, all day.'

'Just hold me for a bit,' Sam told him.

As he did so, clumsily, she thought: No, I can't live here, not like this. Sally wouldn't stand for it, anyway. She'd never like it here. But her thoughts went twisting round. Oh, she'd put up with it. She'd have to. She has to be with her mam. That's the way it has to be. That's the proper way. She'd get to like it wherever I was. She'd have the things she likes, she could bring her books and her toys with her. Bob would build bookshelves. Kids are resilient; she'd soon settle in. Kids change and they can adapt.

Mark had changed Sally. He'd taken her away from her mam. His influence had drawn her away. That was why she was distant, why she found it hard being with other kids her age. Mark worried about that. He told Sam about Sally standing out like a sore thumb at school. It made Sam ashamed. She knew Sally could shake that off once she got back with her mam. She cursed Mark for making her daughter weird.

'Let's go to bed,' Bob said. 'We've had enough of this day.'

'I'm so tired,' Sam said, almost in spite of herself.

Bob asked gently, 'Are you up to it?'

'Hm?'

'Our first night together, under a legal roof?'

'What are you talking about?'

'Well, we've got to take advantage of it, haven't we? And we've got to take our minds off the worry.'

He breathed through his mouth into her face. Suddenly the blush of dark beard on his chin appalled her.

'Mark's on his way to Leeds,' she said, drawing back. 'He ought to be there soon.'

Bob frowned. 'Don't think about it, Sam, love. Remember the night he ran off? When you were expecting? It all gets sorted out. Come on. Let's go and forget it a while; let's go and fuck.'

She shook him off. 'Keep off me! I don't believe you. I'm staying up tonight. I've got a lot of stuff to think about.'

104

'You can't stay up all night.'
She set her jaw. 'I can do what I like.'

Iris said, 'We've been through worse things than this.'
Peggy shook her head. 'No, we haven't. This is the worst.'
'It'll be all right.' Iris came to sit beside her.
The phone was still cold; they caught themselves staring at it, yet again.
'I mean it,' Iris continued. 'We've seen worse times.'
'Like when?' Peggy looked up with dark mascara fingers down cheeks leathered with fatigue.
'During the Second War. We were married then, struggling in Berlin. In the court of James II. When I was Cleopatra and you were Mark Antony.'
'You're insane.'
'But quite serious.'
'You're not starting this living-for-ever shit again, are you?'
'Well,' said Iris, 'the Cleopatra bit was a sensational lie, I admit. But I *am* saying that we've both seen rough times all through history. We've always been in love – for five centuries now – and we've always come through it together.'
Peggy gave a brittle laugh. 'I've not lived for five centuries.'
'No, but I have. You've been reincarnated, again and again. You just can't remember as I can. It's been me who's had to run after you, find you, make you love me, time and time again.'
'Oh, sod off, Iris! I'm not in the mood for this.'
Iris startled her by bursting into tears, heavy, gasping sobs. Her small frame fell against Peggy's. 'It's all true. Don't pull away from me. I couldn't go looking again. I want this to be our last life together, I want us to grow old together this time, and I want us to protect those younger ones around us. I want Sally to come back safe, and for Mark to bring her. I don't want it to break us up in terror. I just want things to be all right. And for you to believe in me, Peggy.'
Her lover gathered her up and Iris sobbed until she fell into a deep sleep. Peggy felt cramp building up in her leg, sitting awkwardly until the night's television finished. This is madness, she thought. We're all cracking up over this.

*

105

Trains are so bright inside. Especially at night, and Mark was all nerves. The blue plush of the seats was like sandpaper against him. Again, he was alone as he travelled, slipping into an unfathomable south. Alone he could believe it was all a hoax. He could see nothing outside. Only, occasionally, an industrial estate would flash by, bristling fuchsia and sodium light, pluming pearl-coloured smoke.

He avoided looking at his reflection. The foundation he wore made him look ill. He looked too blank in this light.

It was the last train. The conductor was fractious as he waited for Mark to produce his ticket.

'My child's been abducted,' Mark told him, by way of explaining his confusion, as the conductor clipped his ticket. 'I'm going to find her.'

The conductor nodded gloomily.

'How far to Leeds?'

'Half an hour.' He passed on to the next carriage. Mark heard the scream of air as the doors opened, leaving him alone again.

How will I know when we get there? Just wait until a sign appears, white and glaring at my window, saying 'Leeds'? Until Tony and Sally are peering in at me? How will I know?

Mark had never travelled far. To stay at home seemed safer; it had everything he ever wanted, or so he told himself in his more optimistic moments. At least, he could make it into any environment he wanted. And so he had; and they were happy, weren't they? They had made a happy family together, successfully, by staying in the same place at the same time.

He knew he had made Sally as nervy of travelling as he was. Somehow the neurosis had been passed on; it wasn't one that Sam had ever had. Sam went out to work daily, thought nothing of catching the bus last thing alone in the dark. Sally had squeezed herself in warily that day they had taken the bus to Darlington to see the pantomime. The sight of strange buildings had been enough to unnerve her. And she had been sitting with her father the whole time. God knew how she was coping with being taken to a strange town by a strange man.

He had fallen into a desperate, headaching sleep, and woke just in time. He found himself slumped, wino-style, and rose up to look out. Floodlights showed the span of conflicting rail lines that crossed and recrossed as they approached the gaping mouth of Leeds Central Station.

Well, Tony, I'm at your mercy. You've got my attention at last. Just make sure you look after my daughter.

Mark gathered up his belongings and started struggling towards the automatic doors as the train began to shunt to a stop.

You've got some explaining to do, Tony.

Fifteen

Once they had been in a rock-and-roll band together. It was when they were fifth-years and most people were leaving school. They rehearsed in Tony's living room because his mam went away at weekends to stay with a newsagent in Chilton. On Sunday nights she would return elated and bearing surplus copies of that day's papers. The house was free all Saturday for the band and friends of the band to fill it with their black, laminated amplifiers, crushed lager cans and blue smoke.

Mark was the singer for a while but they stopped him because he screeched the high notes in songs like 'Rebel Rebel' and spoiled it. Tony played guitar and he was in charge; it was he who had to relay the band's instructions to Mark. Mark didn't mind too much; he was happy simply to hang around on a Saturday, help out with the equipment and chat with the girlfriends of the band in Tony's mam's kitchen, where the dirty crockery would stack up through the long, noisy afternoons.

The other members of the band had already left school. Some were in the borstal up the road, or on remand, or they were about to go into the army after summer. Sometimes Mark thought Tony liked hanging about with boys who dressed hard and shaved their heads. Their girlfriends changed week in and week out, except for Pauline, who was the fat drummer's girlfriend. She wore heavy black eye make-up and her hair was bleached and stringy. She sat nervously at the edge of the settee with her cigarettes, tapping ash into a used beer can, and helped the drummer sort his kit out at the end. Eventually she was consigned with the other girls to the kitchen, after they had spent one afternoon laughing all the way through a version of 'Psycho Killer', which the boys were committing to tape.

Working on the band, Tony was intent and gloomy. Only occasionally would he lighten up and enjoy himself. He was given to messing around, drawing long, blood-curdling screeches out of his guitar in the middle of the songs. These always overrode whatever the singer was screeching. This was another reason Mark had been happy to move over and leave them as a mostly instrumental band. Tony was unequivocally the star.

Mark still thought it unfair that the girls were banished while he was allowed to stay and watch. He had been laughing as much as they that time. Then he saw the reason: Tony had drawn up a band rule that was meant to get them to work more tightly as a unit and make them concentrate. It was a kind of forfeit game: the blinds were drawn down, and for every bum note or mistake they made, the band member had to remove an article of clothing. It would fine-tune their performance and loosen inhibitions, Tony told them.

The lads in the band looked at each other, laughed a bit, and finally shrugged. Yeah, whatever. Might be a laugh. Tony winked at Mark, who was sitting by the rubber plant. This was his leaving present to him. Of course he was allowed to stay and the girls must go out into the kitchen.

All that afternoon the band played hard. Their noise levels were higher than usual and Mark worried about the neighbours sending the coppers round, and the coppers finding the dope that they occasionally broke off to roll into messy, powerful spliffs. The drummer launched into his strained rendition of 'Wild Thing' and it took hours to get through, with elongated passages of drum solos and guitar licks that howled needlessly through the middle of the piece. Mistakes were made and, laughing, the boys stripped off articles of clothing, which were dumped unceremoniously in a pile in the middle of the black cabling.

Tony was in his element. Mark could see him feeding off the slick electricity of the atmosphere. He watched him look up abstractedly from his playing – the best playing he'd ever done, they knew – and stare at the bass player, who was nonchalantly down to socks and underpants. Mark continued smoking and was asked to sing a Banshees song, which he did, quickly, with only one lyrical mistake, for which he was told to take off his cardigan. The drummer insisted, laughing; starkers behind his kit, fat and sweating. Tony started to make mistakes that Mark knew were false until he was playing with his guitar alone covering him. Mark wondered if the others realised what was going on. He started to feel ashamed by the whole business. It was as if Tony were exposing the games that they played together in private to everyone. Tony had an erection, which they could see as he played, and which they would put down to rock and roll. No different from them getting out *Pussy Talk* on video, on a different Saturday afternoon, sitting with the cans and their cocks out, passing the Kleenex round and concentrating on the screen.

Mark left them to it and went to talk to Pauline. She was reading *Smash Hits* at the kitchen table. They talked about the drummer, Simon, and she said they were engaged. He wasn't everything Pauline had dreamed of, but what the fuck else was she meant to expect? It was exotic enough that they had been to different comprehensives.

Just after six the rehearsal finished and Tony led the others out, to find Mark snogging with Pauline over the sink.

'I don't know what it was about,' Mark protested that night in Tony's squalid bedroom. Music was playing quietly, the tape of that afternoon's better-than-usual session. The mattress was on the floor, strewn in dirty sheets. Album covers were scattered and there were envelopes everywhere with bits of new lyrics scrawled. 'I just asked if she minded if I kissed her.'

'You asked her?'

'I don't know why. She looked sad.'

'How do you think she feels now? Her and Simon are engaged, you know.'

'I just wanted to get out of that room for a bit. It was too smoky. It smelled, as well, sweaty.'

Tony stripped off again, waded through the mess past Mark and clambered under the sheets.

'What made you ask them to do that?'

'That was the best rehearsal we've had in weeks.'

'It was risky, Tony. What if they figured out you're queer?'

'It was just lads, Mark. They never thought a thing about it.'

'Yeah, right,' Mark said, though he knew Tony was right. 'But you got a real thrill out of it, didn't you?'

Tony lay back under the thin covering and considered. 'Yes, actually, I did. And listen, I played better than ever, didn't I? You know I did. It does me good to have naked men around me.' He tugged at Mark's shirt.

'I don't think I can sit around and watch it every Saturday,' Mark said, undressing.

'All right. You and the girls can just enjoy yourselves in the kitchen. And, as for them finding out I'm queer, what about me finding out that you're straight, Mark? How do you think that makes me feel?'

Mark slipped off his shoes, sitting on the corner of the mattress. 'I'm not straight, Tony. I've already told you, I don't know why I kissed her.'

'You were just keeping your options open? And letting me know that?'

I could say yes, agree with him, Mark thought. Let him carry that one about with him. 'I don't know how my life will turn out,' he said truthfully. 'I can't see the shape of it at all.'

'So you're saying you're not ruling out going straight?'

Mark slid off his jeans and lay down beside Tony. 'I honestly can't say, Tone. It's so difficult.'

'Did you fancy her?'

'Who? Pauline?'

'Could you have got it up for her?'

'I suppose so. I –'

'What are you after, Mark?' Tony burst out suddenly. Beside them the tape ran out on the recorder and the silence fell hard on them. 'What do you want me to give you?' He looked at him squarely. 'You're mine. You know that.'

Not for the first time Mark felt unnerved by Tony's voice. Strip away all the rest of him, his voice was the strength, the hard core of him.

111

'I can give you anything any woman could. You don't have to go straight to get back at me.' Tony slapped the pillow. 'Jesus, I would've been less bothered if you'd took John upstairs and fucked him.'

John was the bass player. Mark snorted. 'I can't see that happening.'

'Did you see him, though? Was he naked while you were there? The size of him, Jesus!'

'Just stop talking about it.'

'What is it, Mark? Are you ashamed of yourself? This is what it's like, love.'

'I want to sleep.'

'What do you talk to the girls about? Having babies? Is that what you and Pauline were on about? How you could have babies and we couldn't?'

'This is stupid.'

'Is that what you want, Mark? Do you want children? Is that why you want to keep your options open?'

'Look, Tony, I don't know any more. I just want to sleep now.'

'Yeah, right.'

They curled up under the sheet. Tony lay behind Mark, coiling one arm into his chest, gripping him tightly. Mark still had his shorts on; they separated them even though their bodies were clenched as close as they could go. Suddenly Tony felt stupid, vulnerable in his nakedness, with his dick pressed uselessly at Mark's back, his arse in the breeze under the rucked sheet. 'I'm going to put some things on,' he whispered hoarsely. Seeing to it, he was blushing, as if he ought to be ashamed of himself.

Propping himself on one elbow, Mark said, 'Don't bother,' and pulled his shorts off, slinging them into the detritus of Tony's room. He held the sheet for Tony to get back in and curled around him fiercely when he did. This time the closeness was right; they were both relieved, erect and grateful for each other. 'I fancy you, you daft fucker,' Mark insisted. 'I always have and nothing'll stop that. Your body is mine. I know what I'm getting from it.'

*

In Leeds that night it was snowing. He didn't have much money with him. None of them had thought about the expense of all this. What if Tony wanted money? Wanted buying off? I should be keeping what I've got, Mark thought, but as he passed out of the station he went straight to the taxi rank. He wanted to go as fast as possible to the address Tony had given him. Once he had seen Sally safe again, the rest could be negotiated afterwards.

It was such a relief to be in the back seat of the taxi, borne along through the city centre with tall buildings about him, hearing the wheels slash through the build-up of snow. The driver was quiet, too; resentful of working on a holiday. The city was still. Seventies disco played on the radio, as if they had slipped back in time, as if he were in an American city.

This was how cities always struck him, wherever they were. He felt dwarfed and exhilarated, pressed back in his seat and looking up out of the corner of windows.

Soon they were passing through subways and looping main roads, out past the tallest buildings and into the suburbs. Here the shops were less frequent and rougher, their windows barred for the night. They slid through one concrete estate and Mark shuddered. He locked his door just in case. It was probably no worse here than it was on his own estate, but he was taking no chances.

They found Headingley. The houses were older, taller and built of an orange brick that looked dirty in the night and the snow. Packs of students were wandering around, congregating outside off-licences and cinemas. White men and women in dreadlocks were drifting through the sleet with battered pushchairs and Alsatians on pieces of string, past gangs of Indian kids who were playing outside the gleaming windows of their parents' shops, kept open all through Christmas. There were more trees here, more open spaces, but the houses were cramped in closer confinement, as if they had been built piecemeal and were collapsing in on themselves with age.

Abruptly the taxi slewed round one final corner and pulled to a halt before a tall, narrow house with black iron gates and unkempt hedges. 'This is it,' the driver growled and quoted an exorbitant price.

Then Mark was left with his bag on the icy road. Thoughtlessly he rubbed his chin. As he felt the stubble growing through foundation, he realised he must have smeared away parts of his disguise. The tattoos would be showing through. He'd look as if he had a skin disease. He opened the gate and hurried up the slippery path to the door before he got a chance to change his mind about this.

Now that he was here, it all seemed horribly normal. Here he was paying a social call. Was this how kidnappings usually worked? He felt out of his depth.

Grand and lifeless, the house was like a modest slice of cake. In that dark suburban terrace it somehow stood alone, its icing sugar flaking off. An old man answered his knock, fumbling with catches on the double doors. It was like getting into a high-security prison, but the air that met Mark was warm and lit duskily by candles. The decor and furnishings he could see as he shuffled into the hallway behind the old man were rich; opulent, even. A chandelier hung at the mouth of the staircase, its crystal droplets tipped with nicotine stains.

The old man was silent; he nodded to Mark to wait there in the hallway, standing awkwardly by a large glass vase of irises. The man was almost bent double with age. His hands were the colour of corned beef with the jelly left on. He was obviously ready to go home: he wore a long coat and a beret and his hi-tech trainers were laced securely for a walk through the snow. Mark wondered who he was. The sight of those painfully watering eyes when the door first creaked open had caught him off guard. 'Tony?' he had asked, so wound up that he would have asked the same thing no matter who had opened the door.

'He said you have to wait,' the old man had gasped. He took Mark's bag and his fingers were freezing when they brushed Mark's. Mark was about to say he could manage it himself, but with an inexplicable burst of speed, the hi-tech trainers had carried the old man to the top of the stairs. His voice quavered down behind him, 'You're to go and sit in the living room. There's a fire.'

Only one door was open downstairs, so Mark took it. The carpet was thick under the soles of his shoes and the ceilings were high. He didn't shout anything up the stairs in reply. He wasn't sure of his voice at all.

The living room was sparsely furnished but warm. A single armchair sat before the fireplace. He sat right on its edge, as if demonstrating that he didn't intend to stay.

Tony had done well for himself. Mark was amazed. A wide, ornately framed mirror hung above the mantelpiece, complemented with soft lighting. Raising himself to see his face, Mark thought he looked dreadful. On the mantelpiece there was a single avocado resting in a yellow eggcup, a silver teapot and a pile of old hardbacked books.

He couldn't quite work out what was odd about the house, aside from the fact it wasn't how he had imagined Tony living. The silence? The fire crackled and sparked companionably. He noticed a connecting door in one of the room's shadowed corners, and crept over to have a look through. Beyond there was a deep-blue dining room. Its windows were tall, Georgian, an extravagant candelabra alight on the whitewashed sill. But on the floor the scarlet carpet was half rolled up, and dominating the unswept floorboards there was a jumbled hoard of objects. The candlelight glittered on teapots, saucers, cups, bits of statues. They looked like antiques: small, tasteful and just showy enough to be valuable. They looked as if they had just arrived, or were about to be scooped up in a sheet to be flogged somewhere.

That was the look of the house, half assembled or half disassembled. The house was a luxurious stopover point for the accoutrements of whatever life Tony had invented for himself. The whole place exuded both largesse and abandonment, as if it were a bargain basement that declared to its hushed, private guests that this was their last chance to gather what they desired, and run.

Then the old man was at his shoulder. 'I've done out your room and put your things there,' he said.

Mark had had enough. 'Where's Tony? I want to see him now. Has he got Sally here?'

Then the old man really unnerved him by looking him straight in the eye again. Except he didn't; there was something gleaming yellow behind those eyes that made them

115

look directed elsewhere the whole time he spoke. They gleamed with a manic distraction which, had Mark seen it on the telly, would have made him laugh, but here, in a strange house in a strange town, shocked him. He had no idea that eyes really did look like that in the faces of creepy old butlers of old houses. 'I'm to make you a cup of tea in the scullery,' he said.

'*Are* you a butler?' Mark asked.

The old man, still in his beret and trainers and obviously wanting to go home, simply tutted with disgust. He hobbled to the connecting door, saw that Mark had already peeked, tutted again, and led him through that dining room. They went down a few stone steps to a dim kitchen. More candles, more stranded avocados. On the kitchen table there was the most comprehensive canteen of cutlery Mark had ever seen, and five teapots, three of them smashed in unnervingly clean breaks.

The Aga was reassuringly warm. The old man busied himself while Mark went to look out of the window. He couldn't see much of a garden; it looked bricked over, or churned up in the search for archaeological treasures. Stark branches slapped and snagged at the dirty panes.

'I'm Simmonds,' the old man said at last, having, with some effort, slid the heavy teapot onto the ring. The scraping noise went right through Mark. 'I've got some fruitcake some-where.'

'That's all right,' Mark said.

'Yes, fruitcake, somewhere. I think it's dry.'

'Tea will be fine.'

'No, I shall find it for you. I shall.'

'Do you have a phone?' Mark asked suddenly, and in that moment noticed the fifties-style phone at the other end of the table. He had to get in touch with Peggy and Iris, though he wasn't sure what there was to tell them yet.

Simmonds thrust an opened cake tin in his face. 'There.' The smell of stale cake assailed him. 'You'll have some.'

'Would Tony mind if I phoned someone?'

Simmonds shrugged, looking for a plate in a pile of pale-blue saucers. Now he could barely bring himself to look at Mark; it was all or nothing with him. 'It's his phone.'

'Is he here?'

'Take it up with him. He pays the phone bill. Nothing to do with me any more. Here.' He thrust at Mark a saucer with the whole half-finished cake upturned on it. Mark took a bite and found it was dried through. The boiling kettle fortunately distracted Simmonds.

'It'll be tea then,' said Simmonds vaguely, staring at the teapots.

Suddenly Mark felt something clutch at his gut. Where the fuck was Sally in all this? He felt hoodwinked; this wasn't what he had expected at all. But then the kitchen door screeched open and black freezing air rushed in. A bulky Labrador stampeded into the kitchen, pulling on his lead at a young man in a leather jacket. And behind the dog owner, clutching his cold-reddened hand, Sally, looking breathless, laughing, exhilarated by snow.

Mark grabbed at her. He had time only to register the alarm in her eyes, the change from laughter to shock, before he had her lifted to his chest, his face buried in her hair, and he was sobbing with relief.

'Cups,' Simmonds muttered, rattling through a cracked multitude.

'Sally, Sally,' Mark whispered. He had shocked her into tears of her own and now he had to console her. 'It's all right, pet. All right.' He looked up over her shoulder; on her coat snowflakes were just turning to drops of water from the heat of the Aga. A fine haze of steam was rising from her, the young man and the dog. The young man was giving Mark a slow, appraising look, removing his jacket and putting on an apron. He was younger than Mark had at first thought, white-haired and grinning laconically. Tony's houseboy, Mark thought; it had to be. Christ, he's got what we said we'd have at fourteen. The dog lay beneath the table, growling good-naturedly, head between its paws.

'The dog's Duke,' Sally said at last, between heaves.

'I'm Richard,' said the young man in the apron. 'I work for Tony. I have to get dinner on.'

117

'Where's Tony?' Mark asked.

'Richard's nice, Dad,' Sally said.

'He won't be in till late,' Richard said.

It was a relief to talk to someone who seemed to be sensible. 'He's out working a market somewhere.'

Simmonds had his head in a tall, narrow fridge, sniffing cartons of milk suspiciously. 'Antiques,' he murmured.

'I guessed,' Mark said. He and Richard exchanged a glance. 'What's happening?' Mark asked impulsively. He couldn't now imagine calling the police.

Richard shrugged. He said, almost whispering, 'I thought you knew Sally was here. The first I knew different was when Tony phoned you today. I overheard. We fought about it. But, hey – I'm only an employee.'

Mark hated anyone who slipped 'but, hey' into conversation, yet he decided that Richard was all right, really. He turned instead to Simmonds, who was pouring tea, and who had been evasive enough earlier to deserve Mark's asking, 'And are you an employee too?'

Immediately Mark saw Richard cringe, he knew he had made a mistake. Simmonds looked up very slowly. 'I built this business. Tony helped a bit, later on. Bit by bit he took it off me. I'd've given him everything at one time. We bought things for this house together. He had a half share. Eight hundred thousand he's had off me. I totted it up all last night. At least he's still here. At least he's not gone yet. At least he's still selling things with me. Even if he's giving it away to somebody else.'

Richard gave a breezy, overplayed chuckle, and said, 'Shouldn't you be going now? Remember what Tony said?'

Simmonds slammed a cup and saucer down on the table. He had been about to pass it to Mark. Enunciating very clearly, he said, 'I'll leave when I decide, miss. You've not got this place over my dead body yet. I'm making tea for our guests. Then I'll go.'

'I can make tea,' Richard said, entirely reasonable.

'Yes,' Simmonds said. 'I know.' He examined his knuckles carefully for a moment, and reached a decision. 'Make your fucking tea, then.' He turned and walked out of the kitchen. He stopped in the low doorway and hissed, 'Queens!'

Sally was playing with the dog under the table by then, and Richard was happily fetching the sugar. 'What was that about?' Mark asked.

'Mad as a bloody hatter.' Richard shook his head. 'You saw. Resents me, Tony, whatever Tony does. But he's the man with the money. Or he used to be. Jesus!' He wiped his sugared fingers down his apron after spilling the packet into a bowl. He's rattled, Mark thought, worse than he's letting on. 'You'll get used to our ways here. I know it looks completely loopy right now. You think it's all right, don't you, Sally love? We've had a lovely day together.'

'Leeds is great, Dad. Can we move?' she asked, looking up from under the table. Even she was different, brighter, almost vivacious. 'Have I missed Christmas Day?' she added, with one of her more familiar, peculiarly adult expressions.

'Honest, I had no idea what you were going through. I thought she was here on a legitimate visit. Mark, isn't it? Tony's talked about you.'

'Has he?' Mark couldn't keep the coldness out of his voice. Richard was merely implicated, there was no need to freeze him out. For the moment Mark could only look at how he was being construed in all this – the furious, bereft father storming into the antique collector's priceless haven, kicking up a fuss. Richard's shy deference puzzled him, too. Richard saw him as the straight man, vengeful, rightfully so, a breeder on the rampage. Mark was furious at himself for thinking that Richard was actually quite sweet: that offhand shyness was balanced by real concern. Mark was the one being strong, that was how Richard saw it, but all Mark wanted now was to cling to Richard's apron and ask for some comforting.

He was surprised. Richard smiled again gently, handing him the tea. 'I think it'll be all right,' he said, adding, 'The phone's right beside you.'

'Peggy!' The shriek rang through the house.

Peggy was in the bath and came lumbering down the hall to meet Iris.

119

'I've got the address. She's with Mark. She's perfect. I mean, she's safe, happy . . . She's all right!'

Peggy grasped Iris to her and gave her a soaking. 'Oh, God! Oh . . . my Orlando.'

Sam was ashen-faced, exhausted. The phone slipped from her grasp and hit the carpet. Carefully Bob replaced it and didn't dare ask what had been said.

A few seconds passed and then she looked up.

'It's an address in Headingley. We're going tomorrow. Will you drive?'

Sixteen

Sally had been given a room that had once been a sort of dressing room adjacent to Mark's. At first he insisted on keeping her where he could see her.

'She'll be all right,' Richard told him, showing them round upstairs. The ceilings were too high here as well. Mark couldn't help feeling intimidated.

Since Simmonds had gone off into the night, the atmosphere had lightened. Dinner was in the warm kitchen. Richard produced food from the cupboards and the narrow fridge and they sat by candlelight, talking quietly and laughing. They were like three children with the grown-ups away; Sally was pleased she could stay up so late.

Richard had opened some wine and Mark did something he had never believed he would that night: he got happily drunk. After Richard had shown him where Sally would sleep, within his earshot, and they had seen her to bed, they went back to the kitchen, drank some more and screamed with laughter at Mark's story about Christmas Eve, the bits about the walkabout and the orange in the copper's mouth.

The tension had gone. Everything that had tightened and tightened and then burst into disaster over the last few days was suddenly erased. When Mark reflected on the events leading up to Christmas, he marvelled that he had never seen the danger signs. Sam had been flaunting them. He saw that now. She had worn them appliquéd on every word and gesture during the whole month's run-up to Christmas. Even that final, patronising kiss on the chest had been an act of sarcasm. Gradually Mark came to the realisation that Sam had been looking for a reason to leave him. That fitted. It really made sense. The mad letter from Tony she had found gave her the perfect excuse.

He was smiling, confirming this to himself, when Richard ducked back into the kitchen, clumsily uncorking a bottle with the wrecked opener and a teatowel. 'What's so funny?'

'Not funny,' Mark said. He wore the smile of someone about to make a major life change, the sort of smile he had seen on *Oprah* during afternoons home with the telly. 'Just sort of pleasing.'

'Good,' Richard said, pouring.

'So what's the set-up here?'

Richard's face darkened momentarily. Then he blushed, and they both laughed. 'I'm never quite sure,' he admitted. 'But whatever it is these days, Mr Simmonds just isn't happy with it.'

'No?'

'Well, you saw how he was. They got me in about a year ago, to look after the house. They go about all over the place, selling stuff. I don't know much about the business, though I'm supposed to be learning. I was hand-picked to carry on the family firm.'

'Here's to happy families!'

'Yeah, right. To both of ours, invented or otherwise.'

'So what's Tony like now?'

The younger man rubbed his eyes with a sigh. He looked tired. Mark realised that Richard had spent quite a lot of time in Sally's company, and he knew how conversations with her could go on and on, once they started. Once she knew you were interested, there was no letting up. Richard looked wrecked. But Mark needed some advance warning about Tony.

'You do know,' Richard began, 'that the minute he gets back, he'll harass me for the same information about you?'

'But we're not playing bloody courting games,' Mark said. 'He kidnapped my fucking daughter! He's lucky I've not had the police in and –'

'Well, he knew you wouldn't do that.'

Sinking back into his chair, Mark said, 'I thought he was still in prison. He wrote me letters for years pretending that he was.'

'A little game. They're always playing games here.'

'It's just so bloody weird.'

'I suppose it is,' Richard admitted. 'And it's wrong to include people from outside, like you and your family. It's bad enough when it's just indoor games, when they're fucking up each other's mind, and my mind. But we're all willing victims of it, here. Even I am.' Solemnly Richard swished his glass. 'I'm no innocent. I wasn't in the first place.'

'Why do you stay here?'

'It's a job.' He shrugged. 'A bloody good job. You want to see the money going through this place. And if you're on the inside here, there's no question that it's yours as well. It's a family. We've had some lovely times. No, we really have. It's a different world to where I'm from. And . . . I reckon I love Tony a bit, too.'

Mark nodded. 'I can imagine.'

'It's weird, the relationship I have with him. It's like most of the time he takes my personality, everything I am, then raises it to the nth power. He elevates me. Other times, he blasts straight through it and I'm a body, a thing for whatever he feels like doing. I just assume that's how it is with older men.'

'It's how it is with Tony. It was that way with me, and we were together at the same age. I've never had an older man, I must admit.'

'Well, you've been on the straight and narrow for a while now, haven't you? In fact –' Richard's eyes were mischievous – 'you're now in the position to be an older man yourself.'

Mark choked. 'That's a terrible thing to say.'

Sally slept deeply in a cylindrical dressing room whose single wall bore a spiralling shelf. Sally slept surrounded by an interminable coil of books, and she dreamed of a Möbius strip. She dreamed of climbing a friendly gradient, stopping here and there to browse through other people's stories. She dreamed and dreamed so completely, so far from the rest of her life, that images from this night would recur at scattered moments throughout the rest of her formative years. But she would never put them in any kind of order.

That night in the converted dressing room, however, the

world was hermetically sealed, complete and replete with each answer she would ever need.

'Music!'

In the half-dismantled dining room, Richard found a wind-up record player. They danced together for a while, until it was about four in the morning.

Seventeen

Drunk this time, Mark wasn't about to make the same mistake. He hadn't meant to get like this again. At one point, dancing in the dining room with Richard, feet scraping on hollow wood, he thought, I can't handle it if this is another epiphany.

Getting drunk could bring on disaster. You widened out and out and embraced everything; you said anything you liked, did anything you felt, and hoped the world would relieve you of responsibility. This night, too, he could feel his sympathies widening and knew at the back of his mind that he couldn't afford to let them. He was still here on a mission.

Richard was by turns diffident and keen. This night could go any way they fancied, really, with little lost either way.

But Mark knew that upstairs Sally slept in the circular room, and when they reached four o'clock all he wanted to do was fall asleep outside her door. He wanted to guard her room tightly with the full weight of his body, until morning came and they could leave. It was time to shut down and wait until sensible action was called for and could resume. Tonight was not the time nor place for giving anything away.

Richard shrugged as Mark reeled away from him, tangling his feet in the dirty canvas sheet where the assorted *objets* were laid out. Mark explained that he needed to sleep. His 'goodnight' was one of those very polite ones, resolute yet fond, and could be taken by the younger man as a final word on, and even a betrayal of, the atmosphere they had summoned up between them. Richard showed him up and Mark was so intent upon the thought of being a dead weight of protection for Sally, listening in his stupor all night for her breathing through the door, that he was now no longer conscious of Richard as anything but a guide to that resting place.

'In here,' Richard reminded him, patting his shoulder as Mark slid past into the warm room. Richard switched on the bedside lamp and then was gone, the door clicking behind him.

Once in bed, Mark screwed himself up tight in the bedclothes and listened. Nothing; but her room was lined in books, he recalled, and was insulated. With his night vision tilting side to side and his breath rattling in his chest, stertorous as though he were already asleep, he went to her door, opened it a crack and checked she was there. She was: a half-moon of pillow-reddened face showed under mussed-up hair, the fat fingers clutching an opened picture book over the covers.

Mark slumped back into bed and wound himself up secure, making his presence as stolid as he could. When he closed his eyes he felt everything tip slowly into the mattress; nothing would stop the inexorable slide other than keeping his eyes open and lying quite still, in a vigil. He didn't know how far the dark slide would take him but he was sure it wouldn't be into a contented sleep. So he lay still on his side with heart palpitations, able to make out the room's single round window, high up on the wall across from him.

'Let's see what's through the round window today.'

Sally was too young ever to have watched *Playschool*. That seemed a shame. She hadn't seen *The Clangers*, either, *Hector's House* or *Tales of the Riverbank*. She didn't have much patience with what there was on kids' TV these days. Either it was way above her head or way below it. Mark watched with her sometimes to get her interested, but it all seemed to be teenage boys in dance bands parading about with opened shirts and only their underpants on. Sally grew bored and wandered off to do something else. She'd be absorbed in a drawing when Sam came in from work, and Mark would still be watching Take That in action. Sam would tut.

When he heard the patter of tiny feet on the room's bare boards, he thought he was merely inventing it. Then he

126

thought Sally was up and about. But she was heavier than that. Having woken up, she, like her father, tended to lumber about. She had inherited his heavy sleeping; they ate breakfast, mornings, in companionable silence, as if each mulling over the night's images.

These were tiny, deliberate footfalls in his room, and Sally's door was still safely shut. Somebody was being extra careful. They could be the sound of a long, long approach; carefulness from a very great distance. He lay still and vaguely enjoyed the thoughtfulness and respect of whoever it was.

Then, a terrible creak of floorboards. Something was definitely up. He had to do something, now; anybody with any sense would. The sound of weight on old wood was close by him and required reaction. Slowly Mark drew back the covers and lay ready to jump up. His body was knotted with that back-breaking tension of being disturbed in the middle of the night.

He was looking out into the dark, but the round window gave out only a narrow channel of milky light, showing a harmless chair in the corner. Mark felt a hand touch lightly on his shin. He wouldn't look. There was no sound, no breathing yet; nothing palpable other than the hand, and then another, pausing and then pushing a little weight on him to see what he would do.

They were caught in a deadlock; he refused to do anything until the hands declared responsibility by manifesting a full presence. The hands waited there as if for an invitation. Mark could believe, there in the dark, that their owner existed in some other place, in another dimension. The signals he was getting from his body were now so muffled by alcohol and exhaustion that he felt he had no responsibility towards them; it was all a million miles away.

One of the hands reached a decision and moved the length of him, removing itself at his thigh, hovering, pondering; the other was still at his knee, as if waiting to hear from its mate.

Summoning his breath, Mark asked, 'Richard?'

Both hands left him for a second and Mark thought they were gone. Then one palm was pressed down on his chest, fingers slow and questing; the other hand rejoined him tentatively at tip of his erection. He hadn't known he had one; he was so distant by now that it could have been something supplied by that returning hand.

When one touched his face in a caress, he felt the slight brush of fabric; the hands wore gloves. As he arced his spine and it cracked, he was twisting slightly, raising himself. The hand worked steadily, worked him off in a sure, palpating grip. Both hands were stark white.

A slow hiss of suppressed breath could be heard now under the gasps Mark felt himself giving out. One hand roamed his face and neck and pushed him back against the pillows suddenly as he came.

The deep slide into unconsciousness began again and the two hands reunited themselves to smear sperm across his stomach and chest, easing him to sleep with a balm of his own making.

The moon was still out, but Bob was used to early starts. While he waited in the car he had the engine turning over nicely, his first fag on the go and Radio One turned up. He hung one arm out of his window and drummed idly on the paintwork, relishing the cold now that the car was warmed through inside.

He could keep this day in some perspective if only he regarded it as just another day's work. He was trained to cope with emergencies and that was exactly what today was. He was a policeman and knew how to draw himself back from other people's panic and act sensibly. That was all he had to do today, keep a cool head on. He would get them through. He just had to drive, act as a soothing influence and not allow himself to pick up Sam's bristling air of rage and worry. If he got sucked into that, he'd be no use at all to her.

The moon was set in a blue so tender it forced the early starters to squint away. Its fresh resilience shamed their tiredness. Bob felt cramped and knotted up with tension; he had indigestion from bolting his breakfast and leaving the house without a cigarette. Sitting in the car park, he waited for Sam, Iris and Peggy to finish their business in the services, and watched the sky.

Sam had instructed him last thing last night that Iris and Peggy would be coming with them. She had obviously thought it through and decided that she couldn't leave them out. When they pulled up outside Iris's cottage this morning, in the waning dark, Bob had been slightly nervous of them. He needn't have worried; they were much too preoccupied to think anything of him.

'This is Bob,' Sam had said pointedly as they froze on the front doorstep. She refused to enter Iris's house.

Peggy had given him a quick once-over. 'Thanks for offering to drive us,' she said.

He wondered, perhaps she felt as daft as he did. She was the one, after all, he'd seen wandering around starkers. She was probably grateful he hadn't run them in. It was well within his powers. She looked the sort, really, who would respect the police and take well to having one as a son-in-law. At least she would know then that her daughter and grandchild were safe.

Nothing else had been said about or to him. The women spoke to each other or not at all, all this made it easier for Bob to exert his reassuring stoicism.

Would this be how things would carry on when all this had blown over? He wouldn't mind if it was. He knew how families of women worked and knew how to find his place in them. Men were best off keeping quiet and out of it; relied upon, gently mocked but, all in all, respected. In the first half-hour of this morning's trip he had already sussed that this was how this lot worked.

It was much the same with his own family: his mam, the three aunties and his grandmother. They were fiercely tight-knit, in and out of each other's houses. They cooked for each other, took things round, and never quite knew whose crockery belonged to whom. His father had always been there, unassuming but strong. It just seemed the way to be.

Bob had got used to being or not being fussed over by the women. He had gone through a fallow period when he was no longer a child, and felt it resume when he joined the force and moved to his own place. The ladies were delighted by their boy in a uniform. But they did want to know when he would bring home another woman. In the past couple of years he had felt the need for that fond respectfulness that his father had thrived on. Being celebrated as the ladies' clever, brave boy wasn't good enough for ever, really.

He imagined all their lives settling down into another pattern, and hoped he had it right. The way he saw it, it was going to get better, and they would see that he was right.

It gave him a glow of pleasure, anticipating the rightness of how things might turn out. Of course Mark was wrong for Sam; that was one of the things about these lives that was just so wrong. Bob was amazed, really, that they couldn't any of them see it. There was nothing reassuring or stoically strong about Mark. Observed from afar, admittedly, he looked unreliable. Those tattoos of his shrieked his unworthiness, right across the road those few times Bob had caught glimpses of him, while he was sitting out in his car. Oh, Mark might have been doing things like picking up Sally from school, or a few bits of shopping, quiet domestic things, but Bob wasn't tricked. To him Mark was the epitome of a suspected felon. Christmas Eve confirmed it, really. Bob was used to meeting people in strange, calamitous circumstances; that was when the stresses in their characters showed, and that first meeting with Mark had confirmed everything for him. Mark was the sort who needed an eye kept on him.

Bob remembered his mam playing cards once, on a Saturday night. She showed him how to make a card house. He must have been about eleven. His sisters were all at the age when they liked to go out, and his mam had felt sorry for him. She devised things for them to do on Saturday nights. Those were the days when she wore a black wig; they were fashionable then. When he had been quite a bit smaller he had pulled at it carelessly and brought it off. He had run screaming from the room, thinking he had pulled her whole head off. His mam and sisters brought this up for years afterwards, shaking with laughter at him.

The card house had grown bigger and bigger on the nest of tables. His mother watched the telly through it and stacked up storey after storey. When she finished, she had run through two decks of well-used cards. She turned and smiled at him. He hardly dared to move.

130

'Now, son,' she said, 'you knock it down.'

'You want me to?'

'It'll happen sooner or later,' she said. 'The slightest breeze when you open the door. It's best to do it yourself, and then build it back how you want. The fun is in seeing how it all comes down.'

Bob took a deep breath and blew it down. His mam applauded.

The force had changed him, she told him seriously, after his first six months; but she knew that would happen. So long as he remembered where he had come from. His sisters looked at him with new respect, as did his aunties. His father even seemed cowed by him.

Then he started coming in drunk after training. He fell out of the patio window and lay bleeding in the garden in the dark. New, painted veins ran up his arms, down his shirt and trousers when his mother came running down to find him, twitching on the grass. She didn't even have to open the door to get to him; the patio had been done on the cheap and he had wrecked it.

'Come on, then,' she said, looking at him, 'let's see you put this one back together,' before rushing in to phone an ambulance.

And he had. He'd pulled himself together and made a success of his life. Bob felt at times that the only thing in life, the only thing you needed to know, was how to gain a woman's respect. With that you could do anything. As far as he was concerned, women ruled the world. They made you powerful when they were proud of you, and you needed that power to make the world tick. And the world ticked, steady and strong as the motor before him, the rhythm of the song on the radio.

The moon was shading out now, licked over by tatters of cloud. Other cars were pulling out of the services and resuming their journey. His indigestion was settling; he was eager to be getting on.

'At least she asked us. She needn't have bothered. In fact, I thought she would have refused if we asked her.'

'You're right,' Peggy said. 'But I couldn't see her refusing, though. She couldn't've. Not today. Sally's more important than our squabbles. She's part of both of us, Sam and me.'

In her own cubicle Iris sighed and tugged her knickers back up. They had been calling out over the partitions. Peggy felt a bit uncomfortable in this, even though they were both sure that they'd heard Sam clip-clop across the tiles out of the ladies'. She'd gone off to buy Extra Strong Mints for the journey. Her stomach was playing up with anxiety and her breath was vile. Not the best condition for a reunion with her daughter.

Peggy did wonder how Sam would feel about seeing Sally again. She tried to imagine how it would happen. Sally's disappearance had knocked Sam entirely for six. It had been a long time since Peggy had seen Sam so distraught – not since childbirth itself, and before that, the night of the accident when her friend was killed. It took a lot to get to Sam. She flew easily into tempers, but Peggy knew there was a calm about her, deeper down, that hardly anything touched. Sometimes that inner, still resourcefulness could disturb Peggy. It had first appeared when her father, Peggy's husband, died. Sam hadn't really batted an eyelid. But then, she'd hardly known him, really. She'd been so young. Peggy doubted that Sam even remembered her father now. She'd never really missed him.

Peggy had never had any compunction about peeing in front of her husband. Or, indeed, had he with her. When they were first married, they had alternate bath nights and took turns to keep each other company with chat, sitting on the toilet, and never standing on ceremony when nature called. He always said that if you really loved someone, you could watch them do anything. Even defecate, he added solemnly, down on his knees as he asked for her hand and proffered his ring. After all, God saw everything you did. Why, then, shouldn't the person you loved?

The funny thing was, Peggy reflected as they left their respective cubicles and washed their hands in silence, she'd never actually peed in the same room as Iris. She'd never been to Leeds before, either.

'Anyway,' said Iris brightly, 'we're going, and we'll be there by lunchtime.'

Iris had pulled herself together somewhat overnight, and was back in thicker clothes, padding herself out to her usual bulk. She had begun, once more, to bustle around looking organised and busy without actually doing anything. What irritated Peggy slightly was that she was wearing a wide-brimmed blue hat, as if she were going to a wedding.

They went to fetch Sam from the shop. They looked through the glass, past the cashier. Iris picked her out and they watched. Sam was standing awkwardly, her face screwed up in indecision, before rows and rows of cuddly toys. She didn't know what to choose. In one hand she had a ten-pound note, and the other jabbed tentatively at grinning puppies, rabbits, bears, as if she knew she must take one, but wasn't sure how they'd react to being picked out and carried away.

Eighteen

Singlemindedness had evaporated with the frost on the grass through the kitchen window. Somehow he couldn't snap at Simmonds as he ranted and chattered endlessly.

The events of the night pressed a weight of guilt on Mark. Sitting in the kitchen, he smiled and smoked and sipped his tea as he waited for Sally to wake up and come down to breakfast. He couldn't bring himself to yell, 'Fuck off and fetch Tony, I've had enough of this.' He couldn't do anything until she showed up, grumpily awake once more, her face drowsy as sleep and warm as cheese on toast.

So I can smile and smile and be a villain, Mark thought – though he couldn't snag the memory attached to that quotation. It was appropriate enough, however. Did he really feel like a villain? He turned the word over like a pebble, weighing the butter knife in his hand and watching the old man chunter on, obliviously. Did last night make Mark a villain?

Secretly he marvelled at his ability to turn so blithe. It seemed the height of adventure; a sexy foray into a more exotic life. Fancy coming to a house at night in the middle of nowhere, rescuing his kidnapped daughter, and then succumbing to anonymous, extravagantly casual sex with a beautiful stranger.

The breakfast service was the very best. He was being kept like a king this morning. The old man had turned up in a better mood and was serving and supplying conversation, eager to be nice. He was sickly-nice, Sam would say, as she did about many people she met through her work. She knew what sickly-nice was, and warned Mark about it. But Mark fell for it every time. He couldn't see her taking to Simmonds, nor to Richard, for that matter, when she arrived.

They'd be on their way by now. Here he was, buttering more toast, right in the spot where two worlds were about to collide. This was another lull before the storm. He imagined raised voices here in the old, tiled kitchen, demands and recriminations. Nothing would be the same afterwards.

Sam would turn up to find that Mark literally had his feet under the table. She'd perceive him as changing sides, perhaps. His skin irked; she knew how to inject the slow poison of guilt. He'd been sent down here as an avenging angel and, of course, he'd had his feathers ruffled. She couldn't trust him to do anything right. He had fallen badly, feathers crushed under the weight of a single pair of deft and expert hands.

And Mark thought of the white gloves in the room with the single round window, the hands that had played him like a piano, and how perfect that had been. It was a seductively simple model of the way he wanted things to be: protecting and protected, with passion stealing in from nowhere and leaving before first light.

The realisation made him feel even more guilty. A vision of what he wanted was what he could do without when his real, ordinary world walked in through the door. It was time to shrink himself back down to fit the space allotted to him.

Simmonds was gesturing to him. 'Come with me, come. I've got something to show you.'

Mark hadn't been listening at all. He followed the old man out of the back door and up the black metal fire escape that reached to the top of the house, clinging to the very eaves. Again Simmonds proved nimble in his hi-tech trainers, clumping hard on the steps and bringing down icicle showers on Mark as he followed, too perplexed to question where they were going.

At the top there was a platform and from here they could see the width and breadth of Headingley and, beyond, Leeds, expressed in a shallow grey and brown bowl of jumbled shapes. Smoke rolled over, merged with winter clouds, as if the city were crystallising carbon dioxide for fun and relishing the spectacle of its vast exhalations.

When Mark looked at Simmonds with a question on his

face, he noticed the round window of his own room, right by the old man's knees. I was sleeping at the top of the house, he thought, right at the top of the city. But he, in the end, hadn't had to let down his hair to bring up the prince, a skinhead Rapunzel with a fire escape for back-up.

'Yes, that's your room,' Simmonds said quickly. 'Did you sleep well?'

Embarrassed by the old man's wheedling, conciliatory tone, and not wanting to give himself away, Mark nodded curtly.

'No – heh – visitors in the night?'

Mark kept stony-faced, gripped the railing and stared out over the city.

'That room – that whole floor of the house, in fact – used to be a factory, you know. It was bought in 1933 by the men who made false teeth for the whole of Yorkshire. They turned out thousands out of tiny casts and posted them to dentists in immaculate parcels. Somewhere we've got all the casts they used to use. You'd never imagine there'd be so much variety in teeth.

'They bought the floor off the Methodists, who'd been holding services and a Sunday school here since 1903. I used to come here three times on a Sunday when I was small, and here was where I learned to play the organ. When I bought the house from the Tooth Fairies in 1964, I sold that organ for a huge sum. I've even had offers for the Tooth Fairies' cast-off casts. Isn't that extraordinary?

'But people will have anything if you put a price on it. You can, if you are deemed an expert, place value on absolutely anything, simply by privileging it with a single glance. People look to see where you are looking and suddenly they are interested, too.

'Their interest is piqued. That's such a good word. Is *your* interest piqued, Mark?'

He shook his head as if to clear it and spoke without looking at the old man. 'I'm bloody confused, if that's what you mean.'

'But are you intrigued?'

Mark thought. 'I'm too easily intrigued. I get drawn in.'

'I thought so!' Simmonds clapped his hands. 'Then we're alike, you and I. You see, when a value is laid on an object, others follow the gaze, and a conflict of interests is bound to result. And who can unpick the crosscurrents of desires that engulf the poor, stranded piggy-in-the-middle? This is when people get jealous, you see.'

Frowning, Mark looked at him. 'And who, exactly, is piggy-in-the-middle here?'

'Oh,' Simmonds said lightly, 'I'm not drawing an explicit analogy. I hope I have more taste than to be as crass as that. I'm not a didactic man, not at all. Like any connoisseur, I like merely to suggest. If you can impute any meaning at all, set any value on what I imply, then that is up to you. As for who is piggy-in-the-middle . . . Well, my dear, out of each of us implicated in this sorry debacle . . . I would say that we all are, wouldn't you?'

When would the piggies be sent to market? Mark wondered. He had heard enough and wanted to get back downstairs.

'Did Tony come to you last night?' The old man's eyes were bright as a cat's.

'No,' Mark replied. 'I haven't seen him yet at all. That's the point. I haven't seen him at all.'

The old man looked shocked for a moment, as if a plan he had assumed was working had fallen to pieces in his hands. 'I thought he had. I thought that was the gleam in your eye. I thought he was with you last night.'

Mark shook his head and grunted. He turned to go back down the fire escape, not wanting to tell Simmonds anything about it. No sense in giving yourself away to strangers.

At the bottom, in the frozen garden, he came face to face with Richard.

'Good morning!' Richard called out to them both, smiling warmly at Mark.

Simmonds shuffled past them, returning to his usual querulous self, heading for the kitchen.

'What were you doing up there?'

Mark kept his voice low and said, 'He was asking about last night.' Mark was acutely embarrassed. In the daylight

137

Richard looked even younger than he had thought. He was wearing a T-shirt that said 'WILLY CHOP WIFE WALKS FREE' in tabloid lettering. They were strangers again, Richard enjoying Mark's newness. But something had happened in the meantime. No matter how casual, shouldn't there be a kind of recognition?

'Oh.' Richard suddenly grinned. 'So you told him about us getting pissed and ending up dancing like two pensioners to Maria Callas? How could we dance like that to opera? We must have been well gone.'

'I suppose we were,' Mark said thoughtfully. 'But I didn't even tell him as much as that.'

Richard shrugged. 'Wouldn't matter if you did. It doesn't matter what he thinks, really. It wouldn't have mattered, even if anything else had happened, either. Nothing to do with him. Let him be shocked.'

At first Mark could only take in the childish impudence of his words. Then he said, 'But something did happen, Richard.'

Richard looked at him and laughed suddenly. 'Yeah, right. We were so far gone, we'd never remember it anyway.'

Mark froze. 'Are you saying you never came back to my room last night?'

'Mark, I didn't. I wanted to. You knew I wanted to. But you said you wanted to go to sleep . . . you said –'

'You didn't come back? It wasn't you?'

The question froze lightly in the air. Then Simmonds rapped hard on the kitchen window. The phone was ringing.

Sam hated the very feel of the place. She had been in Leeds once before, during a week spent merchandising a new store. All the managers from within a hundred miles' radius were drafted in to oversee and generally work their bollocks off. Too many cooks; it was a nightmarish week working from nine till nine with a bunch of painted harpies in the dust and breezeblocks and plastic wrappings of a new shop. They had been put up in a semi-smart hotel and encouraged to socialise together. Off clubbing in desolate Leeds, shooting each other at Qasar, and bargain-hunting. It had been absolutely vile.

Dawdling through the mystifying roads that looped back and round the tall buildings and closed shops, she kept seeing things that reminded her of last time. She shuddered and told Bob to hurry up and get his bearings.

That had been when Sam was a new manageress, one of the youngest the company had ever had. And the one with the most bloody sense. The rest of them had been silly bitches all week. Sam just wanted to go home to Mark and Sally. It didn't seem right, not going home after work. She liked to come in to find them watching kids' TV, dinner in the oven. Sometimes she even willed Mark not to find a job. She liked him where she could be sure of him.

There was a big gallery with a square extension. In front, an expanse of flagstones with a patio café, its scattering of pigeons, tables, customers and a couple of phone boxes.

'I'm going to try that number he gave us.'

They parked to one side and Sam told them all to go and get a cup of tea at the café while she phoned. Bob and the ladies complied wordlessly. The ladies were gagging for a drink and the toilets again, and Bob saw that look Sam had. He saw it at times when she cradled him between her knees, down in the basement, beside the cardboard crusher. When she decided the shop could do without her a little longer, that was when she got that look. Determination fired by a keen hunger. 'Again,' she would demand and despite the laugh in her voice, the rest of her worked with an urgency that was as serious as it was skilful.

There was a great deal at stake today. A great many irons in this fire. Bob imagined the clinker spat out of today and the havoc it might wreak as it landed all around. In the face of this, all he could do for the moment was scuttle away and buy them all a cup of tea.

'Could you fetch him? This is Sam, his wife.'

'Sam?'

'Mark, we're here. We're slap-bang in the middle of Leeds.'

'That's quick.'

'We were up at the crack of dawn.'

'Sally's having her breakfast. She's fine.'

Sam listened and with satisfaction heard the tinnily distant voice of her daughter asking, 'Is it Mam?'

'We need more directions,' Sam said, almost accusingly, as if he were witholding vital information.

Mark almost told her to ask a policeman. Instead he passed the phone to Sally, who had come to stand beside him.

'Mam?' Sally began.

'Sally! I'm coming to get you.'

'Oh, Mam. I'm sorry. I thought I was going to the North Pole.'

'It's all right, Sal. You were kidnapped. Listen, I love you. I'm coming for you.'

'I'm all right, Mam. It's good here. They've got books. But I'm sorry I ran away from home. I love you, Mam. I love you . . . Mam? I'm sorry.'

Sam's jaw wasn't working properly. It juddered and refused to make proper words. Hot tears worked past her eyelids and scorched her face. She felt they must be audible. When she tried to speak again she gave a hard gasp, which she swallowed, and then a high, keening note that she chewed off quickly. Gripping the receiver tighter until it shook in her hand, she realised Mark was back on the line. She wanted to tell Sally she loved her again. For some reason this was more like loss than Christmas Eve.

'Give me the directions, Mark,' she said. When he spoke, she could tell that he had heard the tremor in her voice. He, too, seemed beaten into submission. Was that a pleading tone, an edge of guilt, that she heard in there? God, we hurt each other, she thought. Then he broke off and she could hear him talking to someone else, a male voice. Sam's stomach lurched. Tony?

'Sam?' Mark asked at last, this quiet exchange over.

'Yeah?' By now she had her tone controlled. She was back in charge.

'The best thing would be if Sally and I met you in a place down the road. It's a bit complicated here at the house. Apparently there's a kind of French patisserie that's really nice.' He waited for a response.

'We're not on fucking holiday, Mark.'

140

'No, but I think it's for the best if we meet on neutral ground.'

Neutral ground. So. Lines were being drawn up. Their lives were changing. In the clicking silence of a bad but local connection, they were renegotiating the lines their lives would take. Tight-lipped, she took down the address of the place, directions, and the time.

'See you then, Mark,' she said.

'Right.' He sounded clumsy. In their worst moments she had never been able to forgive him for sounding so clumsy. If you are clumsy, you can at least cover it up in your voice or appearance for those who have to rely on you. 'I love you, Sam.'

She put down the phone and cried again, forehead pressed on the numbered buttons.

'We could be in Venice, or Paris, or . . .' Iris said wonderingly, gazing about. 'We could be anywhere.'

They were sitting at one of the garden tables with polystyrene cups of tea, on the pavement outside the gallery.

'It's bloody freezing,' Bob gasped and bundled himself up in his coat. He looked to see if Sam was coming.

Iris had a spread of leaflets out on the table. She had picked them from the gallery's foyer on her way to the toilets. 'They had all the picture rooms roped off,' she sniffed. 'It seems a waste, just keeping open for the toilets.'

'I didn't see you complaining,' Peggy said. 'Anyway, we've got no time for looking at pictures today.'

'No.' Iris was glancing through the leaflets. 'There's a Hockney exhibition round here. It looks fabulous. Did I tell you I was in Los Angeles in the late sixties?'

Bob was watching Sam walk slowly across the flagged square towards them. There was such a careless sexuality about her, he realised. When so much about her was deliberate and intent, that was completely natural. 'What were you doing there?' he asked Iris.

Both of the ladies looked at him. They weren't quite used to him yet, and they certainly weren't expecting him to ask questions.

141

'I was having a very expensive affair with an extremely famous man,' she snapped. 'And writing my seventeenth novel while I was about it.'

'What was the novel? I might have read it.'

Peggy's mouth twitched into a smile. She'd never seen any evidence that Iris had written books either. 'I was a different person then,' Iris would say with a shrug whenever Peggy asked to read something she had written.

'I shouldn't like to say which it was,' Iris replied. 'It became a very famous film and if I tell you it was entirely autobiographical, I think you'll appreciate that to tell you would be to breach a confidence.' She sat back smugly in her fuchsia coat and exclaimed, 'Sam! What did he say?'

'More directions.' She flipped the piece of paper onto the table before Bob. 'I meant, get the tea and drink it in the car. You'll die of exposure and get piles out here.'

Bob told her, 'We all think it's quite nice.'

She turned on her heel. 'I'll wait in your crappy old car then. Come and tell me when you're finished, then maybe we can do what we're supposed to be doing here. And that's not a pensioners' bloody day trip.'

They drained their cups hastily.

'Things are astir,' Iris muttered.

'She was the same as a child. Getting her way by going off in a huff. She was taking the moral high ground at four years old.'

'Sally's not like that.'

'We'd better follow her,' Bob said, getting up.

Peggy picked up her bag and fixed him with a look. 'I think you're going to have your work cut out for you with our Sam, Bob.'

She allowed him to lead her back to his car. He did this with a small glow of triumph: he had won her over.

Behind them came Iris, struck suddenly with dismay and the uncomfortably familiar feeling that things were moving on again. She remembered a wonderful merry-go-round in Munich in the 1860s. It was gaudy and beautiful and exciting, but terribly unreliable. You could never tell when it would

142

stop, or start again. Lapses sometimes seemed very close together; at other times, unbearably far apart.

Iris had seen more life changes than anyone she knew, and she could read the signs.

Nineteen

Until now, Mark had thought of Headingley as a bit like Bishop Auckland. Rough as guts, with patches of struggling greenery. As they walked out to find Richard's 'sweet little patisserie', however, he saw that the place had more going for it than Bishop.

It was a reclaimed northern town. Someone had taken hold of the run-down place and injected it with bourgeois taste. It was a prole theme park with added delicatessens, second-hand bookshops and tea parlours tucked away up seedy gullies. Money had gone in with students and young professionals, who'd cropped up among the elderly and the émigrés, and they'd turned the air of the place into slum honey.

On the way they popped into a delicatessen. Yellow light slatted in onto sanded tables and Mark and Sally sat to wait while Richard chatted with the woman serving as if they had all day.

'We need avocados,' Richard said. Mark was about to point out that the house was already littered with them, but Richard added, 'Tony has a craving for them.' That name shook Mark up slightly. He joined Sally in a game, guessing names for all the colourful things on display in the refrigerators.

They still had a while before they were due to meet Sam. In a leisurely drawl, the woman behind the counter was explaining how you could make your own sour cream. She seemed utterly contented with her job. She had purple hair and moles and brown, strapping arms. Perhaps this was a cooperative. A metal whisk and bowl appeared from nowhere and before they knew it she was doing a demonstration with the top of a bottle of milk and half a lemon. 'There's some kind of chemical reaction when you use metal, and it sours up nicely.'

They watched with interest as she worked away, but soon she was frowning, disappointed in herself, because it hadn't come off. 'Well, you can take this for forty pee if you like. It's not proper sour, though.'

We'll hold it under Sam's face when she sees us, Mark thought. That'll curdle it. He stopped himself. I'm just bitter, he thought.

Richard was making it easier to face Sam. Whenever Mark's thoughts veered towards the harder questions – Will she be furious with me? Will she go off with the copper? Whom *did* I have sex with last night? – Walking down the grimy, freezing main street of Headingley, Richard would interrupt him, saying, 'See that newsagent's? If you go in, don't look shocked when you get your change. Bloke who serves you has got two thumbs on one hand!' Passing a junk shop, he would say, 'Art Deco elephant-foot umbrella stands in there. Very swish.' Now he turned to Sally as they left the delicatessen. 'We must take you to this little bookshop right near the house. They've got beautiful old books for children.'

Her face lit up and snared Mark's attention. His stomach was heavy with dread now, as the time crept on. 'Can we go, Dad?'

'I'll take you this afternoon,' Richard promised, 'and buy you a special book for being good while you've stayed with us. Call it a late Christmas present.'

'Thank you, Richard,' she said with a big grin.

'You don't have to do that,' Mark said.

'I'd love to.'

'Dad, Richard's my new Christmas friend.'

'Is he?'

'I met him on Christmas morning. Can he visit us at home?'

They paused at the corner of the street, waiting for a gap to appear in the traffic.

'Of course he can,' Mark said.

Seeming pleased with this, Richard went on telling Sally about the bookshop, hidden up an alley right by their house, and how some of the kids' books there were magical. Nobody had read them since they were printed, years ago, and you'd be finding things in them that weren't at all widely known. Some of the stories, in fact, could turn out to be like shared secrets between you and the person who wrote them.

'Just like real life.' Mark often said that upon hearing something banal. But he was rather touched that Richard could engage Sally's attention like this, knew just how to pitch the conversation for her. And what was more, on this particular sugar-bright post-Christmas morning, Mark fancied the arse off him and wished that it *had* been him in the white gloves the previous night.

'This is it,' Richard said.

They were facing the plate-glass window of a small café. It had only two tables and one was taken by an old person of indeterminate gender and catholic tastes; he or she had each of the morning's papers and three novels fanned out. The window and counter inside were covered with white paper doilies and golden twists of new bread. The air was heavy with cheese and coffee. There were glacé cherries stuck on almost everything that didn't move.

'You've got everything here,' Mark said. Right now he wanted to open and run – Oh, he didn't know – a café? a delicatessen? somewhere just by his estate. This was north, and they managed it here. Couldn't he stretch this boundary somewhat and take this gorgeous continentalism a little nearer Darlington?

Richard and Sally were having milk shakes. When Mark asked for a black coffee, the man with a beard and a transatlantic twang asked if he was quite sure. Mark sighed; he was used to getting hassle over counters. Maybe he thinks I should be ordering lager or superglue. When Mark insisted, he was given a cup with a thin dribble of black in the bottom. He couldn't be bothered with smart-arses this morning and asked for a top-up in a tone that implied he would stand for no shit. The aproned man gave a cultured shrug and filled his cup to the brim.

As they sat waiting for Sam's party, Mark drank the scalding brew and within seconds he was reeling. His eyes flicked back and forth across the stretch of road through the

146

window and his fingers drummed nervously on the stripped pine. That's good stuff, he thought, his mouth lined with what felt like tar, and his brain singing.

Sam was fiddling with the kangaroo's ears in the front seat as Bob ran to pay for the petrol.

'She'll love that,' Iris said, passing the mints back to her. 'She's not got a kangaroo already, has she?'

'She'd better not have,' Peggy muttered.

'Not like this one.' Sam smiled. It had an elasticated pouch with a miniature version of itself stuffed inside. 'Well, I hope Mark's little chum is going to buy us lunch,' she said. 'A patisserie. My God!'

Bob came back and said it was only a couple of streets away. They drove off to look for a parking spot, Joni Mitchell on the cassette player, her voice the exact blue of the morning and the yellow of the light.

It would be, Iris thought, the most pleasant of mornings, if only so much didn't hang in the balance. Then she remembered other good mornings she'd had and reflected that the shadow of a threat always made things more intensely enjoyable.

'We're here.' Bob parked them behind a vast playing field.

Sam clutched the kangaroo to her and felt sick to her stomach. What was she expecting? It was only *people* she had to deal with. Most of these people she knew and loved. Any trouble she'd meet would be caused by people and she had her professional manner; she had the key to working these disputes out. The only things to fear, the only things beyond human intrigue and her control, were natural disasters. Unfortunately, love was a kind of natural disaster affecting the lives of all the people she was dealing with today. She wasn't sure she could handle it.

Joni Mitchell sang 'Strange Boy' and Sam paused for breath before opening her car door. The ladies were already out on the grass, clicking their tongues at the view of Leeds.

'Kiss me, Sam,' Bob said and she did. 'Just . . .'

'What?' she asked, eyes narrowed.

'Remember that whatever goes on today – however all this

147

falls down and comes out – I'm here for you and we can carry on and sort out our lives together.'

Only twenty minutes ago Bob had felt so sure of it, of her, of making all their future lives tick.

She smiled at him. 'We're fearless, right?' When she ruffled his thick black hair, she saw with horror that his eyes were filling up. 'Hey, we fuck right next to a cardboard crusher – nothing human can put the willies up us, right?'

They laughed a little bit over her unfortunate phrasing, got out and locked up the car. The air smelled of cold sunlight and croissants and maybe impending snow.

Twenty

It did snow that afternoon. All that afternoon and on into an evening that turned from a noun into a verb: the evening was a softening and a balancing, an imperceptible change from afternoon to night-time. Leeds seared with a blurring whiteness. It snowed for another three days and the year limped towards its demise with its rough edges smoothed over, its waning light busy with snow and more snow.

The roads were chaotic. Up on the Pennine roads to the west, unwary drivers slowed to twenty in the gloom and bided their perilous time until they found themselves in a geriatric convoy. Nervously they would push on together, the reasoning being that should disaster strike, they would all go together. The radio and the television broke up their festive programming to warn people in the northeast not, if they could help it, to leave their homes. It really wasn't a good idea.

And this lasted into the New Year. Hard luck on those who had got carried away with the Christmas spirit during the holiday and slipped from their homes to celebrate elsewhere. Worse luck on those who were where they shouldn't be. Even more disastrous for those who were somewhere they plainly didn't want to be and were now, for the time being at least, thoroughly stuck.

To some it might be quite cosy. With their feet up, snowed in by the television set with enough food to last, enough wine and fags and good company. The powers-that-be telling them quite categorically that they oughtn't move from their very armchairs if they wanted to live. Beyond the thick curtains, moving with certainty in the dark, a vertical and unceasing ocean was breaking crest after crest onto the ground.

The weight of snow creaks perilously on council house roofs and guttering. Mould on indoor walls freezes over black, like bark. But to be in your own home, even with the pipes cracking and distended and the central heating knackered and the Birds Eye trifle remains in the fridge looking less inviting by the day, even this is better than to be out in the woods and away from home.

Trains stop. Motorways are broken up and sent home. Doors slam. Lights go on but curtains are drawn, futile against the careless paws of snow. The streetlamps buzz on and they stay on.

When you're out somewhere strange, there's an odd comfort you feel, and resent feeling, about the streetlamps. They thread an impersonal, slightly gloomy continuity through your journey. They tell you, You'll see a lot more of our sort before you hit home.

Or they tell you, You aren't going to get home tonight. Come and sit beneath us. Gather your legs up under an umbrella of light, rest your back against the humming trunk. You are like a parody of an old-time wayfarer, travelling the countryside without a care in the world and falling gently asleep beneath spread branches.

No such comfort. This is the way your world ends: disenfranchisement. You're out on the street, out on your own. It's easy to slip from the orbit of your life. You simply stop your journey back home. You sit under a streetlamp. What else might you need to complete the effect except a cup from McDonald's for coins?

And if your stop is forced upon you by circumstances, then your decline seems all the easier, all the better accomplished. If you cannot move heaven and earth and get yourself back on the right track of your life, then a new career in a new and strange town is just the thing. But it's the wrong career. A career in the wrong direction, like a car crash.

So the snow shuffles down to trap people, to make them veer off course and wring dread out of them.

And it begins, quite gently, this afternoon, from a sky which still looked blue when Sam led her party into the patisserie in Headingley.

Scraping the legs of his chair, moving awkwardly for lack of space, Mark stood up. Sam had Sally crushed to her chest, as he had last night. Iris and Peggy were impatient for their turn, and to clasp him, too, in this reunion. By the café door, exchanging glances with the owner, stood the policeman.

As Sam looked up and mutely refused to let go of her daughter, they were locked in a question: What next?

Richard answered them by standing and catching everyone's attention. Mark said, 'This is –' and Sam bent forward and smacked Richard hard in the mouth.

'You're Tony, aren't you?' she yelled. 'You're that fucking Tony?'

He sat back down, hand over his mouth. It was loose and swelling, dripping between his fingers as he said, 'No.'

'It's Richard,' Mark said quietly.

'Who? Who the fuck are you, then?' she demanded, and Sally started to cry.

'A friend, Mam,' she said. 'You punched my friend.'

'It's all right,' Richard said, dabbing himself with a napkin. 'No damage done.'

'It might need a stitch,' Iris pushed in, squinting at the blood.

'Look at the bloody vulture swoop,' Sam said and pulled up a metal chair, hauling Sally firmly onto her knee.

'Shall I order some coffee?' asked Bob.

Absently she nodded. She fixed the still-startled Richard with a glare. 'I'll apologise if you've got nothing to do with all this.'

'He hasn't,' Mark told her bitterly. 'Not a bit.'

'Then I'm sorry.'

'Richard,' Mark added.

'What's your problem?' she hissed. 'I'm here, aren't I?'

'I think we should all calm down,' Peggy said, squeezing in between Mark and Iris. The cups and vase on the table wobbled.

They sat in an awkward silence while Iris fumbled in her bag for a clean handkerchief for Richard. Mark made some quick introductions and Peggy went on, 'Let's just be grateful we're all here, safe, and adult enough to talk this through like adults.'

151

'But Tony isn't here,' Sam insisted, eyes gleaming. 'Don't we need him too? Or has he just pissed off again? Where is he, Mark? Come on, tell us.'

Bob came back from the counter with a tray full of cups, saucers and crisps. He set it down and stood behind Sam, one hand on her shoulder. Sally looked up at him unblinkingly. He smiled at her without reward and looked away again.

'I haven't seen Tony yet,' Mark admitted.

'What do you mean, yet? Where is he?'

'He's back at the house,' Richard said, his head still lowered into the hanky.

'No, he wasn't,' Mark said.

'I mean, he should be, by now.'

'So what do we do?' asked Sam. 'Mark?'

'We're all going back home,' Bob said suddenly. 'We've got what we came for.'

'*Who* we came for,' Iris corrected him, and grinned at Sally.

'No,' Mark said. 'We can't yet. There's still stuff to sort out.'

'Such as?' Shakily Sam lit a cigarette. 'I tell you, I want to see this bloody Tony. I still want to give him a good cracking.'

'I want to at least talk to him,' said Mark. 'Find out why he did . . . what he did. Make sure it won't happen again.'

Sam looked scared. 'She's all right, isn't she?'

'What do you mean?'

'You know.'

'Of course she is. Christ!'

'Look, fuckface, what am I meant to think?'

'Anything you like, Sam, you always do. Anyway, Richard looked after her the whole time. She hardly saw Tony either.'

Sam eyed Richard suspiciously.

Mark continued, 'I think Tony just wants to talk to me. I think that's what this is all about. I have to sort it out. I think I know how I can see him. It has to be on his terms.'

'I'm not listening to this,' Sam said. 'I've had enough. We're going back home and taking Sally. You can do what you want.'

Peggy put in, 'Sam, just listen to him.'

'Shut up, Mam. I let you come here to see Sally. Don't push it.'

'You listen to me, madam. You've had your own way through all of this.'

Followed by everyone else, Sam looked in astonishment at her mother.

'You've had kittens over the whole business – quite understandable – and your wishes have gone over and above everyone else's. Including Mark's. But now you know that Sally's all right. She's with you and safe. Just listen to him. It's time you stopped treating everyone rotten. You were up in arms and being a bitch even before your daughter was snatched. Now, you're about to make changes in your life. I can see that. But remember, Sam, these changes are not just to your life. They're to all our lives. We all have a stake in what goes on now, and you're not going to get all your own way.'

They sat back. Cautiously Mark asked, 'What changes is she talking about, Sam?'

Sam blew out smoke and crushed her cigarette. 'I'm taking Sally home to Bob's house. We're moving in with Bob.'

She felt Bob's grip tighten on her shoulder and took it for support, but it was shock.

Mark stared at her. 'If that's what you want to do . . .'

'There's no "want" about it. It's just what's going to happen.'

'You can't just have her.'

'I'm her mother.'

'You can't just take her.'

'I'm her mother, Mark.'

'You can't –'

Sally was crying again. He stopped.

'Listen to you!' Iris burst out.

'Keep out, you old sow!' Sam told her.

'Listen,' Iris snapped. 'Just listen to the pair of you! You're talking about big life changes, court decisions, right here and now when you should be glad this is sorted! You're in no fit state to even discuss what you'll have for lunch. And – might I add – I'm absolutely starving. Custody is for the court to

153

decide, if it comes to that. And right now you're scaring the life out of Sally. She's had enough of this.'

'She's right,' Mark said.

Sam glared murderously. 'We're still going home,' she said. 'And taking Sally.'

'You're leaving me?'

She just tutted and looked away. The owner was approaching with a menu now, as if his professional manner had expertly located a suitable lull in their proceedings. Or perhaps he had just heard Iris say 'lunch'. When he gave the sheet to Sam, she looked past him, and saw with a shock that it had gone dark outside. The street was dim with a silent storm.

Eventually they took up two full tables and dominated the small café. The adults said very little to each other. They had passed a certain point in their dealings and concentrated instead on eating. And talking to Sally, listening to her talk. The child became their focus. Radio Four played behind the counter, its voices unctuous on the leaden air. The café owner watched the family scene, attempting to work the relationships out.

Sally chatted on brightly as they ate. She talked about Christmas, about travelling on a train, about the stories she had read during her visit, about Richard's dog.

The adults smiled, nodded, urged her on. But she was doing it for them. Sally knew about the times they needed a focus, the times when childish inconsequentiality was all that would stop them fighting.

'We have to go,' Sam said at last, and Mark looked away to see the snow piled high against the door.

Come on, he thought, snow heavier. Bring it all down. I want to keep them here a while. Let it go dark outside; fill in the canyons of the street. Smother us in and make us stay to sort this all out.

'Mark, we're going back home.'

'There's . . .' he began, tapping ash quickly, everyone looking. 'If you go to the newsagents here . . . don't be

154

shocked when you get your change . . . there's a bloke in there with two thumbs.'

'Mark, what . . . ?'

'On one hand. And there's an antique shop that does elephant feet.'

Sam looked at him levelly.

'Ask him,' Mark urged. 'Ask Richard. They've got everything here.'

Iris covered his hand with hers. 'Peggy and I will stay for a while.'

'Come on, Sal,' Sam said. 'We've got to get back off home. That weather's not going to let up.'

Bob was standing. 'Sam? Ready?'

'Sally, get your things together.' Sam started fastening up her daughter's coat. All she was carrying, though, was the kangaroo Sam had brought.

Sally had lost her brightness, but now her eyes shone. 'Aren't we all staying together?'

She looked at her dad.

'I think you'd better go with your mam, pet.'

When Bob opened the café door, the cold wind of the street slipped in. Mark gasped. It gripped him, held him, as he watched them shuffle out.

Twenty-One

'Well, I'm glad we came,' Peggy said at last. 'We needed a trip out. To take our minds off things.'

Iris said, 'I'm amazed we could get anywhere in that weather.'

They had caught the bus just outside the café. It had snorted and steamed towards them, a livid baked-bean orange against the fresh snow. Mark had slumped on the back seat, looking vulnerable and drawn, as he had since Sally kissed him goodbye.

It had been Richard's idea to come here. They had the rest of the day to fill in somehow, waiting until Tony turned up at the house. They all knew that that was the reason for staying, but Mark refused to talk about him. Iris and Peggy set themselves on being supportive, and Richard took the lead in keeping them occupied.

As they skirted through the abandoned streets, Richard was attempting to quell his pleasure in their delay. He wanted to keep them around for a while. He was sad that Sally was gone. He thought it was wrong of Sam just to take her like that. And he could plainly see the effect of it on Mark. Right now, though, all he could do was give them a decent time while they were here and hope that, perhaps, it wasn't only for Tony's sake that Mark was sticking around.

For half an hour they rode through slumbering homes on the outskirts of town, the greenery muffled by snow and losing it in showers as the bus brushed past. Outside it was a winter wonderland spoiled by the smell of fuel and vomit onboard. They were on their way to Salt's Mill, a converted building that was, in these conditions, a foolhardy distance away. But Iris had mentioned wanting to see the Hockney exhibition there.

Richard was a great one for salvaging situations. He would do it for this one, too. He would give them a day to remember. Richard had accepted his mostly contingent role in other people's lives. When these people looked back on this whole event, then at least they wouldn't remember only the bleak bits.

They were sitting upstairs in the diner, at a stainless-steel table. Richard was playing with the cocktail sugar, waiting for Mark to come back from the toilets.

The windows were tall and arched, giving a muted view of Bradford. From up here it all looked clean and swept; the colours that showed were brighter because of the snow. Outside it looked as pristine as it was indoors. There was a gleam similar to the laser-copied 'local snaps' pinned to the walls. Colours here were unnaturally bright. The two ladies were looking about with interest, occasionally dipping into narrow-stemmed blue glasses of ice cream.

'Sally would have loved the ice cream.'

'For God's sake, Iris, don't say that when Mark gets back.'

'Hockney's drawn the menu. Shove one in your bag.'

'He's taking his time,' Peggy commented.

'He's upset. He probably needs a moment to let it all out.'

'Don't be melodramatic, Iris. They've only gone back home.'

'To *his* home – that copper's. Sam's put things in motion now. She's taking Sally away from him for good. For Mark, this is the beginning of the end. That's what he's upset about.'

Iris's voice had turned hard with a kind of recrimination. Picking up on this, Peggy said, 'I know all that. I said to her, didn't I, that she was being too rash.'

A silence dropped between them and Richard was embarrassed. He was already implicated in their lives, and wanted to be, but he was still surprised at the ease with which they allowed him to overhear their difficulties. His family had kept themselves to themselves, hissing politely at each other in private, as in public. This kind of carry-on was common, he knew, but it was also the kind of carry-on he had left home to be part of. He wanted to be in a family that yelled at each other in public when the mood took them. Despite his inbred

157

embarrassment, he admired the frank skill of this lot's interactions. It seemed so much less fraught with misunderstanding than what he was used to.

Sam, especially, had intrigued Richard, even though she had smacked him one. He could see that there was something about her. He still couldn't see why Mark had thrown everything in to be with her – as far as he was concerned, Mark was a Class One 100 per cent fruit – but he still found her impressive for lashing out and protecting her family. Mark listened to Sam; his whole life was dependent upon her decisions. Richard could never hope to exert such an influence, and he reluctantly bowed before anyone who could.

He discovered that he was watching the group at the next table intently. Four stiff-looking men in suits were sitting awkwardly in their chairs, picking over ridiculously large sandwiches. In their midst sat a very professional-looking woman in a similarly smart suit with a short skirt. Her hair was piled up high on her head and she twiddled little bits of watercress under her nose as she laughed, a light trilling note, at her companions' gruff jokes.

Iris and Peggy were watching too. 'Poor cow,' Peggy muttered. 'Fancy having to put up with those old farts. Look at her skirt, too.'

'She's got to be sexier and more brilliant than that lot,' Iris said and sighed. 'You can just see what's going on. So this is what they call post-feminism?'

'Don't, dear,' Peggy said. 'You'll only depress me.' She crammed her mouth with chocolate ice cream, stinging her more sensitive teeth. 'I think it was working like that, in a man's world, that made our Sam hard.'

Iris stared. 'How can you say that?'

'Well, it's bound to, isn't it? You have to harden up to operate in the wider world.'

'She works in a frock shop!'

'It's still a man's world. Business.'

Iris shook her head. 'It's neither a man's nor a woman's. It's what you call patriarchal. That's what your Sam's been steeped in.'

Peggy looked obscurely offended. She wasn't quite sure what Iris was saying about her daughter.

'I know,' Iris added, 'about gender. It's been my business to know, remember.'

Richard perked up, surprising them. 'Is that because you're gay?'

'We never used that word in my day,' she said sniffily. 'The girls wore bunches of violets on their lapels. And anyway, my being gay is not really the point. I know about gender because I've been a woman *and* a man, in the course of a terribly long life.'

'Oh!' said Richard.

'I've done a hell of a lot of field work.'

'Don't let her bore you,' Peggy said. 'Go and see if Mark's out of the toilets yet. See what he's doing in there.'

Vaguely discomforted by being dismissed, as well as by being sent to patrol the toilets, Richard complied.

'Tell him we'll see him downstairs,' Iris cried out, making all the business people look up from their working lunch. 'We'll be downstairs in the main gallery.'

They had slowed right down. It was hard to tell whether it was light or dark outside. It was simply blue, a gloom like the bottom of the sea. Every time Bob seemed about to accelerate, when a relatively snow-free empty patch of road opened up, Sam would seize his arm and get him to slow. She didn't care if it took till tomorrow morning. She wanted them to get home in one piece.

Behind them, strapped tightly in place and clutching her new kangaroo, sat Sally. She was listening to the Top Forty from 1978 on the radio.

'We'll pop in somewhere and fetch fish and chips for tea,' Sam promised.

Bob wondered bitterly how they would do that. He could see hardly anything either side of them. The day was narrowing down to the span of his twin headlights. He was starving and worn out by now. They had the kid and the day's work was done. Strange that he didn't feel pleased or proud, or anything. His triumph had been subordinated to Sam's mood, which was still one of grim resolution. Since setting out from Headingley she had not mentioned Mark, Iris or Peggy once.

'Tomorrow we're going shopping,' she was saying now over her shoulder to the kid, who listened attentively. 'We've got to buy things for your new room, until we get sorted out with your old stuff. You'd like that, wouldn't you, Sally? All new things? We'll make it all posh. You never got your Christmas presents properly, either – so we'll make it special again and buy lots of new stuff. You could have a cassette deck in your room and play it as loud as you like. That's important. And toys. We'll get lots of everything. The sales will be on by now, so it's better, really, to buy stuff now.'

'But I've got everything I need,' Sally pointed out.

'You can never have enough,' Sam corrected, and turned to smile at her, caught in a sudden bar of turquoise light. 'And a girl can never have enough clothes. We'll take you buying clothes. You'll be a trendsetter when school starts again.'

'But we wear school uniform.'

Briefly Bob reflected – and then stopped the thought quickly, guiltily – that this would all come out of his pocket. Only a few weeks ago Sam had been moaning about not being able to afford the Christmas presents she had already bought. Now, suddenly, life had changed, and shopping was high on her agenda. He couldn't help feeling vaguely disturbed that these changes were to come at his expense.

'You'll like Bob's house, Sal. It's bigger than that poky old flat. With a little garden for you to play in.'

Sally leaned forward slowly. Sam could see the tiredness round her eyes, her mouth pulled down in drowsy irritability. She looked as if she wanted to get something off her chest before she fell asleep.

Sam asked, 'You're not going to throw up, are you?'

Bob froze.

Sally shook her head. She asked, 'Is that what you want me to call him, then?' She blinked slowly. 'Bob?'

Sam smiled and looked at Bob. He took his eyes off the road for a second and all three felt the car slide, with terrible slowness, a few inches, then right itself.

'Watch what you're doing,' she hissed at him. 'Well? What do you want to be called? Uncle Bob?'

Sally was sinking back into the upholstery. 'I'm not calling him Dad,' she said, her voice slipping further and further away.

'You won't have to,' Sam murmured. 'Call him Bob. He's Bob. He's not your dad, for better or for worse.'

At times, although much of the time Peggy could forget this, Iris embarrassed her. It was a class thing, she thought dully. Iris wasn't constrained by the same kind of behavioural doctrines. She never tailored herself down to fit into new surroundings. If anything, she turned the volume up. Often Peggy was exhilarated by this. It opened up new worlds and made the old ones less intimidating. It worked wonders in the bank, at the Social Security. There was a brash confidence and assurance that came with anyone who wasn't working class. There was never a temptation to tug the nonexistent forelock and take what was offered.

But then again, that assurance could also be embarrassing. When they walked into the gallery, Wagner was playing and, almost immediately, Iris was whooping along with it and shrieking about Valkyries. Heads bobbed up from the pictures, from behind vases, around the bookcases. Iris was quite oblivious. She explained in a voice twice as loud as it need be that she and Peggy were postmodern Valkyries.

'They're playing our song!' she cackled, and Peggy gave her a sickly smile.

They were inside what felt like an old warehouse, which vibrated along with Wagner. Paintings and drawings hung everywhere on wires, over the wide windows, were propped nonchalantly on antiques. The tender yellow and purple necks of lilies thrust everywhere. When Peggy allowed herself to stop being irritated, and made herself feel pleased that her lover was back to normal, she found that she thought the place was breathtaking. The air was thick and sweet with pollen. The paintings were familiar. Peggy clutched her bag to her chest and stood before a huge panelled picture, resonant with deep, clouded blues. Beneath the spread petals of a large white splash, a boy's pink body wavered, stretching deep across the canvas.

Iris came to stand with her. 'The Valkyries were seer women who judged the fates of warriors,' she said.

Peggy tutted. 'Don't say you were around in those days as well.'

'No, but Valkyries stick around in history.'

'I thought you wanted to look at these pictures.'

'The other thing is that Valkyries had the power to turn themselves into swan maidens. Imagine wearing wings! But all their powers would then reside in the wings, and if a man stole them, then they were lost.'

Peggy shuffled down the room, glancing over the etchings of naked boys, indolent and faintly eroticised. Other faces, less attractive, of all types. The lines wobbled away from a harsh realism towards a cartoonlike facileness. All these faces looked bemused. Their expressions seemed to Peggy to sum up her own feelings at the moment, and it cheered her up. These people, these friends of the artist, she thought; you can tell they're living complicated lives. In the pictures where they're together, you can tell it isn't all a picnic. A pursed-mouth bemusement seemed like the only rational response to them.

She turned to see that Iris had sat down in a high-backed chair next to a potted palm. She plucked a handful of ostrich feathers from a nearby vase and fanned herself lazily. Looking up, she saw Peggy standing over her. 'The Valkyries decided, Peggy. Don't you see? They determined which warriors would fall in battle, or who would get to Valhalla. Isn't that where we are? Aren't we in a battlefield? Aren't all those in our family warriors?'

'I don't think we're as important as that,' Peggy said sadly. 'I don't think it makes much odds to them at all what we think. The younger lot will press on with whatever they fancy doing, regardless.'

'But we can still put spanners in the works.' Iris was starting to look crumpled up again. Peggy felt a twinge of dismay. 'We can still talk sense to them.'

'We're old.' Peggy shrugged. 'They can see better than us, I think, what's for the best.'

'When I write a novel again,' said Iris, rallying once more, 'and I shall, I'll call it *Swanning About*.' She cast a glance back to the painting of the boy jumping into the pool. 'Because that's what we've all been doing, isn't it? We're all dead selfish with each other. But our best moments together, when we love each other most, is when we show off for each other. When we are as fabulous as our friends think we ought to be.'

'I think so,' Peggy said; guilty again that Iris had embarrassed her.

'All we want is for the world to value those we love as much as we do. Not to inflict itself too hard on them. To be kinder. And my book will do that. I want it to show us all at our best and at our worst. It'll be about the warriors I know now. And since I'm a Valkyrie, at least when I'm writing, and since when I'm writing, I can rig all the rules, I'll make sure we all get to Valhalla.'

Impulsively Peggy bent to hug her. For a moment Iris seemed terribly frail in her arms, thinner than ever beneath her many layers. Peggy felt she was embracing a heap of cushions. 'It'll have to be Valhalla,' she sniffed. 'I don't reckon any of us will make it to heaven. Not the heaven my husband used to rant about, anyway. That was just for legitimate family.'

Iris cackled again. 'The Valhalla I'm going to rig up is one for family members of the most illegitimate kinds. Old dykes, tattooed faggots, divorcées, coopted coppers, the lot. Blood doesn't count for much, I don't think. The messy stuff's best avoided.'

Passers-by were staring now at the two old ladies making a scene in the middle of the gallery. The ostrich feathers were spread out, dropped at their feet. Peggy was beyond embarrassment now. When she felt as touched as this, she usually felt sick with love. Her heart seemed somewhere at the back of her throat. For Peggy, the timelessness of lovers meant the minutes she couldn't swallow her saliva. It welled up in tenderness until she swallowed and tears slipped out.

'I love the idea of us being warriors for each other,' she said. 'It makes us seem on more or less the same side.'

'I think, in the end, we are.'

'But some of us have to bear the brunt of it,' Peggy said. 'I think Mark's going under. I've not seen him like this before.'

Richard found him in the smaller gallery upstairs, gazing at the bright, abstract shapes of Hockney's 'Very New Paintings'. One in particular had caught his attention. Richard stood by him and politely looked at the purple, orange and yellow curves and folds, the speckled, swirling contours, graphs on an Apple Mac swollen and distorted.

'Fucking hell,' Mark said, 'I came out of the bogs and walked into twenty-four original Hockneys.'

Richard grinned. The room was like a tunnel, with barred windows running opposite the paintings. He waited until a group of nice ladies left the gallery, discussing cake decorating, as far as he could tell, and asked Mark, 'So how're you doing?'

Mark pointed to the painting directly before him. 'This is amazing,' he said. 'But that's almost what I've got all up my back.'

'You've stopped talking,' Bob said, and looked at her.

She had been dozing off to the radio. Now that Sally was asleep in the back, something had relaxed in Sam and with the loss of her vigilance, her need to stay awake had gone too.

'This takes me back –' Bob grinned – 'to my earliest memories. My mam was never quiet. She still isn't. You'll meet her soon. You'll get on like a house on fire, but, God, she can talk! When I was little, the only time I remember her being quiet was when we were out in the car.'

'Why was that?' Sam was only half-listening. She suspected that Bob was talking for the sake of it. He needed to talk to dispel the claustrophobia. Outside, the snow was falling heavier than ever and they weren't much further on in their journey. The pace was slacker and there were hardly any other cars about.

'Even before I can remember, they used to drive the car out

at night. In the middle of nights, when I couldn't sleep. Mam would sit in the back with me on her knee, hoping the drive would lull me. Dad would be driving, silent as ever. They went on midnight runs out into the countryside, all those rolling hills and tiny, winding roads round the Dales. They went miles. Or they went up round Durham, or the streets of Darlington, through endless, black streets.

'When I got older, too old to need lulling to sleep, really, the trips went on. I think it was because they'd gone off sex. But I remember the smoky quiet inside the car, and looking up out of the window at the huge buildings with black eyes and frightening turrets. That's what ordinary buildings looked like. And in the countryside the land rolled on for ever. Everything outside was terrifying and somehow that was reassuring. Any nightmare you could ever have was out there, externalised so that it could be dealt with.

'Great child psychology, but they never knew that. They were just out for a nice run while the roads were empty. Inside it was a haven and they were peaceful and still. My mam's always smoked like a kipper, and when I was small, you could hear her lungs working, an almost inaudible wheeze. It sounded like someone gearing up to speak and changing their mind at the last minute. We'd drive on for hours on end, it seemed like, in this quiet, as if waiting for the next thing she'd say, but knowing it would never come until the morning, over breakfast, when life was back to normal.'

She looked at him for a moment, thought for a little while, and took the reins of the conversation over to tell him about her early years. About her mam and dad, and how her dad had died. About the mother–daughter fights which were mostly carried out in antagonised silences. She could never associate silence with anything but suppressed anger. And yet it puzzled her that she had carried those silences on when she was at odds with Mark. And she explained that this night was quite different for her, in that she found the silence as they drove compelling, calm, healing, even. It was a new experience for her. She thanked Bob, said she was glad he was driving them.

She passed the Extra Strong Mints and hunted out a tape to play when they slipped past the range of the local radio

165

station. When she opened her window a crack to smoke, there were thick snowflakes and the wind's low moan. Quickly she shut it again and filled up the car interior with smoke. A new doubt crossed her.

'Do you think we'll make it tonight?'

'I was hoping to get the traffic report on the radio before it went off. I've no idea. And the trouble is, in these conditions, none of this looks remotely familiar. I don't know how far we've got to go.'

Sam sank back in her seat. She was beyond frustration or anger. There was a weird lucidity about her rising panic. It was there, along with the doubt in Bob's capabilities for getting them home safe. But its rising was a slow, slow process. It seemed as if it would take as long to reach its catastrophic height as this snow would to cover and bury their car. Fighting the panic down was a sheer and stealthy battle, one as dogged as the car's own unrelenting progress. We can't be buried, she thought, diffidently, if we're still moving. It's as simple as that.

The gallery seemed to be open till quite late. It's so civilised and so restful with it, Mark thought as he sat and just looked. Open all hours, free to get in.

The warehouse windows were black now and in response the colours here indoors were sharper. He felt as if he were bathing in sheer colour. It's like being inside my own body, he thought, oddly. Someone's sorted this all out for *me*, he thought. Someone who knows me better than I do.

Iris and Peggy were looking at the prints and cards for sale at the other end. Everything seemed disordered. Mark couldn't tell where the originals ended and the cheap reproductions began. It was, he decided, in the nature of this art, and was pleased with the thought.

Eventually they decided that it was time to leave. Puccini was playing while they had one last drink. They inhaled the smell of coffee, of pollen, of cigarette smoke, and prepared to store it, to meet the rare, frozen air outside.

Richard led them across the Mill's car parks, over the roads to the bus stop. 'We were daft, really, for coming. I hope they haven't taken the buses off.' Leaving him and Mark to keep an eye out for their transport, Iris and Peggy popped into the off-licence across the road.

'It's coming!' Richard yelled as they appeared in the snow-clogged doorway, gripping carriers on their way out.

As they bustled on board, Peggy thrust a bottle-shaped parcel into Richard's hand. 'Whisky,' she muttered, as he stared at the neat twist of paper covering it. 'As a thank you.'

It took almost an hour to reach Headingley again. They sat on the front seat on the top deck and got through two bottles of red wine, passing them back and forth and slugging it back. Iris always kept a bottle opener in one of her capacious pockets.

Wine jolted in the bottle as it knocked against their teeth when the bus rode unsteadily over hills. Up here they had a cinema screen of a window, and Leeds was dark, inscrutable in the snow. They smiled drowsily, warmed by wine, and exchanged glances when Mark began to sing. He had a terrible voice and no one could quite tell what it was he sang. But they joined in anyway.

Twenty-Two

Should we take a look at the inner man?

Mark sits in another of Tony's living rooms, slumped on a sofa. His feet worry at the woven mats and he weighs a glass of whisky in his hand.

He doesn't believe in the inner man. Were we to draw out such a thing and wave it under his nose, he wouldn't be convinced. Imagine saying this to an unbeliever: here is your soul. Here is your essence.

The white marble fireplace is streaked in grey veins and here rest two shining violins. Not just for effect, it seems. They lie as if recently put down, as if the air hums still with their interrupted music. Maybe that is the effect intended. Mark shrugs. They're taking up too much of his attention. People do daft things with interior decor. They make features of all sorts, and expect you to admire them.

He is surlier as the night goes on. That fragility has gone out of him. The slow evening, the company, the emptied bottles on the carpet, all of it has first pulled him together and then put him out of sorts.

Peggy and Iris have withdrawn to the kitchen for a little while; the drink has dissolved their reserve and they are raiding the absent Simmonds's pantry. Richard has nodded his assent to them and he still sits across from Mark, watching his mood darken.

Mark is barely aware of his presence. Yet, when he stares at the french windows that lead to the patio and its herb garden, he laughs aloud and says, 'I like your conservatory effect.'

Richard smiles and sips his drink, unsure.

Mark doesn't believe in the inner man. If he did, he certainly wouldn't want one. It's like those razor-blade adverts where they sing about not wanting to hide the man inside. Who's that supposed to be, exactly? Mark would laugh if he didn't suspect it all leads to something sinister. 'The man inside' sounds rough, chest-beating. It makes Mark feel uncomfortable. He succumbed to life with Sam only because she seemed to understand. Despite everything, she seemed to understand. Although she looked the sort to want a big, strapping, sexist bastard, she settled for Mark. She has never – not even in their worst times – demanded the presence of Mark's man inside. Never has he felt obliged to fabricate such a thing.

Then what does he believe in?

He believes that we all have pasts. He can't quite see himself with an interior world of essences and memories, arrayed in neat little bottles on shelves. Somehow Mark can't think of himself as a human minibar, the sum of what he is, jiggling and chinking inside.

Hearing the slow tick of the clocks, Richard's occasional impatient sighs, Peggy's and Iris's distant giggling, he now thinks that his past is rather figured out upon him. When he thinks of his history, he is a silhouette-Mark and his past is a Mark-shaped continuum dwindling back to a still point: his beginning as a plain full stop. The point of no return. If he had a man inside, that point would be inside, too, and he could return to it when he liked. He could stare within and pore over that point of innocent origin.

But people do. They believe they carry within themselves simple, smiling children, untouched by experience. They fondly think they can regress. Mark scowls. He decides that they think this way only because they can afford to. Just as they can afford to leave violins lying about for ornament and effect.

Peggy and Iris return with biscuits, bread and cheese, and set them out on the carpet, laughing still over some private joke. They have been drinking and eating since their arrival here. The pair of them fell in love with this house straight away. Simmonds took one look at the new guests, told them that supper was simmering on the hob, and fled into the night. They sat down to a perfect bolognese in the stony kitchen and the atmosphere warmed up.

'Look at me,' Richard says now. He wants to start the talking up again and draws their attention by plucking at his stained white T-shirt. 'If I went walking in the Antarctic, I'd still come back covered in tomato sauce.'

Peggy pours him more whisky and they laugh. Having appropriated the house, Iris commandeers the discreetly hidden hi-fi and puts Billie Holiday on. So at ease is she that she has shed some of her layers of jumpers and cardigans. Yet she is wearing her blue wedding hat again, holding it down with one hand as she dances alone, on the spot.

Mark finds he has been staring at Richard, who is now deep in conversation with Peggy and grateful for it. Across the room drift fragments of their exchange and Mark stares into his glass, trying to block it out, knowing he will get cross if he listens in too much. He hears 'drama school', 'college' and 'father', before he manages to distance himself enough. Richard has a veneer of capability, shiny as his expensive leather jacket. He appears to think that the world is there for him to move through unimpeded. Look at how he took control of their day today. He derailed them entirely and forced them into having a good time.

He succeeded, too. The disasters of this morning now seem like half a lifetime ago. Richard had sorted them out. No wonder he gets on so well with Peggy. It's the same assurance that Iris has and it's all down to class. It is a veneer and yet Mark knows that Richard will believe in his man inside. Just as Iris believes in her own man or woman or God knows what she keeps locked up within.

When Mark thinks about Richard's body, he thinks of cool, white flesh, well-fed middle-class flesh, softened with talcum powder. It makes Mark feel scrawny. All that whiteness, with muscles he has no pressing need for.

One moment he is looking at Richard, his profile in the lamplight, that startling white at the start of his collar bone, seen at the loose neck of his T-shirt. The easy way he sits slumped back, one leg folded beneath him, even the shape, the fold of the crotch of his jeans. Then Mark bites back with another thought, troubled and cold, about who still has the luxury to put their pasts behind them, or inside them, or put it all down to experience.

I'm drunk, Mark thinks. Poor Mark's a drunk. And self-pitying; nobody has it as hard as I do. They've all got *essences* and I haven't! Here am I surrounded by soft centres; I'm an empty shell and nothing in my life will be resolved.

He is resenting the other three so steadily that he is alarmed when Richard gets up suddenly and flees the room.

Iris looks at Mark as if from a mile away. At first he thinks he sees reproval in her face. Perhaps she has heard him thinking. My thoughts, he thinks, must be written all over my face. But Iris hasn't heard or read a single thing. She smiles and shrugs and says, 'I think the poor thing's gone to throw up. Bless him.'

Peggy is lying on the pleated mat at Iris's feet. Mark notices she has trodden Stilton into the carpet and has some stuck to the bottom of one shoe.

'He's such a sweet boy,' Iris adds.

Upstairs a door bangs.

The keen glare of the service-station restaurant was like walking into a headache. They had decided they must stop somewhere because Sally had woken up and, although she never said anything, Sam knew she must be starving. It was late. Sam didn't want to think of herself as a bad mother. When the sign came at them out of the gloom, blue with a knife and fork, she told Bob they ought to stop for a bite to eat before pressing on.

It was bleak inside and the restaurant was high up above the desolate, near-invisible fields. The skeleton staff were weary and obviously convinced they wouldn't see home tonight.

Sam slid their trays down the self-service counter, determined to sod the expense. Bob and Sally sleepwalked after her down the yellow tiling. If adults had a full meal, apparently, children could eat their fill for just a penny. It seemed a good deal.

The baked beans had grown a thick, overheated skin and the fish-shaped fishburgers were slumped in one corner of their sweating glass cabinet.

'It looks lovely,' Sam said. 'I'm gagging, aren't you?'

Tiredly Sally smiled and pretended to ask her Kanga and Roo what they wanted to eat. Heartened by this, Sam quietly asked Bob how much further they had to drive.

He grimaced. 'Bloody miles yet. We're not even half way there. We've done about a third of the trip.'

'But we've been driving hours!'

'Slowly. And –' his face darkened – 'while you were napping I took a couple of wrong turnings.'

'I wasn't napping. Fish, chips and beans three times, please. One's a child's portion. I was wide awake the whole time.'

Bob shrugged. He was too tired to argue. By now he knew Sam well enough to know that it would become something to argue about. She was no longer the demanding manageress beside the cardboard crusher. He was learning how that demanding, demonstrative nature exerted itself in all areas of her affairs. So he gave in.

But as Sam shunted their trays up the line, and stung her fingers on the hot plates as they were passed across the counter to her, she realised that he was right. She had been dreaming that she was on a boat. A strange sort of boat, low down, on black water. More of a raft, really, and she was lying down, with two others. There was room only for three of them and they had to paddle with their hands. It rocked wildly and for some reason they were in a hurry to get somewhere. Sally was beside her, fast asleep, and so she had to paddle harder. Someone else was on Sally's other side, but Sam couldn't see. She had to concentrate. The water was oily and the night was grim. The dream went on without rhyme or reason, without narrative. They paddled and held on for dear life.

When they sat at their table and Sam did her usual trick of packing her handbag with packets of sugar and the cheap, bendable cutlery, Bob said, 'We might have to turn around.'

'What?' Sam was thinking about how she always ended up in motorway services. Wherever she went, no matter how much of a good time she thought she might have, she always arrived somewhere like this. They went, not on holidays, but on coach trips for the day. And days always ended with a sleepy cup of tea and fiddling under neon strip lights with cartons of UHT milk. The plastic lips always broke off in her fingers and she had to risk a nail to puncture the lid.

'We might have to give up. Turn round and go back to Leeds for tonight.'

She looked at Bob and she realised he looked hounded. What would he be doing, she thought, if he weren't here with us? Beside him Sally was suddenly alert, listening. But was she distressed or hopeful? Sam couldn't tell.

'There's a motel-thing here,' Sam said, hitting on a brain wave. 'If we can't go on.' She wasn't going back to Leeds. What was the bloody point? She certainly wasn't going to that Tony's house and knocking on the door. Not back to the enemy, because that was what he was. And not back to where Mark was, either, because . . . because Mark had suffered enough.

The thought was a novel one. She knew Mark would be delighted to see them, cold and soggy on the doorstep, asking to come in. It wasn't to deprive him of his joy or triumph that she wouldn't do it. It was because, she realised, she couldn't bear to wrest Sally from him again.

'A motel?' Bob was saying, an edge to his voice now. 'Sam, I'm not made of money.'

She felt this like a slap. It hit a raw nerve. Of course she never thought that, never assumed that, never really wanted that. Now the look on his face said he thought she had. That all she wanted was a nice motel. The sign outside had said *en suite* bathrooms, continental breakfasts and satellite TV in every room.

She wanted to tell him, I'm not with you for an easy ride.

'All right then. If we can't go on, if that's what you reckon, then we go back. Motels are a waste of money.' She couldn't keep the rancour out of her voice. Even though it would make Bob think badly of her. 'So we go and find Mark and beg for a place to stay.'

Bob stared at her and she saw stirring in him vague pulses of anger, hurt and disappointment. Beside him Sally's face was unreadable. But under the table she felt the swishing as her daughter kicked and swung her legs.

*

173

Tony's bathroom was full of clutter. On one side of the toilet was a wooden armoire with a marble top, littered with shells and oddly sprouting plants. A slim volume of poetry pointed one corner politely at the sitter. To the other side and on the floor squatted a dirty fish tank, whose inhabitants moved through their green gloom in contemplative silence. The walls were plastered with Art Nouveau prints. Mark took all this in as he entered, bursting for a pee, thinking, Tony's tastes have really changed.

He swayed on the spot over the toilet bowl aiming and was disconcerted by the fish peering out of the top of the tank. They looked as if they expected to be fed. Pissing was a great relief right now, as if he were emptying his body of all the toxins accumulated in the last week or so. It kept coming out long enough.

Like Peggy, Mark was peculiar about whom he let see him pissing. It seemed a funny thing to want to watch. Men did it communally all the time, although generally Mark kept out of that. He was always the one, when faced with the jostling at the urinals, to slip into a cubicle. He wasn't sure why. In case someone made a move, in case they looked down at him, came shuffling up – or, worse still, in case he looked at them.

So at the sound of the tap being turned on, the gush of water, he jumped. Richard was standing at the sink, rinsing vomit from his mouth, pale and shivering. His look was deadly serious, as though he were equally shocked to be disturbed. Yet he must have seen Mark first.

Mark felt a fool, planted over the bog by the fish tank, dick peeking out and pissing as he stared round at Richard. Richard had even more bolognese streaked down his white T-shirt now. His long hair dripped with icy water.

He took one step hesitantly, and then appeared to decide something. Richard strode across to Mark and gripped his upper body, one hand at the back of his head, and kissed him fiercely. Mark fumbled to keep his cock still trained in the right direction, resisted at first and then, feeling suddenly supported, relaxed into the kiss.

The last few drops fell and he could taste a blend of whisky and tomato from Richard. He thought, But the dirty bastard's

174

just thrown up! How can I be doing this? Yet it didn't matter. Now, at last, Mark was getting a taste of the inner man and he loved it.

Richard pulled back, gently flushed the toilet, took a tissue and carefully dabbed Mark's prick. When he kissed him again, stronger this time, he pressed his palm down upon it as if both to provoke and repress its erection. Mark was shocked more by the bristle of Richard's beard. It wasn't the same, kissing a man. He remembered now. Under the rustle and clash of stubbles, you never quite expected that soft whiteness. Mark felt himself pressing his mouth to the side of that face, sensing the complexities of that flesh. And he felt grateful. He gave a kind of half-sob of relief and shock, and because now Richard was wanking him steadily. He seemed much too easy and practised at this. Obscurely, this shocked Mark too. He's barely in his twenties, he thought.

Fuck. This is everything I thought I'd left behind. Now Richard seemed like someone Mark had always known. Mark was getting to know the whole of him, all at once. The whole of him: this was the illusion he fell for every time.

And he had left falling for it all behind.

But God, it felt good.

Richard stopped. His hand slipped away and he stared over Mark's shoulder.

'Christ, I'm sorry,' came Iris's voice. 'I just wanted to use the loo.'

Hurriedly Mark tucked himself in.

'It's all right,' Richard said. 'We've finished in here, I think.'

He smiled at Iris as he took himself off downstairs. Mark washed his hands and left Iris to piddle in peace.

It seemed such a comedown, such an anticlimax. Sam hated giving in. It wasn't her.

The journey back, however, was identical to the way home. She could almost imagine they were going the way she wanted.

Perhaps the snow was a little easier this way. Leeds was opening its clogged arteries and drawing them back in. It made it easy for them.

In the back, Sally was wide awake. She was waiting.

Sam said, 'We'll have to phone Mark at some point. Warn him to make sure we can find the house.'

'Yeah,' Bob said. He was perturbed and she didn't feel like asking him about it. Naturally he wouldn't be happy about throwing himself on the mercy of Mark and Tony. Male pride.

Mark and Tony. As if, suddenly, they were an item.

This is our great triumph and our fabulous procession home. All of it gone to pieces. This is the way all my plans go, she thought. She dreaded this feeling that all her fire and energy meant nothing in the end. That in the end she fell apart in the teeth of the storm.

The car was still pressing gently on, as if relieved and pleased, like Sally, to return to Mark.

Sam was concentrating on a separate rhythm. What was it? A slow rocking, side to side.

The raft on black water, and she felt it threaten softly to overturn. At either side the city's walls thrust in to jar their progress and sink them. They ploughed on unsteadily. Rarely did Sam's dreams pursue her like this. She was a woman of practical means. Life was clear-cut and dreams did not impede. Tonight Sam was, on all fronts, in between states.

Downstairs Mark made the mistake of drinking from another bottle of red wine.

Peggy sat with Richard and they were attempting to pick up their conversation from some time before. But Mark could see Richard casting glances at him, only half-heartedly chatting away.

Mark wasn't sure what was going to happen now. Earlier the evening had been winding down towards that disconsolate, close-down blip on the screen that follows the national anthem. Now everything was up in the air again. Mark was having to pick himself up, stir himself for whatever the sequel to the bathroom would be.

Iris reappeared, simpering and drunk. Peggy took one look and suggested some coffee. She slipped out to make it and

Mark sipped more wine. It was coppery in his mouth and he felt a vague regret. It washed out that brief taste of Richard.

Richard and Iris were talking in a half-playful, half-hushed tone. Mark wasn't sure what about. He stretched back leisurely, unwilling as yet to commit himself to the night's unfolding. He had time to sit back and pick carefully over the precise pleasures of what had happened. Richard's warm, sure and only slightly clumsy hand had been quite different to anything that had touched Mark recently. He smiled in premature nostalgia at the thoughtfulness of those gestures; that quick dab of the tissue and the practised running of the finger up his cock's tender underbelly.

Mark had forgotten how he recognised a good lover, those who acted from the first as if your body were as familiar to them as you were. When their curiosity is accompanied and rewarded with a delighted recovery of what they always, surely, expected, then you know you have them, hook, line and sinker; and they have you.

'So what did you see?' Richard was jeering in a louder tone. Mark saw that he was drinking again, too.

God, this is decadence, he thought. Like the Borgias. Nipping out to spew and snog and wank and then back in for a chat and more booze. Fabulous.

'I didn't see much. But it was a surprise!'

'I'm sorry,' said Richard. 'I don't know what came over me.'

But Mark thought it wasn't directed at him. If it had been, it would have signalled the end of the matter. It would have been saying, I'm sorry, but it was a silly mistake. Mark blinked. Perhaps it did mean that. He knew now that he wanted Richard tonight. He had done all along and he was pissed enough now to admit it. The thought that it mightn't happen set up a prickle of disappointment. A surge of panic, even.

'Well, I saw enough,' Iris was saying. She looked at Mark and giggled. 'Nothing I haven't seen before, anyway.'

Mark lurched to his feet. 'Excuse me.'

Iris and Richard looked up in concern as he hurried out to the kitchen. Peggy was thoughtfully plunging the filter through a cafetiere as he dashed to the sink. She watched Richard follow him and lovingly pat his back as he threw up. Fastidiously Mark managed to direct the spew between the washing-up bowl and the taps. He didn't want to disgrace himself and make a mess for anyone.

Peggy picked up on the tenderness of the scene and left them to it. So they've bonded, she thought, with some satisfaction. She took coffee in to Iris.

When Mark had brought up the whole lot, Richard silently plied him with pints of cold water, then black coffee. They had a quiet exchange of 'sorries' and supportive back-pattings and shoulder-rubbings. Mark was shuddering and streaming with tears.

At last Richard said, 'So we've both thrown up tonight, love.'

Mark stared at him. He was horrified by the words. Inappropriately, of course. Richard was just being sweet. But they recalled irresistibly the disastrous night Mark had first met Sam.

Here he hit another hinge in his life.

His chest seized with a series of dry retches. Richard hugged him and Mark had to struggle free.

Quietly Richard walked to the kitchen door.

'Listen, I've got to go round and switch everything off. You'd better go up to bed. We need to rest.'

Mark wanted to say, That's not what I meant. That's not what I wanted. Not at all.

Now Richard could reverse yesterday's roles. With satisfaction? Mark wanted to ask. But Richard had slipped out to do his housekeeping bit. Mrs Danvers, Mark thought. Burn down Manderley; bring it all down. I've had enough – but to tide me over, I still want you. It was terrible, pathetic of him, but he wanted to depend on Richard now, on his sometimes eager, soft, cool, warming flesh, to give him a separate space to play upon. If only he could take him to bed. Now. But Richard had gone.

The night had been jump-started into something exciting, waking Mark from his stupor and self-absorption. Now abruptly it seemed to have ended and no one was happy.

178

Mark had never really used sex to forget. It had never seemed the thing to do. Tonight it had and he was starting to suspect he'd chucked it all away down the sink.

Never mind. With nothing to regret, he decided he'd better get himself away to bed.

This house was labyrinthine. All these half-assembled dining rooms, sitting rooms. In the front hall connecting them all, he found Richard standing pissed and nonplussed before two familiar, abandoned heaps of clothing.

'I was going to lock up the front door,' he said. The key was ready in his hand.

'Oh,' said Mark. 'They've gone out. They do this sometimes.'

'They've taken the spare key.'

'They can look after themselves.'

'It's weird,' said Richard and they both laughed.

A tense moment hung between them.

The phone on the table beneath the chandelier started to ring. Mark looked at it and so did Richard. There was a spread of recent glossy magazines fanned out. As the ringing went on he found himself fascinated by the grinning faces of their covers.

Richard said, 'I'd better answer it. Get yourself up into bed. You've had one fuck of a day.'

Mark complied and thudded up the stairs. He was happy to have instructions and it was only when he groped his way into his room, with Richard's low voice on the phone fading out below him, that he realised he still didn't know what was happening tonight.

He shut his door, left the light off and, quivering like a teenager, threw off his clothes. In the dark, alone, he even felt embarrassed by his erection. Might all be for nothing. The frosty moonlight still came down from the round window. So here he was again, waiting in the dark.

He pulled the chair to the window and looked down at the snowy city. The weather was worse than he thought. The park beyond the houses was like a mixing bowl of wet meringue. The trees were picked out in irritable black exclamation marks. And there were two human figures, arm in arm, quite a distance away but distinct all the same. Their walking was easy, easy.

Mark put the antique chair back in place and lay on the bed. The house was still, silent, and he shook with fatigue and wretchedness and the threat of anticlimax.

He closed his eyes a moment. When he opened them he saw that perhaps that trick with time was happening all over again.

Because the white gloves were hovering in the air above him. At the foot of the bed they spread their fingers in greeting. He seized up in terror, having forgotten this point in the previous night.

He had forgotten so much. So much.

And here they were again. One reached down to stroke his foot. With an elegant gesture the other turned a pirouette in mid-air and landed on his stomach, gave a quick caress and returned to its mate.

Mark found he couldn't speak.

The hands pressed fingertips together and seemed to think. This was like watching a magic show.

The room was about to spin round, he felt. He pushed his own hands down on the mattress to weigh it down. And he watched. Watched as, just like a magician, one of the hands apparently reached into the other's invisible cuff and produced . . . a bright pink disc, the size of a fifty-pence piece.

It roved about the air in circles, to make sure it had Mark's attention. Then deliberately the hands brought the pink disc down until it was level with Mark's head as he lay. He looked down the length of his body and the bed as the white fingers worked dexterously.

There ought to be musical accompaniment, applause and a spangly assistant. Because surely this was magic?

The pink disc turned inside out. It was swelling out, a stretched luminous pink. Now it had an odd strawberry shape. The fingers tugged and rolled and the shape grew. At last it described a thick, long-familiar cock erect in glowing fuchsia.

180

The hands displayed their palms in triumph, back at their natural height. Ta-dah!

You must remember this, the gleaming cock implied as it bobbed through the dark toward him. A kiss is still a kiss . . .

Stealthily the hands reached out to him and with them, following inexorably – since there was indeed some invisible connection between these members – came the cock. Mark was thinking, This must be real. The way the erection swayed and dipped and slapped against the invisible stomach. Only a real one looks this absurd.

The hands clutched his shoulders, then there was a weight on his chest, the warmth of a body, as the luminous pink thing jabbed its way blindly towards his mouth, shuddering as it nosed up to him.

Mark reached his hands up to the empty air and touched it. It pulsed and squirmed under pink rubber. He gently stroked at the dark and felt solid, stiffly haired legs. The chest was taut and clenched for his explorations, but he could see the doorframe through it.

Insistently the cock wavered under his nose.

Not yet, Mark thought. Not by a long chalk. First he wanted to ask something.

'Tony?'

The question fogged the air.

And then there was a knock at the door. It opened and admitted a shaft of yellow light. 'Mark?' Richard asked and stepped quickly inside. 'The phone. Sally's been calling us from –'

By the hall light Richard could see Mark stretched out in his gaudy nakedness. And then he saw the hands and cock poised above him. He fell against the doorframe.

Mark felt the bedsprings jolt and sing as the body on top of him launched itself across the room. He sat up stiffly to see the gloves double themselves into neat little fists and knock Richard flat with two quick jabs.

The hands turned to survey Mark. The condom had sagged by now, hanging dolefully. One hand snatched it off with a snap and flung it angrily at the bed. And then the hands were gone, slipping out of the door, into the light.

Mark jumped off the bed to see to Richard.

He was bleeding and gasping and had to be helped over to the bed. 'So you saw him,' he said. 'You saw him, after all.'

'Sit down,' said Mark and hugged him to him.

In the mussed-up covers they embraced. They were both shaking badly. When Richard scraped his back with his watch, Mark remembered he was naked. Between them, between his own exposed tattoos and Richard's new bruises, his erection was back and squashed uselessly. It didn't seem to matter. With a sudden certainty and blocking out whatever other doubts he had, Mark said, 'He's not coming back tonight. I know Tony of old.'

Mark got up from the bed and clicked the door to. Gently and mindful of the fresh bruises, he stripped Richard off, wiping the blood from his chin with the already stained shirt.

Then he wrapped him under a sheet with his own body and, quite slowly, he made love to him with a relief and gratitude they had worked out between them and shared equally by now.

Twenty-Three

'Of course, a Valkyrie's natural element was never the snow . . .'

Iris and Peggy made their way through the park back to the house. They never thought themselves lucky to avoid getting arrested in the dead of night. Bob in his panda on Christmas Eve had been a shock, but at the time they had been more shocked to see Sam sitting behind him. Their nightly exhibition struck them as something justly beyond the bounds of law and order.

The still-falling snow was gentle on them, and warm because of the whisky. They ought to have drunk vodka, Peggy murmured at one point, to feel that needlepoint warmth brewed for burning flesh free of ice. Its lingering savour might have suited the scene. Vodka rinsing through the body sets up a clatter of sleigh bells, a far-off baying of hounds.

'And what is a Valkyrie's natural element?' she asked Iris, gripping her arm harder than she need to. The ground was becoming slippery; the grass was a black pelt matted with slush. And Iris seemed nostalgic tonight, wistful, so that Peggy was reminded of the sea-change her lover had promised.

'Well . . .' Iris began. 'The Valkyries only crept about in snow in the line of duty. Battlefields were often in the far north. With the sun never setting and blood freezing in the veins, armies would battle for long, long hours on the glaciers. The combat was slowed down almost into stop-motion animation. For some reason the men liked to fight that way. Sometimes the glaciers would shake out their bedspreads and freeze the combatants to the spot. Even wounds blossomed gradually in those wars. And the pain of bloodshed was postponed by cold.

183

'These were the places Valkyries had to visit. But to get there they had to travel back and forth across the North Sea. That iron-grey sea which rides up high, impossibly high, it seems, to meet the horizon, is the natural element of the Valkyries.'

'I see,' said Peggy, who had grown up in North Shields and knew all about the sea there, thank you very much.

She used to take the young Sam to the fish markets on Sunday mornings. Clutching the bundle of Sunday papers, Sam stared into ferocious maws until she told her mam she didn't want to go any more. Peggy was pleased that at last Sam was expressing an opinion. She didn't mind stopping the trips. They never bought anything anyway. They went because Sundays at home were just dire; the old man coughing, praying, coughing.

Iris said, 'Surveyed from above, those currents seemed a symbol for possibilities. When a Valkyrie looked at the patterns made by the thrashing sea beneath her feet, she could still say to herself, Well, anything might happen. The thrill of predestination went through her when she realised that everything was still up in the air.

'But when she came to the bleak fields of snow, the pattern was already set, she could no longer fiddle with the outcome. All she might do then is pick up the pieces. A Valkyrie prefers things in flux.'

They had arrived back in the street.

'I always think,' Iris added, 'of snow as a signal that things are virtually settled. As if it were raining plaster of Paris.'

They stopped under a streetlamp, watching with perfect equanimity as a single, exhausted car slewed to a stop outside Tony's house. As the doors on either side creaked open and its amber lights popped on inside, the ladies saw that Sam had returned.

For a moment Peggy felt like diving into the nearest hedgerow for cover, but Iris urged them on.

'Let's see how the plaster hardens,' she said determinedly, bustling onwards to meet Sam and Bob, who was carrying the sleeping Sally.

Peggy didn't like the sound of this plaster hardening. She

could almost sense it inching along her skin, bringing up the gooseflesh. She thought of the slow, cool clasp of plaster dragging over her face. She pictured herself and Iris frozen in their tracks by the hedges, a statue of two linked old dykes. It would make life so much easier simply to adopt one decorous position and hold it for ever.

But Peggy still had the salt and ice of the North Sea in her veins. Coming from a town battered into submission by its exertions, she knew that if she stayed still, she would freeze. So she was determined to keep going, even if it led her into disaster.

'Hullo, dear,' Peggy said. 'So the weather was too bad, then?'

Sam looked her mother up and down and rolled her eyes.

Bob said, 'We almost got stuck.'

'Let's get Sally inside,' Iris suggested.

I'm never going to sleep again, Mark was thinking.

Richard lay crooked in his arms, like a baby. Mark lay slumped against the headboard. You couldn't trust the night these days. It had brought so much unexpected stuff his way recently. Visitations of the worst sort, which he had brought upon himself.

And he thought about the years of taking every night for granted. Despite everything, with Sam he felt safe. With a grim determination, a Lego-building look on her face, she had protected him and Sally from the world. He was learning to give her credit for that. Even reading Tony's letters, secretly, before he got them, could be seen as part of this protective process now. Furious and with accusations flying, Sam had been protecting Mark nonetheless.

Richard murmured in his sleep, shifting position, seeming to want to roll away and lie by himself. With a twinge of regret Mark let him. It almost feels like betrayal when someone does that, he thought. As if, with sleep, a selfish negligence sets in, and their body can feel free to cast you aside.

Of course you only get that feeling if you lie awake all night, thrumming with tension, like a violin set aside, and alert to signs of anything less than slavish devotion. Mark didn't expect that from Richard

How many nights had Sam laid awake, watching Mark's body inch away from her?

He remembered now, those nights of knowing full well that she was awake and knowing she wondered whether he was. He would be pretending sleep and fiercely thinking of ways to extricate himself. How he could make it seem natural to be turning in his sleep towards the coolness of the further part of the bed.

Thinking it over now, it struck him that any glimpse of a new life, any whiff of change in the air, brought him the exact prickle of pleasure given him by turning to lie on the fresh side of the pillow.

On him Richard was stirring awake and Mark almost forgot to breathe. He was suspended, waiting to see where a conscious Richard would turn.

When Sally opened the door a crack and crept in, on her way to her own room, Richard shook fully awake.

'Goodnight, Dad and Richard,' she whispered, and Mark saw she could barely keep her eyes open.

''Night, love,' he said, and Richard looked up, shocked.

Sally was like a sleepwalker, flat-footed across the carpet, opening the dressing-room door.

'Hang on,' Mark said. He couldn't trust the night these days, but Sally seemed real enough.

Richard was sitting bolt upright, gripping his shoulder. 'Shit, I forgot; the phone! They said they were coming back tonight!'

The dressing-room door clicked shut and they listened to Sally stumble through her scattered books and drop with relief into bed.

Sam knew what posh was and she was determined not to be in the least impressed by Tony's house. Not being impressed had been a key element in her refusal to acknowledge Iris's impact on Peggy's life. So Sam sneered at the chandelier in the hallway and the ornate mantelpiece in the living room, where they sat, shivering with fatigue.

Iris and Peggy dressed quickly in the hallway.

'Sally knows where her room is,' Peggy called out. 'There's no sense in keeping the poor thing up any longer.'

Sam was too tired to argue. Bob was no support. He was stretched out on a scarlet chaise longue and snoring. She had never heard him snore. With a jolt she realised she had never slept with him before. He made the same noise snoring as he did fucking and that revolted her. She was thinking, He's always on the job, just like a bloody copper. He's never off duty, never out of uniform. If they were always together, those stertorous groans would punctuate her every move.

Peggy sat by her. 'I'm glad you're back. We can sort things out now. It didn't seem right, you just storming off like that.'

'We had no choice about coming back. This isn't with my tail between my legs, Mam.'

'I didn't imagine it was.'

'I never do that.'

'I know you don't.'

'We're going to be snowed up. Snowed in. It's outrageous out there.'

'Well,' Peggy said. 'At least we're all safe.'

Sam snorted. 'In his house. Have you seen him yet?'

'The mythical Tony? No. I don't think he exists at all.' With this Peggy stood. 'I'm going to find you a room upstairs. I think Iris went to hunt one out for you and Bob. We all need to rest just now.'

Sam looked at her. 'Thanks, Mam.'

Peggy smiled.

'Mam? Just . . . would you tell me . . . I haven't acted like a kid in all this, have I? I've not been like some big daft bairn stomping about and shouting the odds, have I?'

'Oh, Sam!' Her mother knelt to hug her and was surprised when Sam hugged back. 'If you have, then I reckon it's a lesson to the rest of us, frankly. It doesn't do any harm to know what you want. Out of any of us, you've at least had the guts to broadcast it.'

Sam pulled back and looked at her mother. 'That sounds as if there's something you want and daren't say.'

'Ah,' said Peggy. 'Your professional manner. You sniff

things out. Yes, there's something I want.' She stood again and looked at Bob, at Sam. 'I want things to stay exactly as they are. But knowing that they won't, that they can't, I daren't say that. I daren't say that's what I want. Because nobody else wants that.'

Peggy went off to find Iris, to allocate the rooms. It was as if the house had somehow become theirs and they were playing the competent hostesses.

Downstairs Sam cast one disappointed look at Bob and, to keep herself awake until she had found a bed to fall into, went hunting around the other rooms.

The detritus of the evening before lay strewn around: crumbled cheese and biscuits, empty bottles overturned and glasses smeared in fingerprints. Vaguely Sam wondered whether Richard had copped off with Mark. It oughtn't to make any difference now. Well, they all seemed to have had a nice night, at any rate, to judge by the remains. A better night than we had, she thought, blizzarded in Bob's crappy car.

Could Sam have consented to a safe and pleasurable night, even to see her husband seducing – or being seduced by – a stranger? She didn't know. Unless pushed, Sam never knew how possessive she would be.

She happened upon the dining room where the candelabra was pasted to the whitewashed sill by wax drips. Nothing had been done with the china on the tarpaulin. The pieces still waited, gleaming, to be hauled like swag to market: teapots, Toby jugs, figurines twirling painted skirts, dead clocks and toast racks. Both desolate and exotic, this tableau drew her attention for a few moments.

The moonlight was such that she could see only half a room. The remaining furniture was bisected by the slant of the light. In the dark half floated six avocados. As her eyes accustomed themselves, she could pick out their green skin and then, as they whirled slowly through the air, two stark white hands flexing and waggling underneath.

Tony juggled avacados for Sam's benefit, suppressing his giggles, and Sam didn't know what the fuck was going on. Unwilling to trust her own imagination, she fled the room.

She left Tony to sink to his knees in hysterical laughter. He let it out in long, whooping bellows as the avocados fell with six ripe thuds on the floorboards.

I'm just making mischief, he thought as his giggles subsided. But I don't really care right now. I deserve some fun.

It was his first recent glimpse of Sam and he was reassured by the fact that she behaved, meeting him, as if she were in a horror film. It made her seem less of a threat.

Twenty-Four

Early, very early, Richard decided he should wake. He knew Sam, Bob and Sally were there. Things would have to be discussed.

When Simmonds came in to go about his daily business, Richard would have to make the introductions and decide who was related to whom and how. That seemed like a moment of daylight clarity and one to be put off. Richard wanted to stretch the deft ambiguity of the night into the day. He knew that everyone else would sleep in till late, but he wanted Mark conscious and around him, with him until the last moment.

He woke him, almost brusquely, and urged him to dress.

'I want to take you to that bookshop. It's not far.'

'What for?'

'Because it might be fun.' Richard didn't know why, but he wanted them to do something. He wanted a peg to hang this morning on. He stripped the sheet off the dozing, still complaining Mark.

Whose body was bright blue in the morning. Mark was oblivious to his own spectacle and Richard was half-ashamed by the shock of it. The alarm clock on his chest. An eagle flying between a unicorn's belly and a stretch of Icelandic coast.

Richard could see no connection between the skin and its cautious oils, the taste of it, and this incredible jigsaw. He felt hoodwinked, as if he had eaten a Mars bar with the wrapper still on. And yet . . . He thought about food dyes and how once, for a joke which backfired, he'd done a blue curry for Tony and old man Simmonds. It was meant to be tasteless, that odd midnight blue, but dinner was bitter that night and the old man gloomily suggested that Richard was trying to poison his mentors.

Mark stretched and yawned, eyes squeezed shut with those fake eyes squinting unseeing at the ceiling. His William Morris prick stirred feebly and Richard wondered why he hadn't at any point tasted the design. Those violet anemones and blue arum lilies. Oughtn't pollen have come away on his tongue from Mark's stomach? Shouldn't his morning breath be complex with the juice of crushed fruit? Yet all Richard could taste still was whisky.

He watched the silent Mark haul himself from the bed and tuck this ensemble, piece by piece, back inside his clothes. It seemed touching that he exposed all this to Richard. Richard watched him dress with fascination.

Why was the sight of roman numerals on the clock a man had painted on his chest somehow more intimate than taking his cock into your mouth?

They crept down the corridor on their way out for the morning. Everyone will sleep in, Richard consoled himself.

But behind them, in her circular room, Sally was sitting up in bed, turning page after page of the book she had been forced to leave unfinished. On either side of them in that thinly carpeted corridor, Iris and Peggy and Sam and Bob were awake also, and yet engaged, buying time of their own.

Something about snow and being snowed in, perhaps.

But early, very early that morning, Tony's house creaked in its icy coat with the secretive and relieved sounds of its visitors loving each other.

It was the morning you were told not to leave your house.

Unless absolutely necessary, you were warned to stay indoors. Outside it was risky and you ventured into its deep and even crispness at your own peril. This morning was strident and blue, offering the slightest respite in terms of snowfall, but you were told more was gathering. The sky was, as it were, drawing in the deepest of breaths, making temperatures drop, preparing to unleash itself once more. The already fallen snow developed a gleaming crust and declared its intention to remain.

If anyone in Tony's house had been watching TV this morning, they would have heard these warnings. In the grim dawn they might have watched the concerned, puckered faces of presenters on plush sofas urging their viewers to go back to bed.

Why don't you just give the day a miss? It is too hazardous out. Go back to bed, pull the covers up to your chin, and enjoy the rest of the show? You can spend all day, should you wish, entirely passively, taking in the odd magazine article and quiz show and perhaps, occasionally, apprehensively, spare a glance at the window. The dropping snow casts moving shadows on your curtains.

On the TV news, images remind you how wise you are to avoid snow chaos. Images of a country knocked into a standstill.

A postman being discouraged on a long, long, slippery street. The wind snatches letters from his hand and valiantly he attempts to retrieve them . . . gives up.

Eager lambs totter, slump, sink and are never seen again.

A train has derailed itself. The black swathes of churned earth make the snow look wounded.

Cars shunting slowly, filmed in infrared, still not getting home, batteries ticking down. The frazzled AA men get soup at motorway services.

As it happens, nobody in Tony's house watches the TV. There isn't one, anyway.

If Sam knew, she wouldn't be surprised. She couldn't imagine the inhabitants of this house sitting round to enjoy *Blind Date*. It was another reason to despise them. Sam would quite enjoy spending this morning in bed with the telly on and Richard Madeley and Judy Finnegan at her feet. It's one of the things you miss when you work in a shop. The newsreaders and presenters – our current Lords of Misrule – would demand that she embrace the novelty of this solstitial decadence.

As it is, she is relishing quite another morning novelty: waking up with Bob. Whether it is TV deprivation and the mistaken tang of spring in the air, or whether it is the subversive cosiness of a wintry carnival, doesn't matter. But she finds that she has Bob chained to the brass bedstead by a twined-up sheet. She has him bound hand and foot and is thoughtfully getting herself in a position to straddle him. It's such a faff on, really. They should be doing something sensible instead, like giving Tony a hiding.

But at the moment this is much more fun and with Bob thrashing gently beneath her, making half-hearted feints at escape, it seems as if they are in a different time; the morning has shanghaied them.

Sam slows down, grinding in small, clockwise circles, screwing him down to the lavish mattress, and it is then she sees it is snowing again outside. She sees the shadows on the curtains, dropping almost lazily, their soft penumbra touching now and then.

Bob gives her an impatient nudge with his pelvis and unthinkingly she reaches beneath them both to provoke him, squeezing a finger up his arse. The policeman's eyes go wide and inside her, his cock goes off abruptly in a spasmodic fit of surprise.

Mark and Richard were caught this morning when the snow came down again, tripping and sliding their way through a series of alleys and abandoned streets. The junk and bursting bin bags set out after Christmas were half disguised by now and thrust themselves out like mantraps.

'Really,' said Richard, 'I wanted to show Sally the bookshop. But we'll buy her a present there. I must show it to you, though.'

Dully Mark reflected that he could now hear the snow. It stripped Richard's voice of echo and all Mark could hear was Richard. In all the frost Richard's voice was pure and uncontested.

More alleys, more tripping.

'Are you sure there's really a smart bookshop here? It seems a bit unlikely.'

But there was, and it was open. The doorway was low, into one of those buildings constructed for a smaller working class than the present one.

Inside, dust and greyness and that insinuating smell of crumbling paper. The woman at the desk stacked high with newer books gave them a quick look, then ducked her head back into the span of honey-coloured light from her lamp. Her fingernail scratched down each page as she read.

Mark and Richard went to look at the shelves and when they had something to say they said it in whispers. In here, dust sapped them almost into silence. Mark found the books disordered and dirty to the touch, some of them jammed backwards, or upside down, into any available niche. He shivered as he browsed and his legs were shaking. Just the aftershock of good sex, he realised, and remembered those sensations of anti-anticlimax.

Mark had almost given up poking around and peered over the top of his shelf to see Richard, who squatted by the art section with a picture book of tattoos from all around the world. Sighing, Mark prepared to return to his unenthusiastic perusal – the whisper of covers' withdrawal from close-packed shelves, the aromatic flipping of pages – when he saw one particular book at the top of the pile. The mottled golden cover suggested itself to him, slyly drawing him away from Richard and his thought that it was time to leave.

A hardbacked novel, the span of his hand, perhaps sixty years old, with Art Nouveau stencilling and design.

'*Three Cheers for Retrogression*: A Novel by Iris Margaret Wildthyme, Author of *The Youngest Monkeys*.'

Mark's heart bossanovaed as he looked for an author's photograph and sure enough, in the back flap, there was Iris, looking quite bohemian and yet not much younger, draped upon a deck chair on what seemed to be the *Queen Mary*.

Peggy used to have a dog whose leg had been shattered in a car accident. It could no longer scratch behind its own right ear and was grateful when Peggy did it, the ruined leg making useless, sympathetic jerks.

When she made Iris come with her own right paw, it always reminded her of that poor dog. The way Iris bucked and jounced irresistibly suggested Sheba's compliance.

They lay clasped for some time afterwards. Peggy was constantly astonished by the heat coming off Iris. Maybe that's why she's so small – she burns everything off with the heat of her cunt. The word 'metabolism' popped into Peggy's head. Metabolism: the archaic, chthonic goddess of the fevered morning. Peggy had had God knew how many years of cool, distant couplings with a dying husband. Since being with Iris she had never known such heat, and never become used to it. She lay still touching Iris, unwilling to leave the warm centre.

When she did she found a loaded, steaming tea tray left outside their bedroom door. With a glance up and down the passageway – no one was in sight – Peggy picked it up and they settled down for a gentle breakfast before their frozen window.

'Richard must be back on houseboy duty,' Iris said.

'I can't see that, somehow.' Peggy took her tea black, or rather a deep orange. When she sucked at the cup's rim, its heat stung her mouth. 'He was in an extreme state last night. I expect this is from that little man we scared out of the way last night. Simmonds, or whatever he's called. It looks like he's decided to like us.'

'He gave me the bloody creeps,' Iris said.

'It's not like you to take against someone.'

'No, it's not, really.' Iris considered. 'I think it's because he's a bit of a rogue element. It's the novelist part of me speaking. The Valkyrie in me. Simmonds gives me the bloody creeps because I don't know yet what part he has to play in this. And he looks weird wearing hi-tech trainers.'

'I see you've dropped the Orlando business and you're sticking to the Valkyrie stuff?'

'It's all the same. It's all about having a long enough, wide enough view to see how people work and fit in.'

'What makes you think Simmonds has a part to play?'

Having watched Peggy drink her tea scalding and orange, Iris overcompensated and poured herself too much milk. 'I like a tidy ending, that's why. If I'm swooping down on Valkyrie wings to pick up the pieces and cart them off to Valhalla, I don't like the idea of rogue elements throwing me off balance. It puts me off my stroke.'

'This isn't Cluedo, dear.' Peggy sniggered. Miss Scarlett was not about to be smacked about by a crowbar in the billiards room. But Peggy wasn't to know that Sam had been menaced by avocados outside the pantry.

'Anyway,' Peggy added, 'what do you mean by a tidy ending?'

'I mean, precisely, How Things Turn Out. Despite the weather, I want to be able to say, it's turned out nice again.'

'Again?'

'This isn't the first little drama I've been involved in. I've had more lives than you've had hot labia, dear.'

'And we're approaching an ending to your involvement in this one, Iris?'

Peggy put her cup down and it struck a loud, clean note. She had wanted to ask this question and now it was out. Really she wanted to shout at Iris, or beg her to stay. Are you going? What about me? Where are all your clues leading?

Iris looked at her seriously. 'I might have to go somewhere, yes. I'm sorry, Peggy. It's the way my life always works.'

From outside in the street there came the groaning and clash of engine and gears, startling in all that enforced quiet. They rubbed holes in the window's condensation to see a green furniture van parked outside. In his beret and trainers, Simmonds was climbing out of the cab, flanked by and busily instructing the burly removal men.

'Here comes your rogue element, Iris.' Peggy smiled.

And suddenly Iris looked as if she were indeed playing at Cluedo. Weighing the crowbar in both hands, adjusting a peacock feather in her hat, tightening the noose strung ready in the kitchen.

Twenty-Five

'Sam?' Peggy tapped on the glossy white door. 'Are you up?'

In the corridor, two of Simmonds's overalled men were removing a wardrobe. She flattened herself against the wall to let them past. 'I think we'd all better get up,' she said, knocking again. 'Things are happening.'

The door opened a crack and Sam slipped out in an orange kimono she had found. She laughed when she saw the wardrobe turning the corner, on its way down the stairs. 'Everything's being repossessed!'

'Iris has gone to find Richard and Mark,' said Peggy. 'They weren't in their room. It's eleven o'clock.'

'*Their* room? Where's Sally, anyway?'

'I'll fetch her. You get yourself sorted out.'

Peggy dashed off and while Sam dressed, Bob was watching her, spreadeagled on their beautiful bed. 'What's happening? Don't just leave me trussed up here like a dick!'

'Sssh,' she said, buckling her jeans. 'I'll be back in a minute.'

Sam had a feeling that everything in this house not strapped down was about to walk off. From below there came the muffled thumps, bangs and curses of the removal men. It seemed fair enough for her to rush downstairs, leaving Bob where she knew he couldn't run off.

On the stairway she passed by a small window and saw four of the grim men carrying the stretched tarpaulin between them like a safety net, carefully balancing the arrayed *objets*. Simmonds was barking at them, toddling behind in the snow, carrying the six avocados.

'This is fucking bizarre,' she said as her mother came hurrying down the stairs with Sally in tow. Language, Sam thought to herself and swiftly picked her daughter up.

'Are we moving house?' asked Sally.

'This isn't our house,' Sam said. 'But they could have given us some warning.'

At that precise moment Simmonds looked up from the van's lowered tailgate and gave them an airy wave.

Iris heaved open the french windows and snow tumbled onto the carpet. 'Where have you been?'

Mark and Richard came running out of the garden, stumbling across snowed-up rubble. Mark was clutching a small parcel.

'What is it? What's happening?'

She pointed across the living room, where the men were kicking back pleated mats and last night's spilled bottles, getting a grip on the chaise longue. Richard looked horrified.

'Where's Tony?' he asked.

'You're a bit late asking that, aren't you, love?'

Mark pressed his new-bought parcel on Iris. 'Hold these. I've got to get Sally and all our stuff . . .'

He met Simmonds in the hallway. The old man was collecting up the sheaf of recent magazines and unplugging the phone.

'Good morning,' the old man said. 'I hope we're not disturbing you?'

'Does Tony know you're doing this?'

'Of course he does,' Simmonds cackled. 'Why, did you think I was just reclaiming everything that was mine as revenge?'

'I don't know what you're up to.'

'I'd be well within my rights, even if I was doing that. Even the dentists' antique casts are mine, should I ever find them. And the Methodists' organ in the cellar. I'm taking it all, but it's under the instructions of your precious Tony. Now, if you'll excuse me . . .'

Peggy, Sam and Sally appeared on the stairs.

'Dad, we're moving house!' Sally called.

Sam broke in. 'Mark, I want to speak to you.'

'Come on, love,' said Peggy as she took Sally's hand. 'I think we can still get some breakfast, if they haven't already started on the kitchen.'

Soon there were only Sam and Mark standing halfway up the first flight of stairs. Simmonds beetled about below, but they were oblivious to him. He whistled to himself through his teeth.

'It looks as if we're all going to have to go home today, anyway,' Mark said. He spoke hesitantly, almost politely, as if to a stranger. Sam resented this. 'The trains should still be going.'

'We've got ourselves into a bloody mess, haven't we, Mark?'

'You could say that.'

'Did you fuck that lad just because you found out about Bob and me?'

'Come off it, Sam. I wouldn't do that.'

'I thought you might.'

'I wouldn't sink that low. I couldn't give a shit about Bob.'

'You're a conceited bastard, Kelly.'

'How do you make that out?'

'Any other, normal man would be furious and fuck someone else out of revenge. You just please yourself.'

'Right.'

But by now they were grinning at each other. Sam smacked him hard in the face.

'You see,' she said, 'if that had been the case, it wouldn't have been so bad. But if we're both serious about going off and . . . Well, if you're set on this Richard like I'm on Bob . . . and we decide to break up our happy flat –'

'You made that choice before I did, Sam. You decided to move out yesterday. You went.'

'And I'd still be gone if it wasn't for the snow.'

'Maybe there's nothing else to say to each other, then.'

They looked at each other and found it hard to synchronise their expressions. Just like old times. They had never known, when they looked at each other, whether to laugh or cry.

'I think there's a fuck of a lot we've still got to say to each other,' she said.

'Yeah?' He shook his head, still ringing with her slap. 'I'm going to get my stuff and see Sally.' His daughter didn't seem quite real to him this morning. He hadn't expected to see her

199

so soon. He was more surprised to see her today than he had been last night, finding her apparently patrolling his dreams.

'I don't think I can do it, Mark.'

His feet kicked at the next step up. 'Do what?'

'Do you know when I was happiest?'

'Go on.'

'Each night when the bus pulled up outside our flats. When I'd finished work and our place was warm and you and Sal had already been in for a few hours. Or when I could watch you sleeping at night. Fuck. What am I saying?'

'What are you saying?'

'I don't know.'

'I think I do.'

'Bob's a boring fart,' she exploded. 'And he thinks I'm after his money!'

'They get quite a bit, coppers.'

'Come on then, Kelly. Tell me you don't really like fucking boys.'

'But that's not true, Sam. You've always known that.'

'I can't fucking win, can I?'

'Where's Bob now?'

'Oh, I left him tied to the bedposts.'

'Bob, we've been talking . . .'

Sam let herself into the bedroom to find it close and dusky. Bob was snoring again, his limbs flung out. Mark peered in and Sam shook her policeman awake.

'Big cock,' Mark commented. 'Is that what you were after?'

'Fuck off.'

Bob woke with a shout and stared in dismay at the two of them standing there.

'It's all right. I'm not sticking around,' Mark said, sitting on a corner of the bed.

'Mark's seen it all before,' Sam reassured him.

'What are you going to do?' asked Bob warily. Throughout their training, policeman are warned about compromising themselves. And here he was.

'Bob,' Sam began. 'Do you love me?'

'I . . . Of course I do, Samantha. Look at last night.'

'Enough to want me and my daughter living in your nice house?'

He stammered, 'Yes. You know that.'

'But more than Mark does?'

'Mark doesn't want you at all, Sam. You've said as much. He just wants the kid.'

'"The kid"?' asked Mark.

'I've done a hell of a lot for you already, Sam . . . I don't believe this. Get that faggot out of here and let's discuss this –'

The door shot open and two removal men appeared. 'Oh. Sorry. We've got to clear this stuff out.'

'In a minute,' Sam said in her best manageress voice. 'Two shakes.'

The removal men exchanged a glance and retired.

'Mark and I are evolving an outrageous plan,' she told Bob.

'Sam!' He was shouting now. 'I'm sick to the back teeth of fucking outrageousness. Why can't we just go home – to my bloody home – and tell this twat to piss off? Why can't we just be *normal*?'

Despite her careful equanimity, something in Sam stirred. It was a memory of her father's barking rages and how she had been forced to watch them from a similar position. She never did have a good bedside manner.

'Sam,' Mark said. 'Why don't you get your policeman to define "normal" for you? If he comes up with anything interesting, let me know. I'm off to pack before those men get all my things mixed up.'

Mark's belongings had already been disturbed. There wasn't much to go through. Sure that this would be a short trip, he had brought only one bag with him. Beside the rumpled double bed in the room at the very top of the house, this bag was being turned inside out and a swift ransacking was under way.

And who was the perpetrator, breathless and busy?

As Peggy, Iris and Sally ate breakfast, flinching every time someone nearby dropped a vase or banged furniture against a doorframe, items of Mark's clothing were being strewn.

As Sam untied Bob and told him to shut his mouth and dress

so that the men could take his bed away, the perpetrator was choosing, with careful deliberation, what to wear.

And, as Simmonds wrapped pieces of china in fuchsia tissue paper, looking up at the ceiling as if in expectation, this perpetrator made himself apparent.

In the top room he pulled on Mark's spare jeans, easing into their cool, creased legs, fastening the buttons with fingers that trembled.

The shirt he slipped into bristled with static. A cheap shirt with threads dangling, buttons missing, but it was charged with Mark's presence. Tony breathed him in.

When the door swung open, Tony turned to face it.

Mark stopped dead. He stared at his emptied bag because it was easier to look at that than at Tony. It gaped at him.

At one time they had delighted in wearing each other's clothes. Turning up places dressed as the other. The thrill of unwashed things, to wear the other's essence.

And here were Mark's clothes now. The striped shirt that was his warmest, his most comforting, the jeans that fitted him like no others. The shirt wasn't properly fastened and where it hung open – Mark forced himself to look – there was nothing underneath. He could see the back of the shirt.

Tony's arms were raised in a gesture of welcome. No hands. Only the cuffs of those familiar sleeves.

'Here we are then,' came Tony's voice. 'In the daylight.'

A headless man. The shirt's collar was loose and open about nothing. From here the voice welled up, the first time Mark had heard it in years, though it had echoed through letters and ploys and the silent hands. Tony's voice had a timbre that raised the shaved hairs at the back of Mark's neck.

It threatened to pull him back. Tony was beseeching. An amputee.

'You've gone . . .' Mark whispered, ' . . . fucking crackers.'

Tony produced his white gloves with a magician's flourish. He put them on and, with a curiously tender gesture, caressed his own invisible face. 'Have I? Quite honestly, Mark. I don't know where I've gone.'

And Tony gave a low, regretful, yet thoroughly sane chuckle.

'What's happened to you?'

'Don't know.' The shirt shrugged. 'It's good to see you, Mark.'

'What did you want? Why did you lie?'

'About being in prison?'

'Yes. All of it. Why take Sally like that?'

'It's good to see you, Mark. You look so good, I could eat you. You always did that for me. I loved you, Mark.'

Mark went to sit on the bed, by his opened, upturned bag.

'Oh, I know,' Tony went on. 'This isn't the time or place to go into all that now. I thought it was. I didn't see at first. But now I've had you all here and I've seen how you go on, seen how you work as a *family*.' Tony's voice was tinged with scorn when he said this word. 'I see how things are. How complicated. Should I really thrust in my love, my old, decayed, long-lost love, to further complicate matters? If I loved you truly, I'd quietly step aside and give you an easier ride. I'd be discreet and kind and let you forget me.'

'Tony –'

'Hang on, Mark. What I'm saying is that I made it seem, in my own mind, all too simple. I just had to storm back into your life, make you notice me. Such as I am. I thought I was enough for you to love. But when now I look back to all that stuff in the past, I see that you never really loved me. I'd forgotten. I could see then more clearly than you could. You tried so hard, but you couldn't. And I never stopped wishing that one day you'd wake up and realise that you could. That you could commit yourself to my protection.

'But Sam is the one that protects you, Mark. You know that. I, on the other hand, scare the shit out of you.

'We created each other. But you can't love me because you know that we can destroy each other, too. You're like a dam, brinked before the burst. All I need do is pick away one motif in your overall design – pluck away that clock on your heart – and you'd fall to bits. I oversaw the construction of your bricolage, Mark. I was the proud father watching the tattooist's needle work as she brought you to birth. I'm too implicated in your birth – as any parent is – to bring you up safely.

203

'But Sam can take you all at once, can't she? She has veneered that tender skin of yours and kept all the pictures together. You're a whole man at last. I see that now, and it's all down to her. There's no chink in that armour for me to find.'

Mark was shaking his head.

'In my early on, transparent reasonings, I thought it was a simple matter of sexual politics. How dare she take my man? But it's not an issue of your bisexuality, or your selling out. It's me. I just wasn't right for you, was I? Sam is, and maybe Richard is, too. Perhaps you can engineer a way to have both? You deserve that. I can say this because I do love you and want to see you get what you deserve.'

The empty figure bent to kiss him. Mark felt the swift brush of Tony's cheek.

'I'm fucking noble, aren't I?' Tony laughed. 'And you thought I was insane and demonic!'

'But what about you, Tone? They're taking everything out of the house, you know –'

'I'm clearing out. It's all my idea. I've got the money now to chuck all this crap away. Disperse the fragments of this shitty life and start up again somewhere. It's quite exciting, I suppose. I want to prune away the loose baggage, the extra elements, and transform what can be transformed into something more useful. Without all the belongings, I'm literally nothing. I had to put on your clothes in order to talk to you just now. Just think, I can put something else on and allow myself to be anything I want. Oh, you needn't worry about me, Mark. I'll crop up somewhere, unexpected. As something unexpected. It's in my nature.'

'You were never going to hurt Sally, were you?'

Tony sighed. 'No. Actually, in the end, I went through with it all because I thought you might like to meet Richard.'

Mark looked shocked. Tony went on.

'That was a lie. But it makes me sound clever, doesn't it?'

Mark stood up, unsure. 'Tony, would you let me . . . ?'

'What?'

Mark went through his bag and produced the make-up set given him by the ladies. 'I want to see how you are now. I just

204

want to. Whatever you think, Tone, I did love you when we were sixteen. We made each other. And it may be dangerous and impossible to carry that on. I don't know. I don't believe in rules, in essential truths. We might have made it. But life got in the way. Circumstances stepped in and they changed us all. We can't regress . . . can't take it back to how it was, start again. That's why I want to see your face now. If we're moving on, I can't go on thinking of you as you were when we were younger.'

Tony sat on the antique chair, white hands harmlessly on his knees. Clumsily, inexpertly, Mark set to work with the make-up. Tony came up, gaudy in purples, blues, pinks. His cheekbones were too sharp and his eyes slightly startled.

And Tony sat bewildered as Mark made him up. As he always had, he sat passive and let it happen. It struck him then, This is how it always was. This is how it worked. And why, in the end, after all the pontificating, it was no good. Not for Tony. Tony could be as sensible about Mark's life as he wanted, but in the end Tony knew that the involvement with Mark was bad for *him*. Because here he sat, letting Mark do this to him.

He felt the delicate scrape, brushing and tweaking of cosmetics. No one had touched his face in years. These parts of his body were brought back into existence.

Once more he was in the position of being grateful to Mark for making love to him. Tony was back where he had been at sixteen: full of relief and gratitude that Mark had risen to meet his challenge, in whatever form.

Mark was oblivious, as always, having been gently probed and manipulated into this position of reciprocation. As far as he was concerned, he was being nice. He was doing something for Tony, making things better. It was that innate child-rearing instinct in him. He was, after all, a breeder. But Tony was angry. Mark could be provoked to make the significant gesture and give the kiss-off to this life in a perfect, epiphanic scene. But it's always got to be me doing the provoking, Tony thought.

I sit here passive, being painted on, for Mark.

205

As I lived here for years, pretending to be in prison, selling antiques, being shat on by Mark.

And as I was sent down, in the first place, taking on Sam's culpability for manslaughter, all for Mark.

At the outset I was the one to let Mark know his potential. I tempted him into looking at me, at my body, and led him to what his inarticulate desires were clamouring for.

I didn't create you, you bastard; I was the raw material you took yourself from. You're a thing of shreds and patches, a snatched-together, botched-up man, and you've left me behind. But I am your inner man, Mark; you have me inside.

'There,' Mark said at last. 'So that's how you are.'

He sat back on the bed to survey his handiwork.

Through the colours Tony's face rose up to meet him, through the false accentuations, the pouches, the changes worked over the years. With the face of a clown, a drag artist, an embalmed corpse, Tony looked out through a complex, unreadable mesh of emotions. But Mark looked and he thought, This is Tony. Changed, yeah, but so have we all. So this is what the years do? And it's good to get the update. But this is Tony after all. At least as close as you could ever get.

'Go now,' Tony told him, with some difficulty. 'Just go, Mark.'

Mark went.

And when he went, at last, Tony walked to the window. The snow was coming down, thick enough to give him a reflection. He saw himself once again.

'Simmonds!'

Anger does strange things to people.

When circumstances get too much, when they crash down like portcullises and you are expected to become something else again. And you're tired, tired of hauling yourself up out of the mess gratitude and relief have made you into. When your self-respect has scraped too thin and you're not sure there's enough left for you to reinvent into yet another, hopeful self. That's when anger does strange things.

Tony attacked the bed. It was, after all, the root of his problems. He stripped the sheets and shredded them with his gloved fingers, and the bits fell in a mock snow shower. Then, gathering all his resentment, he took a deep breath and hauled the bed around on its castors. With a final burst of righteous adrenaline he sent it crashing through the bedroom wall.

'Simmonds!' he screamed. 'Simmonds!' he howled at the old man who had rescued him from penury once before. He had one more use for Simmonds and, furious, he waited for the patter of hi-tech trainers.

He stared in the meantime at the destroyed outer wall. The snow was falling thick beyond and coming into the room. The crash of the bed into the garden below still rang in his ears.

Tony didn't question how he could have managed such a thing, how he had gathered the strength. It seemed entirely reasonable. When you're as impossible as I am, Tony thought, you learn not to worry.

Impossible he might be, but the wind coming in through the trashed bedroom wall was freezing him as he stripped off Mark's clothes.

'Simmonds!' he yelled again.

Like a smashed window in an aeroplane, the gash in the wall let in the sky and it fought for possession of him. Tony stood with his handfuls of Mark's clothes whipping up around him.

The old man had been standing in the doorframe for some moments. Mark had pushed past him on the way out, almost startled to see him in the same room as Tony. Somewhere in the back of his mind Mark had expected them to be the same person. Anything was possible. But Simmonds was real, just an old, old fuck of Tony's. The cast-off older man, a withered shell Tony was good enough to keep about the place.

'Why didn't you come when I shouted?'

Simmonds looked to where Tony stood, where he was visible by virtue of the mess he had made. Simmonds was used to the ways of his one-time golden boy, his only love. He was used to his invisibility. Talking to Tony was like spot-the-ball. Simmonds played the game with the dogged optimism of a lonely pensioner and he knew how to field Tony's anger. Today, though, he would play a dangerous game with it.

'He's told you no, hasn't he?' Simmonds sneers.

Mark's clothes are wrung out in mid-air into a thick knot, eloquent with fury. Tony answers stiffly, 'Yes.'

'I know rejection. You can't hide that's what you're feeling. Not from me.'

They are quiet a moment.

'How did you manage to push the bed through the wall?'

'Shut it.' The clothes begin to unwind, as if purposefully, like a serpent's coils. Tony is sloughing Mark's jeans and shirt. 'I want you to do one more thing for me, Simmonds.'

'Tony, please. Say Peter. Say my name.'

'Fuck that.'

Tony is standing right by Simmonds and before the old man knows it there's a razor blade taking a neat line down his soft cheek. He falls flat on his arse. With his gloves off – as they are now – no one can see Tony coming. Simmonds begins to howl.

'Shut the fuck up!' Tony hurls Mark's clothes at him. 'Put these on. Now. And then we'll put on some nice make-up, shall we? You used to enjoy dressing up in the old days, didn't you?'

Simmonds clambers to his feet, bleeding. 'What for?'

'You're going to stand in for me. Just for a moment. You can be my best man. You'll like that.'

Simmonds regards the empty air. 'I'd give anything to be you, be your best man. You know that.'

The razor transfixes him as it forces him to change. Mark's clothes are cool and damp with the snow blowing in. The old man struggles to do as he is bid and Tony says, 'Yes. It's a reason to despise you. Now hurry.'

Twenty-Six

'The car's fucked.'

In the hallway Bob had the look and the tone of a man whose only concern was his fucked car.

'It doesn't matter anyway,' Sam said. 'We'd never get home in it now. We'll all have to take the train.'

'Together,' Mark said. 'Where are the others?'

'Having breakfast.'

But they were out in the garden, standing around the fallen bed. In the centre of the garden it sat on four wrecked legs, its bedsteads only just holding on and its mattress rucked up in alarm. A light dusting of snow already covered it.

They were looking in astonishment at this, and then up at the hole in the wall, far above. The fire escape gave an occasional groan of complaint and steadied itself.

'This is madness,' Richard said and sat down on the bed he had slept in last night. 'I just want to get away from here now.'

Inside, the removal men were working swiftly. Tony's house was emptying out.

Peggy picked up Sally and sat them both beside Richard. 'Never mind, love. You're welcome to stay with us, you know.'

Iris touched his knee with a wink. 'You don't get out of this family that easily.' She looked at her lover. 'Peg, I'm going in to get our things. Check that no one's nicked them.'

'That's not all, is it?' asked Peggy archly.

'I want to find Simmonds.'

'He'll have pissed off now, with all of his and Tony's belongings.' Richard was disconsolate. And how could they blame him? He had watched, this morning, the break-up of his happy home.

His Labrador came bounding up out of the shrubbery to

cheer him up and amuse Sally. Iris took the opportunity to slip into the house. Peggy watched her go, her feelings mixing. She wanted to warn her not to be Shelley Winters in *The Poseidon Adventure*, knowing that she would be.

Soon, Sam, Mark and Bob came out to the ruined garden to survey the damage. They sat on the bed and, as if expecting a fairy tale, they all drew up their legs onto the mattress.

'It was Tony who did this,' Mark said.

'So you saw him?' asked Sam.

'At last. And it's all sorted out. He's out of our lives.'

'I've never been on a train,' Sally said brightly. 'Is that how we're getting back?'

Sam nodded and kissed her daughter. She looked at Bob, who sat awkwardly on the bed. He seemed to be having some difficulty in looking at either Sam or Mark. Reminded, possibly, of his last adventure on a bed.

He said, 'Sam, tell me. What's this outrageous plan?'

He sounded weary. Poor Bob, she thought. Just an ordinary bloke. An ordinary bloke who wants our lives to be normal. And I've got to sell him an outrageous plan. But if he wants to be a part of our lives, then he's got no choice but to swallow it.

Sam took a deep breath.

'Mark and I are going to stay together, with Sally, in the flat. And, part-time, at least, I have recourse to you, Bob, your nice house and your bed. And Mark, if he wants to, has Richard.'

'Cheers,' said Richard bitterly.

Mark gave him a swift hug. He promised him. 'We'll discuss this.'

Valkyries decide who gets to Valhalla. They come swooping on ruffled and vengeful wings and what do they do then? Arriving at another Ragnarök, how do they stack the dice?

Iris came backing into the attic room. Some memory of Cheryl Ladd in *Charlie's Angels* lent her posture a cautious authority. The cold air through the new hole in the wall was like a slap in the face. It framed a man dressed in Mark's spare jeans and shirt. She saw his face was smeared in glistening colour.

'I'm Simmonds!' he shouted, dismayed as Iris advanced. She mistook Tony's amused chuckling for the beating of her own imaginary wings behind her.

'I don't care,' she said grimly.

'What are you going to do?'

She wasn't sure but she advanced on him anyway, with vague thoughts of stamping out a rogue element. It would make the ending of the tale neater, safer.

Simmonds quailed, 'That's Tony behind you.'

Amazingly Iris fell for it. She turned and saw Tony's lurid face hovering alone at her shoulder. A horrible, wingless, grimacing bird. And she saw his stroppy razor as it flensed into her thickly padded side.

But shock made her shoot forwards, through the hole, onto the fire escape, where she smacked her head on iron bars and went flying, taking the old man with her.

Tony's face swooped after, lilac, like a terrible familiar.

'I think that should satisfy everyone,' said Sam, looking about and wondering if she'd missed anyone out. 'In fact, it's almost the way it was before.' Sam smiled ruefully at Peggy. 'And that, Mam, if you remember, is what you asked for.'

Bob pulled a face. 'That's not *too* outrageous, I don't suppose.'

'But will it stand the test of time?' asked Peggy, who was the oldest and yet the least jaded of them.

'No idea,' Mark said. 'But we'll hold it together for as long as we can.'

Peggy realised she was still holding Mark's books from the shop that morning. Iris had given them to her for safekeeping. 'She's taking her time,' she said.

'*The Emperor's New Clothes* for Sally,' said Mark, opening the parcel. 'And a novel by a certain Iris Margaret Wildthyme.'

As they crowded round to examine the gilded cover of Iris's long-forgotten novel, Iris's voice called down to them.

She was shouting for help, although she never meant to. In her long life Iris had prided herself on never really needing anyone's help. But at this moment she was perched on the perilous fire escape, held tight in the grip of someone wearing a garishly made-up face and Mark's clothes.

'Tony!' Mark shouted, jumping up, the others following his lead.

Iris, thought Peggy steadily. Don't be Shelley Winters. Be Orlando. Be a Valkyrie. Just this once.

The next few moments stretched on for hours.

Time was playing its tricks although none of them was pissed.

Mark had never thought to see Tony again. He thought now that he was being betrayed.

They all cleared the bed and stood round, helpless, looking up, as if instinctively knowing they must provide something to break a fatal fall.

For in those endless moments the figure wearing Mark's clothes launched itself and Iris off the fire escape and into the air. They jerked into life as if pulled on strings, or pushed by a hand unseen.

And then they flew.

The sky was that flinching blue again and no one in the garden could stop their eyes watering in order to see how they fell. The bodies tumbled and soared, seemed never to descend.

Then came, amid the gentle snow, a patter of sharp swan's feathers onto the mattress. They fell, fresh and inexplicable, as around the bed dropped Iris's many layers of clothing. And finally, in their midst, with shocking suddenness and no harm done, fell a bright pink child, about the size of a rabbit.

The body in Mark's clothes hit the wet, stony ground nearby with a hideous crunch.

Peggy took the baby up, picking the feathers out from between its limbs. 'She said she was going somewhere . . .' There were tears down her face. She looked at Richard. 'Well, Mr Houseboy. How are you with kids?'

Sally smiled at her. 'He was brilliant with me. He'll look after Granny Iris.'

Ever the vigilant policeman, Bob was tending to the not so lucky, the also-ran.

Simmonds's made-up face was smashed on the ruined

foundations of an outhouse. But they could see plainly who he was.

'We'll have to report this, Sam,' said Bob as they clustered about, appalled.

She shook her head. 'The country's having snow chaos. We can't make a fuss. The police have enough on their hands.'

All that afternoon they dug the iron-hard earth and at last buried the old man in his hi-tech trainers.

Then they caught the train back home to the north, back to separate homes, in the same town, as planned.

Twenty-Seven

I'm south, now. In a railway station, in brand-new drag.

Remember, Mark, when I told you about Anna Karenina? Well, for a while I was tempted to pull her stunt. Remember Garbo being her, bless her? I want to be alone, too.

I watched your patched-up family board the train at Leeds, happy and contented. I thought about interposing myself, throwing off my disguise bit by bit and making myself apparent. There's the irony, of course – the more disguise I shrug off, the less apparent I really am.

I could have done one final, self-vindicating disappearing act. I could have been Anna, or Garbo, shedding my coat, my shoes, my hat, leaving only a made-up face, a Cheshire-cat grin, and I could have forced you to watch me mangle it on the railway lines as your train pulled out. Just as you went off home to figure out your new, complex lives.

But I sat there instead and pretended to be corporeal.

And you went and I came south.

I don't know where I'm going yet. This is a stop-off point. I've been travelling for a few days now, choosing a place. I can see the Tyre and Exhaust Centre from here. Tired and Exhausted. I think we all are by now.

That's how the wild woods in winter make you feel. But winter is relenting today. The sky has pink and blue shreds drifting through it. Complementary, not quite oppositional spring shades. It's fucking cold, though. Here I am on one of those metal seats that make you shudder rather than shiver.

If *Frankenstein* were written today, would the monster and creator dash about the country on British Rail? They could never be sure of finding each other. If Frankenstein and the monster had an AwayDay now, even if they did come across

214

each other on a dark, windy, romantic platform, they'd never tell who was who anyway.

This red-bricked station occupies many contradictory states: desolate and busy, orderly and chaotic. On the bench beside me sits an old woman in bright red shoes, who rocks herself and stares and stares. Involved in her own drama, whatever that may be.

In these stations we have only one role: the quiet traveller, the bit-part player. And no necessary relation to each other. In stations, we needn't connect.

Oh, Mark, I'm writing to you again. The lilac paper is resting on my knee. Already written, abandoned sheets lie about my feet on that pockmarked concrete of the platform. Fags are squashed out in the pockmarks like killed beetles. I just feel the need to write again, although I shouldn't, I suppose.

Across from me there is a disembowelled train, resting on an unused track. Its undercarriage has large white letters stencilled upon it: NOT TO BE LOOSE SHUNTED.

Rest assured, Mark, I will *not* be shunted loosely into that good night.

Here's my train.

Love,

Tony.

Twenty-Eight

Miss Kinsey was rattling the staff-room blinds once more. It was home time, the end of the first week of a new term and a new year. This was the hardest time with children – with anyone, really – the deepest months of winter. Her teachers were shattered already. This was the time that the best-laid plans frittered away into disaster. Pipes had burst. The school hall had been flooded.

Behind her Doris Ewart washed out the staff-room mugs, complaining that no one bothered to wash their own, and went on with some interminable story about young Miss Francis's affair with a pet-shop owner. That was, apparently, where all the terrapins came from.

'Well,' said Miss Kinsey. 'I wonder who we'll get tonight.'

She was watching the mothers collecting their children. The kids looked so sweet, dashing about in their crumpled uniforms of red jumpers, grey trousers or skirts. To be met by, frankly, mothers who had let themselves go. Who smoked beside the main entranceway, their hair unwashed.

'What do you mean?' asked Doris, and came to see. Then she realised.

Sally stood, clutching her lunch box, waiting to be collected.

'We could run a book on this,' said Doris.

'I hope you're not advocating gambling on the school premises,' Miss Kinsey purred.

'Oh, no. But I bet you a fiver we get her mother tonight.'

'You're on. A fiver says it's that nice young man again.'

Because, so far this week, Sally had had different people to meet her from school each night.

Monday, a nice young man with wavy hair, a Labrador and a leather jacket. Miss Kinsey and Doris Ewart were a little

216

concerned, but on Tuesday night Sam – the legitimate mother – had picked Sally up and explained that Richard was 'a friend of the family'. On Wednesday came Sally's grandmother – whom Miss Kinsey had met before – with a pushchair and a squawking brat. (Miss Kinsey liked children to be between the ages of five and eight.) And on Thursday there was a police car for Sally and a beaming, handsome policeman. The other kids will be getting jealous, the headmistress thought.

'We've both lost a fiver,' Doris Ewart said.

Miss Kinsey sighed. 'What a shame!' And she went to close the venetian blinds.

Because on Friday night Mark came to collect Sally. She ran to him and grasped his blue hand. The crowd of mothers and kids, waving thickly painted posters and tugging on anoraks, didn't move apart for this casual reunion. Sally and Mark had to fight through the mass, standing out for anyone's inspection only by virtue of the tattoos and the especially vivid pink of Sally's lunch box.